Poppy's Revenge

BOOK 2 - THE PAIN SERIES

To Dad

Enjoy

Love you loads

Lynda
xx

LYNDA THROSBY

Poppy's Revenge
Copyright © Lynda Throsby Publishing 2021 All Rights Reserved

Editing by ellie @My Brother's Editor
Proofread by Rosa @My Brother's Editor

This book is licensed for your personal enjoyment only. It may not be resold or given away to other people. If you do, you are STEALING.

I only distribute my work through Amazon and Ingram Spark. If you have received this book from anywhere else, it is a pirated copy, it is illegal, and you've really spoiled my day.

Thank you for respecting the hard work of this author.

Lynda Throsby has asserted her rights under the Copyright, Designs, and Patents Act 1988 to be identified as the author of this work.

This book is a work of fiction. Names and characters are the product of the author's imagination and any resemblance to actual persons, living or dead is entirely coincidental. The characters and names are products of the author's imagination and used fictitiously.

All rights reserved, no part of this publication may be reproduced or transmitted in any form or by any means, electronic, mechanical, photocopying or otherwise, without the prior permission of the publisher and author except for the instance of quotes for reviews. No part of this book may be uploaded without permission of the publisher and author nor be circulated in any form of binding or cover other than that in which it is originally published. All rights reserved.

Cover design by Sybil @Popkitty
Formatted by Champagne Book Design
ISBN: 978-1-9993150-8-5
Lynda Throsby Publishing
Email ljtpublishing@gmail.com

Warning

This book is not intended for anyone under the age of 18.
This is for adult reading only and contains counts of violence and sexual content.

This one is dedicated to my mum—who I have sadly just lost.
Rest In Peace Mum
Astrid Glassbrook
12/02/47 to 19/02/2021
"Love You Loads"

Poppy's Revenge

PART IV

Poppy

One

Poppy

I'VE BEEN WATCHING THEM FOR WEEKS. PLAYING HAPPY FUCKING family. They attend the deaf and hard of hearing school each week where Prim has been teaching deaf people to sign, including that fucking ass Nick. I watch each week as they leave and head to the same coffee shop. I'm standing here watching them now. I see the minute he spots my reflection in the shop window, his shoulders tense and he turns around to look at me. I'm standing on the other side of the street, knowing I can make a run for it. He's seen me fleetingly the last few weeks, but only because I've allowed him to. Making him think he's going crazy, trying to work out how I could be there, I'm supposed to be dead after all. I watch him jump up from his chair and he steps to the edge of the sidewalk, he's going to make a run for me. I notice the bus out of the corner of my eye. He won't make it. I start to run toward the bus, knowing he will miss me once it's passed by.

I'm on the other side, the coffee shop side, watching his back as he looks up and down the street, looking for me. I turn and see Prim coming out of the shop with a tray of coffee. That bitch deserves everything she gets. I move toward her, making sure she doesn't see me. I look over to Nick. I see as he turns and notices me, the look of horror on his face at me near his precious Prim. He shouts out to Prim, who isn't looking, asshole, what use is shouting to her? She can't hear you, fucking moron that he is. I start toward her, quickening my pace, not giving him a chance to get back across to us. I take the blade out of my pocket and as I approach her from behind. I discreetly stick it in her side and push her. She has no idea what just happened. I start to move away quickly, quickening my pace into a jog. I hear him screaming as he runs back toward us from across the street, car horns are blaring at him. I start to run. I don't have time to look behind me in case he's chasing me. I'm struggling a little. I feel nauseous, and I hold my back as though I'm in pain, but I know I'm not. It's Prim and the pain she feels. I hear screaming. I glance back over my shoulder, no one is following me.

I stop, I'm far enough away that I could outrun him if he tried to come after me, but close enough that I can see them. I see the panic and anguish on his face. He's trying to talk to Prim, she's facedown, so what good is that, he's a fucking dumbass at times. I see him look up and around, then he spots me. I see a lot of blood around Prim. Good, the bitch deserved it. I feel so nauseous I hold my side. I feel like I have a cramp, only it's more painful.

He glares at me. I smile at him, and then because he can't hear me, I sign, "Revenge will be sweet."

I watch for a minute, I can hear sirens getting closer. Time for me to leave, I don't think he would leave her lying there to come after me, so I have no danger of him following me. He saw what I signed, and I meant it. I will have my revenge. I've already started it, getting her gets to him. I didn't kill her, at least I don't think I did, unless the knock to the head when she went down killed her, but I know exactly where to stick the knife. What do you think I've been doing all this time? Revenge will be very sweet.

Two

Poppy
Present

I'VE BEEN WATCHING HIM THESE LAST COUPLE OF WEEKS, COMING and going to the hospital. He hasn't seen me. I didn't want him to. She's obviously not dead, I'm sure I would have felt it if she was, and him being at the hospital all the time tells me she's still alive. I just don't know what the damage is. I thought about going in, but I don't want to be on the CCTV. I think I may just call and ask, I'm her sister after all. I've seen Aunt Cassy and Uncle Trevor coming and going and I saw Trixie and Pixie. I can't believe how grown-up they are now. It's been over twelve months since I've seen any of them. I suppose everyone was happy for me to disappear after attacking the princess like I did. There's no doubt she told them all it was me, she told him after all.

I'm sitting on a bench on the hospital grounds far enough away from the entrance but close enough so that I can still see it. I know he'll be arriving soon, it's his routine. I hear a familiar voice shouting, "Blaine, Blaine, wait up." It's Aunt Cassy and I see him, Nick, turn to her? Why is she calling him Blaine? Don't tell me that fucker lied to me all that time. He lied about his name. That fucking bastard. I watch as he turns around and they hug each other, well isn't that cozy. She links his arm and they walk into the hospital together. It's hot out, I'm sitting here in a hoodie with the hood up over my head. I light up, yeah, I smoke now. Who can blame me after what I went through? He left me for dead in that grave. He thought he had fucking killed me, but he was wrong. So, so wrong.

———

A year ago

I wake suddenly, I'm disoriented, I feel like I'm suffocating, like I have an elephant on my back. I try to open my eyes. They feel swollen, I can open one to a slit. Just. I can't make out where I am, it's dark, there is no light. I can't remember where I was. I try to move, I can't, something's weighing me down, my body hurts all over. I try to focus through my one eye, nothing. I can barely breathe. It smells earthy, like dirt, but also a nasty rotting smell. It's making me feel nauseous. I want to vomit. I can't lift my head, it's being pressed down along with my body. I feel claustrophobic, I'm going to start to panic. I can feel it start to build in me, panic, I need to stay calm. I need to try to focus and try to remember where I am.

My eyes focus, I can't see what's beneath me, the smell is so strong and rancid. I'm really struggling to breathe, whatever is on my back is weighing down my entire body, preventing me from taking in any deep breaths, I just take in small shallow ones, I nearly swallow something that is in my mouth, I manage to push it with my tongue and spit it out. I try to take in a deep breath. It hurts so much. Whatever is holding me down is stopping my lungs from expanding to get the breaths I need, I try again and this time I get a mouthful of something. Eww, it's stringy and horrible, it must be my hair. I try to move my head. I manage only slightly from the weight on top of my whole body, my forehead smashes down as I try to lift it. Oh fuck, that hurt, it was hard, and there's more hair, not mine though, that's someone's head underneath mine. It must be a skull. I'm on top of a fucking body. That must be what the smell is from, I want to be sick, bile comes out of my mouth, leaving a nasty taste and I suck in dirt.

I definitely start to panic, trying to move, trying to wriggle my head or my body but it's no use, I would be hyperventilating right now if I could, but I can't breath and I feel I'm going to suffocate. I try to wiggle my fingers. They move slightly. I need to do it more. I start to scrape and scrape with my nails. I seem to be moving dirt. I'm buried, oh my god, I'm in a fucking grave, with a body beneath me. Panic sets in again, and I try to wriggle more, I need to take in a breath, some deep gulps, but I can't. It's no use, I need to breathe. The earth on my back seems to be getting heavier and heavier. I continue to scrape with my nails, each time I manage to move very slightly, but it's wearing me out far too quickly, the air is getting thinner and thinner, I'm really struggling to breathe. If I don't fight it, I will die here, there is no doubt. I struggle, trying to gulp in air, not wanting to suck in the hair again. How can there even be air if I'm buried?

I rest for a few minutes, trying to catch my breath, I'm getting so tired and weak. Then I try again, I'm moving my hands more, I'm in so much pain as my nails rip from my fingers one by one, suddenly one of my finger's pokes through the dirt, I feel the breeze on it. I can do this, I need to dig with my hands. I don't care how fucking tired I am, or how much pain I'm in, if I don't then I'm gonna die here.

I keep at it for what feels like hours. I have to keep resting then trying again, all the while trying to take very shallow breaths. I'm so dizzy, it's getting harder and harder the longer it goes on, I just want to sleep each time I rest. I close my eyes each time. I don't know if I actually sleep during any of the times I rest. It only feels like minutes before I know I have to keep going. I can do this, I have to do this. My fingertips are raw, the dirt stings at each stroke, but I keep going. Once I get my hands free at my sides, I dig around me more, making the holes bigger at each side. I don't feel as constricted now. I wriggle my body from side to side. Now I've managed to move more of the dirt, I start to move my legs, doing the same thing, wriggling. I have to stop so many times to try to breathe. I have no energy for this shit, I'm getting weaker and weaker with every second that passes. I just need to rest a while. I wake suddenly, trying to breathe, trying to gulp for air. I have to keep going. I have to get air in here. I don't have much time left. I feel myself suffocating. I really dig in trying to wriggle myself out of here.

My arms are finally free, I can lever myself up, it takes everything I have to push through the dirt. I feel it all falling around as I push my body up. I use my hands as leverage to push my body upward, higher, just a little more, higher and higher. It's a slow process and my chest is hurting, but there is air getting in, I can breathe a little better now. I do it. I fucking break through the earth. It started to get easier as the dirt fell away from my back, making the weight lighter. Eventually I get on all fours and manage to lift my head up, raising my face to the sky, and breathing as best I can. I take in a few shallow breaths. It hurts and burns with each breath, I take a few more breathes, before trying to open my eyes. The one opens slightly, it's dark but getting light. I look down and I see I was resting on a blanket, but where my head was, it was resting on someone else's dead head. I take a closer look. It freaks me out, I can make out it's a rotting head, I think it saved my life. Because of the hollows from the rotted flesh around the head, I think there was trapped air in the skull, probably from when the hole was reopened by whoever it was that threw me in here. It gave me the air I needed to survive and free myself. I call that a fucking miracle.

I ache badly. I can't catch my breath enough in the cold morning air, I feel like I may still suffocate. I'm still on all fours, I try to straighten up, my back kills as I do, putting my hands on my knees for support, trying to take shallow breaths. I need a big gulp, but my chest won't take it. I'm taking shallow breaths, but I need to take deep ones. I feel like I'm going to hyperventilate. That won't help, I'm trying to gulp. I need to move. I need to find someone to help me. I start to stand. I hear a noise and I freeze. It's a grunt, and what sounds like breathing and sniffing. I don't move, but I need to breathe more, taking tiny breaths. The noise isn't getting any closer. I turn very slowly, there's nothing there. I start to move, hopefully in the direction of civilization so I can get help. I can't see clearly. I feel my face and it's swollen, my eyes are all puffy, my head is killing me with a splitting headache and my whole body aches, I feel like I've gone ten rounds in a boxing ring and lost.

I hear the noise again, but louder this time. I try to see where it's coming from, but I don't see anything. Just then I take a step, or at least I try to, but the earth moves from under my foot. I fall back onto my ass as I'm off balance. It knocks the wind out of me, I try to gulp, holding my chest. It's no use. I need to move. I get on all fours and I start to crawl slowly, each move of a knee or a hand hurts, my hands sting so bad. I want to scream but don't have the air in my lungs to do that. It takes me ages just to move a few feet.

I move some more, but my hand gives out this time and the dirt moves from under it, I manage to stop myself catapulting down by moving back slightly. It's then I see a hole in front of me. I lean forward very slightly, and I see breath coming up. I move forward some more, cautiously testing the ground, and peer down into the hole, there's a fucking bear in there. That's what the noise is. Fuck, I nearly ended up in there with him. What are the fucking chances? I escape from one hole, being buried alive, only to fall into another hole and be eaten by a bear? I scramble backward away from it and sit on my ass and take slow, shallow breaths.

After a few minutes of sitting on the cold dirt, I get on my knees and then try to get to my feet. I do it. It took a lot out of me, but I've done it. I start to walk around the hole, my feet are killing me, they sting as I walk, I'm trying not to get close to the edge of the hole in case it gives way and I fall in, I look around and can only just make out in the dim light that there are more holes around me as I walk farther on. I notice something in one of them, it's a car, I look and it's my fucking car. It's coming back to me. NICK. He fucking did this, he tied me up. I hit him then he hit me. He must have thought I was dead, and he buried me. That fucker. He buried me alive. He beat me, then buried my body in that grave.

I remember his cabin wasn't far from here, I'm fucking freezing, I'm naked. I look down and I see fresh blood on my tummy. I wipe it away and see there is a hole there that must have opened up when I was trying to get out of the grave. That fucker stabbed me. I need some clothes. My car has my bags in it, I wonder if I can get them and my cell phone? I need to get some water. I stumble, what the fuck is wrong with me, I have aches and pains everywhere. It's a lot lighter out now. I stand and look over my naked body, it's black from all the dirt, I look at my feet to see what I stumbled on, it's then I notice my little toe is missing. That's what must have been in my mouth in the grave. I remember him putting something in my mouth before he knocked me out. I start to heave, bending over, putting my hands on my knees. I fear I'm going to collapse. I try to take in breaths and steady myself, ready to carry on. I make it to the cabin, it's not locked, there's nothing to lock up, I remember he said he wasn't coming back.

I search for water, there's some in a bucket, at this point I don't give a shit what's in it, I drink some and choke. This must have been the water he used to wash himself, I can taste the soap. I look around and see a pan on the wood burner, there's water in it. I drink that. My throat is sore and dry from all the dirt, and my lips feel all cracked. I go to his room, the bed's gone. It wasn't in the front. He must have thrown it away. I'm shivering, I'm that cold. There are no blankets or anything to wrap around me. I need to get to my car and see what I can retrieve from it. I just need to rest first, I feel so tired. I see a pair of dirty jeans on the bathroom floor. They'll do. I pull them on. They are huge and come up to my chest. I don't care how dirty they are, is that blood on them? I look closer, it's really dim in here but that's blood. Is it mine or did I get him good with the bedpost?

I curl up on the floor and close my eyes. I forgot to shut the door and I'm woken up sometime later by the sound of scurrying around me. I don't move. What if the bear got out? Suddenly a rat appears right in my eyeline and I scream like a little fucking girl. It scared the shit out of me. I sit up quickly and see there are a lot of them rummaging around. Probably thought I was their next meal. I swipe them away with my hand. I get up, I need to get to my car. I step outside into the bright sunlight. It hurts my eyes. Well, the one I can open slightly. I feel dizzy again as though I'm going to pass out. He hit me hard. I remember that, over and over, he was doing what I did to Prim. He was paying me back for hurting her like I did. I left her for dead, just like he did to me.

I see where he chopped up the deer to the side of me and wonder if there's any left. I take a look, but the rats have finished it by the looks of it. I head to the hole where the car was. I just hope I can get into it and out of it. I suddenly remembered I fell into one of the holes and struggled to get out of it on my own. He had to get rope to help me out. I approach with caution in case there's something in it. It's empty, well empty of any animals that is. I can climb into it no problem, he's thrown a lot of stuff in, including his missing bed. The car is on its roof, but the rear end is raised slightly, resting on something under it. I think I might be able to open the trunk and get my bags, not sure I will find my purse with my cell. I move some of the branches and rubbish out of the way. I don't have the keys for the trunk. If I can open the back door, I can pull the back seat down to access my bags in the trunk.

The door opens, it's not locked. It's creaky and a little bent out of shape, so it's hard to fully open. I open it just enough to crawl in. I pull the back seat down and my bags are in there. I pull them out one at a time. I struggle holding my stomach where he stabbed me, it's opened up again and is now bleeding. I crawl into the front to see if my purse is there, but I don't see it. He must have gotten rid of it and maybe took my cell? I drag the two bags out, one at a time, I manage to get them on the top of the upside down car, but it's agony lifting them. I climb up and out of the hole.

I take the bags one at a time back to the cabin. I know he said there was a creek somewhere. Do I have the energy to carry water back from wherever the hell it is? No, I'll use the water he used to clean up for now. Just so I get all this dirt off me and don't look too bad. I get my clothes out and decide wherever I have to walk to there is no way I can drag two bags along. I'll sort out what I really need and just take the one bag with me. I search around to see if I can find my purse just in case he has thrown it somewhere nearby. I don't find it. Fuck, I have no money, no cell, no cards, in fact, nothing. Just some clothes and toiletries. I don't even know what time it is. I don't know if I should hang around here for the night or if I dare chance making a move. I have no idea how far the nearest civilization is, and he already told me there were wild animals around these parts, hence the bear in the hole. I kinda feel sorry for it, but I'm in my own mess right now.

I have a missing fucking toe. I managed to tear up a shirt and tie some of it around my foot to cover the missing toe, as a bandage, and put a sticky bandage over the top. I still managed to get sneakers on, although it fucking hurt. Then while washing I realized why my chest was really sore and I saw that he cut my nipple almost off. I taped my nipple up with another sticky bandage. I looked at the hole in my stomach. It didn't look too bad, but it keeps opening and bleeding. I wrap that up, putting some of the torn shirt into the hole and a sticky bandage over it. I hope it holds. Thank god I had that stuff in my bags. My face feels a mess. It feels so swollen and I have cuts all over it and my head. This headache still will not go away even though I took some Tylenol, but it doesn't surprise me after the hits it's taken. My palms and soles are cut, they sting like crazy, along with my fingertips and missing fingernails from digging myself out. I found a bottle of water in the car. I've drunk half of it. There was a bag of potato chips. They didn't last a minute. I decide I'm going to attempt to find someone to help me. There's no way I'm sticking around here tonight. What if he decides to come back? What if he is only out at the creek or hunting or whatever shit he did around here. I can't take the chance he will come back.

I'm on the road. I've been going for what feels like forever, my toeless bad foot is crucifying me, and I already walk with a limp because of the cuts on my feet. The cars that have passed me wouldn't stop to help. There was one truck driver who stopped but I didn't like the look of him, so I took my chance to keep walking. It's getting dark. Maybe I should have gone with the trucker and taken my chances. What could be worse than being beaten and then buried alive? There are no houses or any signs of anyone around and I've been going for hours, I swear I have. I've passed a couple of dirt tracks but there was no way in hell I was seeing what was on the other end, if they're anything like his place. I'd probably end up murdered and raped for sure.

I have to stop a few times, to rest my feet mainly, but also because I'm so tired. I have no energy and feel so weak. I don't have any more water. I made it last as long as I could. I rationed that last half bottle, but finished it a few miles back. Everywhere hurts and aches. I just want to curl up and sleep, but I know I have to keep going. I need food and water. I have no energy and I know I've lost a lot of blood. My tee is wet from the stab wound. I don't have any more sticky bandages. I just have to hold it and keep pressure on it.

I finally see lights up ahead, I'm real sluggish and at this point I'm dragging my feet along to get me there. I have zero energy and I'm in so much agony all over, I've fallen a few times. I need water and painkillers. Finally, I reach a small town, I have no idea where I am or in which direction I even went. I step into the diner, I feel like I'm an alien as the people inside stop and stare. I ask if I can use the phone and if anyone has a few bucks I could borrow. They all look at me like I'm crazy. I tell a waitress I've been kidnapped, beaten, and buried alive. She looks at me like I have two heads or something and won't help me. She can see the mess my face is in, she looks at my clothes, which are now dirty from walking for miles and falling over. I look down and see what she sees, a young woman who looks like she lives on the streets.

I stand with my head hanging, wondering what to do. An old man must have heard me, and he offers me his cell to use. I smile and go to take it from his held-out hand, I pause, who am I going to call? I don't have any numbers for anyone, they were all programmed into my cell. Should I call the police? Tell them what? I was kidnapped, beaten, and buried alive? The waitress didn't even believe me. I don't think I could even tell them where the cabin was. I only know him as Nick, I never knew his last name. I'm screwed. I need to get to a hospital to be looked at.

"Thank you, sir, but I don't have any numbers to call. Can you tell me where I am or where the nearest hospital is, please?"

He smiles and offers to drive me to the nearest hospital. At least there I can tell them my name and they can check my insurance. I have no choice but to go with him. I don't have any money for the motel or any food. I lick my lips looking at his plate. He calls the waitress over and orders me some food and coffee. I'm so grateful to him.

It's 4:25 a.m. when he drops me off at a hospital. I asked for his number so I could send him some money. He told me nonsense, he didn't want anything and he was happy to be able to help me. He was a nice old man, said he'd been traveling all day after visiting his grandkids in San Francisco, which means I've headed in the opposite direction to where I wanted to go. At this point, I don't care.

I had to run through everything at the hospital. Telling them how I was kidnapped in my car and taken to a remote wooded place and that I didn't know where it was or who it was that attacked me. I gave them my social security number so they could look me up. I didn't have an address or a home to go to. I had nothing on me. Not even any ID. As it was, the hospital I was dropped at didn't need insurance. My social security number told them I was who I said I was. The nurse who took me in to check me over said I was lucky he didn't rape me, and that I was lucky to be alive after the injuries I had sustained. I had lost a lot of blood from the cuts to my hands, feet, the hole in my stomach, the loss of my toe, and my head injuries. She said she was amazed I had made it there. The stab wound hadn't done much damage. She said I was lucky with that too. I really don't feel fucking lucky. I had a concussion and as I had no one to look after me. I was admitted to the hospital with a nice warm bed for a few days to recover, along with hot meals and drinks.

The hospital called the police which made me fucking annoyed, but it was protocol they told me. I couldn't tell the police any more than I had told the hospital. I didn't want to give Aunt Cassy's details. Not after what I had done to Prim. They would probably have me arrested for attacking her. In all honesty, I'm screwed. Until I can get out of here and get some ID, even the bank won't give me any money without my ID. I will have to sort it out once I leave here.

Three

Poppy

AFTER BEING DISCHARGED FROM THE HOSPITAL, I HAD nothing. They made sure I was well enough, then kicked me out. I was in downtown LA, not the best or safest place to be. I've never been to this side before, but I'd heard about it. I wander around, not knowing what to do or where to go. There's no one I can contact. Not even Don or Tilda, I don't know their numbers or even their addresses. I don't have any friends, and the only family I have will probably want me dead anyway, and I have no money. The only possessions I have are in this bag I'm carting around with me.

I've been walking around for what feels like hours with bad feet, they smart from the cuts that are still not quite healed and the missing toe, the nurse told me to stay off my feet and rest up, yeah like that's going to fucking happen. I sit on a bench in a park I come across, watching people come and go, that was me once, not giving a damn about the people around me, until I started to work on the streets looking out for the young girls, when I was doing good with Don and Tilda, I learned a lot from that time. I learned about people and real life situations they go through. I sit watching, wondering what each person's story is.

I watch men in suits on cell phones, totally oblivious to their surroundings.

I watch young people rushing around, mostly chatting with each other or on cell phones.

I see young moms, some struggle with the children, others seem to be in total control.

I watch homeless people begging for money or food.

I watch some people sit just like me, watching the world go by.

I see others rummaging through the trash cans to see what scraps they can find.

I watch everyone, so much diversity in this one little area, all ethnicities going about their day-to-day business.

I watch everyone, mainly because I'm nervous sitting here on my own not knowing where I am or what I'm going to do next. Not knowing where to go. I have no idea where to start for ID, money, or accommodation.

I must have sat for hours watching, or at least that's what it felt like. I'm hungry. I pull out a Jell-O cup, one of three I took from the hospital, and I start to eat with the little plastic spoon, I also took. I eat it slowly, keeping my eyes on everyone around me, not trusting anyone. I watch as a young girl eyes me eating the Jell-O. She must be about eighteen or nineteen or she could be younger, she's on her own sitting on the curb, she looks homeless. She has that look about her, the sallow, pale face, long brown hair that from here looks loosely matted under her hoodie. Her eyes are dull, her clothes look like they've seen better days. It's hot out, but she wears a hoodie that is too big, which tells me she's hiding and doesn't want to be seen. She has torn jeans, but that's fashion these days. I see the pitiful look on her face as she watches people pass her by. She's looking pathetic, hoping someone will give her money. I then see her nod ever so slightly and I follow her eyeline. I don't see anyone else, just lots of people milling around. She looks back to me with a hurt look on her face and she licks her lips.

I stop eating and look into my cup, I've only had a couple of bites of Jell-O, but I look back to her and hold out the cup. I see her eyes go wide, I nod, she gets up and walks over to me. She pulls her sleeves over her hands and she stands in front of me.

"Take a seat." I motion with my head to the bench next to me. She looks around warily as though looking for someone, then sits next to me. I hand her the cup, but not the spoon. "It's not much, but it's all I have."

I watch her use her fingers to scoop out the Jell-O and put it in her mouth. It's gone within seconds, but I notice her hands are clean and her nails nicely manicured, not dirty like I would have expected them to be.

"When was the last time you ate something?"

She looks at me but doesn't speak.

"How long have you been on the streets? How old are you?"

She's still watching me but doesn't say a thing. She tosses the cup to the ground.

"You got any more food in there?" She motions to my bag between my feet.

I shake my head but watch her face. Trying to work out what she's thinking. She doesn't sound American. She has an accent, but I don't know from where. She's eyeing my bag, I close my legs tighter around it. I watch her closely for any sudden movements.

"How long have you been out here?"

She shrugs. "Long time now, maybe months." She looks away watching other people pass by, but I watch as her eyes scan everywhere, she looks terrified, and looks like she's looking for someone.

"Where are you from?"

She looks back to me and frowns. "Why, what is it to you?" She's very defensive.

I used to deal with girls like her all the time on the streets. The ones that were abused by boyfriends like I was. I used to be just like that. Very cagy, not speaking about my business to anyone, too scared to. I wouldn't tell anyone about being used as a pawn for a drug dealer. For him to abuse me or have his friends and clients take me at his command. He would have two and sometimes three on me at a time. I was so pumped with drugs, I hardly knew what was happening most of the time, and I didn't care. I was off floating in my own world somewhere far away from the situation I was in. I used to see Mama, Pappy, and Prim, all of us laughing together. Then I'd remember she took them from me, and I would hate on her even more. I'd get so angry and lash out at whoever was in me at that time, only to be punched in the face or stomach or knocked out. I used to wake up sore and in pain from whatever it was they did to me.

He had me drugged, but just lucid enough to cooperate for the sex. It got so bad I used to crave it, the drugs and the sex. I would ask to be pumped, literally, by both. He would shoot it up for me, sometimes injecting it between my toes so it wasn't noticeable to the outside world. Sometimes I would be so high, I used to beg him to stick his cock in me and if he didn't then I would ask whoever was in the room at that time to do it. Every night and day were the same. I would get fucked by so many, with so many watching me. I never told anyone the actual details, I couldn't, I was too ashamed.

When Uncle Trevor came to 'rescue' me, he walked in on three men sticking it to me in every hole. I don't think he ever told Aunt Cassy, he was too embarrassed, and we never spoke about it. He always stayed away from me when I went back to live with them. He made sure never to be in the same room as me, so it was never just the two of us alone. I don't know what he thought I was going to do, but he made me even more paranoid than I already was. Time helped and I became more normal, well the normal me. I still hated Prim. I couldn't stand seeing her and that meant looking at myself in the mirror. It's one of the reasons I used to dye my hair all different colors and wear outrageous clothes and makeup, so I never looked like her.

I'm lost in my own thoughts on the past when she suddenly jolts forward and grabs my bag. She's up and running with it before I know what's happening. I take off after her. One thing I also learned after my time with a drug dealer was self-defense, just in case I ever got into the same predicament again and with working out on the streets.

Catching up to her, and I grabbed her by the hood, yanking her back. She jolted to a stop, dropping the bag. She grabbed the base of her hair trying to ease the pressure I was putting on her scalp. I had her hair caught in the hood. I have her arm around her back and twisted upward, putting pressure on it knowing it will be hurting her.

"Please, stop, I am sorry, please, you are hurting me."

I ease up a little on her arm and let her hair go. "What the fuck did you do that for? I was being nice to you. Why would you do that? Did I look like an easy target to you?"

"No. please, I am sorry, I did not mean it. I am hungry."

I let go, pushing her forward and bending to pick my bag up before she has a chance to grab it again. She turns suddenly and before I know it, she's kicked me in the stomach. That winds me and I fall backward. Fuck. She reminds me of me. There is no way I have survived the attack from that bastard Nick to be put down by some foreign homeless bitch. I get to my feet quick before she can do anything else. I drop the bag to the ground, and I watch as she watches it fall. I take the defense stance with my arms in front of me and my legs positioned, ready to react.

"Think about this before you try to do anything stupid. I already got you once and I can do it again. There is nothing in my bag apart from some clothes. That's it. I don't have any money or anything else. I am like you, homeless."

"Puh, I do not believe you. You do not look homeless to me. You are clean, your clothes are clean, your hair is clean, your face just looks like a mess."

Gee thanks, but she's right.

"I just got out of the fucking hospital, that's why I'm clean. I was taken, beaten, and buried alive. I managed to escape, and I've been in the hospital for a few days. I don't have any money, ID, or a cell, and I have no way of getting anywhere." I would never ordinarily tell anyone things about me, but I guess there's no reason to lie.

"So, you are alone, with nowhere to go?"

I nod. I bend to pick up my bag, keeping my eyes on her the whole time as I do. I then look around and I can see we are attracting a small gathering around us.

"Look, these people are watching us. Let's just go our separate ways. I will forgive you for taking my bag."

She laughs at me, then she scans everyone around us. She's searching for someone, I watch her eyes scanning every face. I watch closely, and I manage to catch the very slight nod of her head. I scan the faces around to see who she's with, who she just acknowledged. Maybe there are a few of them that work together, to steal from easy targets. I step back a few paces.

"Wait, you come with me," she says sternly, as though giving me an order.

Like hell, I will.

"Um, fuck no. What, so you can attack me again, you and whoever else you are looking for or working with."

She tilts her head to the side and there's a wry smile on her face.

"I like you. I will not hurt you. Now come with me. I take you to get some food and somewhere to sleep. It's getting darker now."

She's right, it must be early evening, I've been sitting in the park for a long time, wondering what my next move will be, or where to go. Being new to the city, I have no idea where any shelters are.

"Come, now." She's very stern, very authoritative, maybe it's the accent.

"Where are you from? What is your accent?"

She furrows her brow. She's thinking how much to tell me. I look at her and she has brown hair with high cheekbones. I can't place her ethnicity.

"I am Russian. I come to LA to be a model. It did not turn out well." That's all she says as she turns and starts to walk away.

I don't move, I stand contemplating what to do. Fuck, do I follow her? What choice do I have, she offered to help me. She turns back to me.

"You come," is all she says and starts to walk away again.

I follow, but I keep watching everyone around me. I see people looking at us. I follow behind her gripping my bag to my chest, not walking as fast as she is but enough that I don't lose sight of her. Every now and then she turns slightly to see if I'm following. I see why she could have been a model, she's tall, skinny and I suspect had beautiful silky hair. Now though, not a chance looking the way she does. I want to find out how she got like this, but I don't think she would tell me at this point. Her English is good, I could understand her perfectly, but she is very harsh with the way she speaks and her words. No feeling in them at all.

We walk for a while, my feet are hurting me, I notice there aren't as many people where we are now, and it's gotten darker but not quite completely dark yet. I'm not sure I like where we're going but then I have no idea where we are or where we are headed. She turns down an alleyway. I stop. She turns to me.

"Come, it is okay. You will be safe with me."

I don't know her, she's already attacked me and who knows where she's taking me. Who knows what awaits me wherever we go? I don't trust her, why should I when I've only just met her? Do I turn and leave and head for the nearest church to try and get help or do I go with her?

"Where are we going and who will be there?" I ask. The last thing I need is trouble after just getting out of the hospital. I'm still not right, my head hurts, my chest hurts, my tummy hurts and I wouldn't be surprised if that's opened up now from her kicking me, my feet smart when I walk, and my palms are sore from the cuts, oh and I have a missing fucking toe. Yay, go me.

"Just my friends, just up here." She nods ahead.

She and her friends, yeah that's what I'm afraid of. They could over-power me, especially if they are all like her. I'm standing, contemplating what to do when I feel someone come up behind me. I jerk my head around suddenly to see who it is, ready if someone attacks me. It's a man, he's a lot taller than me and he looks well-dressed, he looks clean, not homeless. He's probably a little older than me, maybe in his early thirties, but looking at him, although I'm fucking scared, his eyes put me at ease. He smiles at me showing his white teeth, but he has the bluest eyes, they almost look like mine. I can't stop staring at them.

"Hey, are you okay? Do you need any help?" He smiles at me, but I hear a slight accent in his tone but only slight, not as prominent as the girl I'm foolishly following. He takes a step closer, he's so close I can feel him against my back.

I start to turn to face him, but he holds the top of both my arms gently to stop me. He's touching me, I should feel scared, I should run, but I don't, I feel sparks shooting through my body from his touch. Why am I not shitting myself at this point? Why am I feeling fucking turned-on with him touching me? I don't get it. I should be shoving him away from me and running from them both.

"Svetlana, who do we have here?" He speaks over my head.

I feel his breath on the top of it. I look to her, she's looking at him, but she looks scared. If she's scared of him, then I should be fucking terrified.

She just shrugs. "I do not know her name. I did not ask." She looks to me.

"What is your name?"

I scowl at her. Why can't he ask me instead of asking her? I shrug out of his hold and I step to the side. I'm now sideways to them both so I can watch them. I look from one to the other. She looks terrified and he looks hot as fucking hell. I look at him from bottom to top.

He has smart black polished shoes, a dark blue pinstripe suit, with a hand in his trouser pocket, but I see an expensive Rolex watch on his wrist, the other hand is on his face where he is scratching his smooth chin. He has the most beautiful face I have ever seen, his eyes are blue and kind looking. He has dark eyebrows but his hair is a dirty blond that doesn't match them. Maybe he dyes it. His hair is kind of long for a man it's wavy and messy but in a hot way. I could imagine running my fingers through it. He's smiling at me. He is beautiful, I feel like he's cast some kind of spell on me, I'm just staring at him with his chiseled looks.

"ебать (fuck). What is your name?" she asks me again in part Russian and part English, sounding angry, but I don't turn to her.

I can't, I'm mesmerized by him, he's still smiling, he has beautiful full lips that are heart-shaped, and I'm sure any woman would envy.

"She will not answer me. You ask her." I hear her saying, but I don't acknowledge her.

He takes a step closer to me, he's in my space and I have to look up into his face the closer he gets.

"What is your name, little one?" He runs a finger down my cheek, and I don't even flinch. Instead, I melt at his touch. I close my eyes, I suddenly feel his breath at my mouth which I didn't realize was even open. "Are you going to tell me, or do I just call you мой ангел (my angel)?"

I open my eyes and he's right in my face, looking deep into my eyes. I have no idea what he just said or called me but I just nod. I can't speak at this point. Who the fuck am I? Since when has anyone ever rendered me speechless?

"Come with me, I will make sure you are safe." He stands up tall and speaks to Svetlana. "Светлана, иди и приготовь комнату с горячей едой (Svetlana, go and prepare a room with hot food)."

I have no idea what he just said but she turns with a huff and walks off leaving him here with me. I'm like the Jell-O from my cup earlier, I think I'm going to collapse. I feel all funny, kind of weird like I'm having an out-of-body thing, but I don't think it's anything to do with him being close to me and more to do with me being in so much pain and being hungry.

I wake up in a bed. It doesn't feel nice, it's hard and the covers are itchy against my body. Fuck, why do they scratch my whole body? I lift them up slowly and see I'm naked underneath. What the fuck. I look around the room. Where is this? I have no idea, the room is pretty bare, not much in it, the walls are clean to some degree, they are all whitewashed with nothing on them. There is a small, high window, and the door is closed. The light coming through the window is enough to tell me it's daytime and illuminates the room enough for me to see. I sit up and look around. There's a small basket in the corner of the room that has my clothes and my bag in there, there is a bucket in another corner which I can only imagine is my toilet.

I sit, trying to remember what happened. It's then the beautiful face of the man comes into my head and I remember Svetlana and him. I remember she turned and left and then I looked at him and that was it, I don't remember anything else after that. But that beautiful face.

I pull the cover off me; I need to get dressed. My head is killing me, I go to stand up but I fall on my knees. What the fuck is wrong with me. The hospital cleared me. They said I was good to go. I need to pee. I crawl to the bucket in the corner, managing to get up using the wall and I crouch over it and pee. I get up and get dressed, throwing on yesterdays clothes, I assume it was yesterday. I notice I have fresh dressings on all my wounds. I don't know how long I've been in here. I notice the small table next to the bed with some water. I rummage through my bag for my painkillers to take, but they're not there, neither are my two cups of Jell-O.

I head to the door to find out where I am, turning the handle, it's locked. No fucking way. I did not survive being buried alive and cut up by Nick to end up being held captive by some Russian lord, I just presume he's Russian because Svetlana is. I bang on the door.

"Let me out," I shout, slamming my fists on the door.

This is doing nothing for my head.

I sit back on the bed up against the wall with my legs tucked up and my chin resting on my knees. I don't know how long I've been sitting here when I hear the door being unlocked. I dive off the bed ready for who-ever comes through it. As it opens, I see him, it's those eyes and that hair, in fact, it's just him. Him with the most beautiful face, dressed in a suit as he was when I first saw him. I couldn't tell you if it's the same suit or not, this giant of a man that rendered me speechless. Well, speechless no more.

"Why am I locked in here? Where am I? You can't keep me locked up here. Who are you and who got me naked? How long was—"

He puts his finger to his mouth. "Shhhhh, I will answer your ques-tions after you have eaten."

I look and he has a tray in his other hand with food and orange juice. My tummy rumbles and he laughs.

"Мой ангел."

I frown at him. I don't know what he's saying.

"My angel, that is what I said, it is in Russian which is where I am from."

Ah his angel, I think I actually blush. I take the tray from him and sit on the bed against the wall with it on my lap. I start to eat. This is the first decent food I've had. There's bacon, scrambled eggs, sausage links, biscuits, and coffee as well as the orange juice I spotted. I eat all of it. He just stands watching me, leaning against the doorjamb with his arms crossed over his chest. I look up and he's smiling at me.

"Are you going to answer my questions now? Who are you?"

"I am Igor, you met Svetlana yesterday, she is my ward, I am her un-cle. You fainted in my arms yesterday and I carried you in here. I did in-deed undress you, and I tended to your injuries, I have to say you have some interesting wounds on your body. Now, you must tell me how you got them."

I feel so ashamed, how could he undress me, and he doesn't even know me. I've never fainted in my life, not that I can remember, anyway. I'm embarrassed, I can't look at him.

"Мой ангел. Look at me. Do not be bashful, I have seen it all before." He motions to my body with his hand.

I look at him and he's now got his thumb at the side of his mouth and he's smiling at me. I bury my head in my hands. I hear him move, then feel the bed dip as he sits next to me, he pries my hands apart.

"Мой ангел. Please do not worry. You are safe here. Do you want to tell me about your injuries and why you were out on the streets with nowhere to go? I promise you are not in any danger."

I look at him, I mean really look at him and as weird as it sounds, I feel I can trust him. He seems caring but that could just be a front. I open up to him and I tell him everything about Nick and what he did to me. I only looked at his face a couple of times whilst telling him and I could see his jaw tensing and him balling his fists up. By the time I've finished telling him, he's taken me in his arms and is pressing my head to his chest. I didn't realize I was crying while telling him what had happened.

"Shh, Мой ангел. You are safe now. I will help you."

I look up into his face. "What do you mean you will help me? What will it cost me for your help?" I'm not a fool, I've been there before and there is no way I am going back to whoring myself for anyone. Svetlana seemed afraid of him, maybe I need to be careful here. If he's a Russian mobster, which I know exists, then I need to be very cautious.

"I will help you get some ID, that is the first thing I can do for you. It will not be legitimate, but it will be enough for you to then get your official ID back. That way you can do as you please. It will not cost you anything. I do not want any money for helping you. мой ангел."

I don't believe him. Nothing is ever free.

"Igor, thank you for what you have done for me, but I think it would be best if I just leave now. That way I will not be indebted to you and we can part on friendly terms." Maybe I'm playing with fire here, but I will not be held captive ever again.

He kisses the top of my head. He's very over-friendly. He doesn't say anything as he leaves me in the room, locking the door behind him. Fuck. That means I've upset him. I sit on the bed and I wait. It feels like hours pass before the door opens again. I wait, expecting Igor, but it's Svetlana.

She doesn't smile. she closes the door behind her making sure no one is there. I watch her as she comes and sits on the bed next to me.

"I shouldn't be here, but Igor has left, I needed to come and tell you to be careful. He is a dangerous man if you cross him. I will help you escape him but it may take a day or two. He is due to leave in two days and head to New York, he has a big family gathering to attend."

I frown at her. Do I believe her? Do I trust her? She was, after all, the one who brought me here in the first place.

"Why would you help me, Svetlana? You don't know me, and you were the one who brought me here."

She looks down.

"Why are you not going with him, to New York? I mean, if he is your uncle and it's a big family gathering he is going to. Is that not your family also?"

She looks at me but it's not the hard look she kept giving me yesterday, this is a much softer look.

"He is not my real uncle, he found me on a trip to Russia and he promised me the world back in LA if I joined him. I was only fif… sixteen at the time, so my mama said he could be my ward. She trusted him, he gave her so much money, he basically bought me. I have never done any modeling jobs for him. He used me as his whore for a short time, until he got a new ward. He then put me to work on the streets for him. I am his lookout when he is doing business. I have to pretend to be homeless, I saw him watching you yesterday and I knew he wanted you. It is why I came over. He was watching me and wanted me to befriend you. I had to make it look like we were fighting, hoping you would get away, but you didn't, and he was watching everything. I had no choice but to offer to help you. He followed us until he showed himself to you." She hangs her head.

I look at her closely. I don't see track marks on her arms. She took her shoes off when she sat back on the bed next to me. I look to her feet. It's hard to tell from here, so I edge forward on the bed and I grab her feet and spread her toes. She has needle marks between them, as I suspected. That is why she looks as bad as she does. I was in the same place she is, and I've seen so many young girls in the same situation since.

She pulls her foot away from me. "What are you doing?" she shouts at me, then remembers she's not supposed to be in here and lowers her voice. "I have no choice. He does this to me."

"I've been in your position before, Svetlana. You can get out of it. If you help me get out of this then I will help you once we are out."

She looks at me quizzically. "You would help me?"

I nod and smile at her. "We need a plan though. I don't have any ID or money and he said he could get me a fake ID so I can at least get my driver's permit back and some money. If we wait till I have the new ID then make a move—"

"No, you cannot wait that long. He will use you." She looks worried. I have to think about this.

"I don't want you getting caught in here. You go and think of the best plan. If he wants me as you say, and if he doesn't drug me, then I can play along until I get my ID. Once I have it, we can both get out of here. Is he likely to keep me locked up?"

She shakes her head. "He will have you stay with him. He has a suite in this building. He owns the building. You will be free to wander around his floor, but he will not let you go anywhere else without someone following you. Once you are with him, it may be harder to escape."

"We can do this. Hang tight. Now you need to leave so you don't get into any trouble."

Once she has locked the door with me inside, I sit and think about my options. At this moment, I don't see I have many. I need to see how he is going to treat me and deal with my American ways, rather than his scared submissive Russian girls' ways. I will get out and in one piece, I have to, I'm a survivor.

Four

Poppy
Present

I'VE BEEN SITTING ON THE BENCH WATCHING THE HOSPITAL FRONT door forever now. It's a good thing I've learned to be patient. The old me would have gone in there and killed Blaine by now. I see him come out with Aunt Cassy. I put my head down as he looks around. I'm too far away to hear what they are saying, but when I take a peek from under my hood, he's looking up to the sky as though praying. Aunt Cassy is rubbing his arm. He looks like he's crying from here. I wouldn't have put him down as a crier. I wonder if something's happened to Prim. Has she finally died? Be good if she has. Then my revenge will just be on him for what he put me through. I'm sure she is still alive though, I think I would have felt something if she had died.

———

A year ago

Igor came back for me that night. He took me to his suite as Svetlana said he would. What an amazing place, you would have thought royalty lived in it.

"Igor, this place is amazing. So big and luxurious. Do you live here, or do you just stay sometimes?"

He smiles as he watches me move around the apartment. He's leaning against the wall with one leg crossed over the other and his thumb at the side of his mouth. That smile is to die for, and it makes me want him no matter the circumstances.

"Мой ангел. This is my home, I own the building."

I must have looked a little crestfallen.

"Why the sad look on your face, мой ангел? Did I say something wrong?"

I just shrug then turn away from him. I feel it when he comes up behind me. He puts his hands on my shoulders and turns me to face him. He smells divine, I could just eat him. I blush thinking those thoughts. I've never blushed before, maybe he intimidates me, and I like it. He places a finger under my chin to make me look him in the eye.

"What is wrong?"

"I just wondered, if you own the building, why was I locked in a little room with no toilet and a horrible bed? Why was I not put in a nicer room?"

He laughs and pulls me into his chest and hugs me. I feel the rumbles from his laugh throughout my body and I need to get away from him before I embarrass myself further.

"I would have put you in here, мой ангел, with me, but I didn't want you to think I was being forward. We don't know each other, but I feel you are special. I don't even know your name. Tell me, мой ангел, what is your name?"

"Poppy." I almost whisper it. Who the fuck am I right now in front of him? I've gone all timid and shy and that's not me at all.

"Ноппи, that is Poppy in Russian. I will just call you my angel, мой ангел. Come, let me show you where you will stay. Please make yourself at home here, anything you need, just let me know and I will have someone fetch it for you."

He takes my hand and leads me to a bedroom down a long corridor. I need to pay attention to which door I'm led to, there are so many. He opens the door and lets me enter first. Wow, this place is amazing, I gasp, it's like something you would expect a princess to sleep in. He comes up behind me and wraps his arms around my waist, placing his hands on my tummy very gently and rests his chin on my shoulder. He's so forward, we don't know each other, yet he's always touching me in some way, maybe it's the Russian way. Dare I say, I like it though?

"You like мой ангел?"

I nod my head. I don't want him to think he has me because it's beautiful. It's not like I'm from a poor background or anything, but I have never seen richness to this extent before. There is gold everywhere, it wouldn't surprise me if it's real gold. He takes my hand and leads me to one of the two double doors to my left. He opens the doors then takes me inside and I gasp again. It's a closet, filled with clothes, beautiful clothes, there is everything from normal jeans and sweaters to T-shirts then long ball gowns, some very sexy ones. There are rows and rows of shoes. Heels to sneakers. I bet if I took a real close look, they would all be expensive.

"They will all fit you, I checked your size when I undressed you last night and had my people go shopping today for these. I hope you like them."

I wander around the inside of this huge closet. This closet alone is the size of my last apartment, almost. There is an island in the middle.

"Look inside," he prompts.

I open the top drawer and it's filled with jewelry, expensive jewelry, there are rows of Patek Philippe, Rolex, and Cartier watches. There must be hundreds and thousands of dollars' worth.

"These are for you, мой ангел," he says, coming back up behind me and putting his arms back around my tummy. "Open the next few drawers."

I do and in the next one which is a deeper drawer, there are rows of underwear, some very sexy ones. The next drawer is full of lace basques and corsets.

"They are my favorite, мой ангел, I hope to see them on you very soon. Do you like?"

I nod, how can I not like? There he goes again, being very forward and presumptuous. I must have the biggest smile on my face though, I like it. He takes my hand again and leads me out and back into the bedroom. He heads for the next set of double doors and opens them both to reveal the biggest bathroom I have ever seen. He takes me inside, there is a double vanity in gold, another separate room which I presume is the toilet, then there is a huge shower room with seats and power jets. In the middle of the room there is a huge claw-foot bathtub, the claws and taps are all in gold.

"I will leave you to get cleaned up. You take a bath or a shower and I will have some dinner prepared for you. I will join you for dinner in one hour. Do not be late and wear something nice." This is said more as a command rather than a suggestion, he's telling me, not asking me.

I stand and nod my head. Since when have I been so fucking submissive to any man, he just has this aura about him, this authoritative aura that makes me want to do as he says. He once again comes up behind me and wraps his arms around me. He leans into my neck and kisses it gently and I melt into him. He has me pressed against his front and I can feel he is hard. He peppers my neck up to my ear with kisses.

"Get cleaned, you smell, мой ангел."

I freeze, the fucking nerve of him. He feels me go rigid, kisses the top of my head, then leaves. I wander around the rooms, looking in all the drawers that are filled with things. I check the door to see if I am locked in, but it opens. I close it, but I lock it from the inside. I don't want just anyone to walk in. I take a long hot bath and just lay in the hot soapy water. It's been a long time since I took a bath, it feels so good. I then jump into the shower and wash my hair. I'm sure I have taken far longer than an hour, but I don't care. I'm at the vanity in the bathroom, bent forward to blow the underside of my hair when I feel a body pressed against my ass, and someone gripping hold of my hips. I jolt up, grabbing my towel to make sure it doesn't fall off me, dropping the hairdryer in the process, as I try to swing around.

"What the fuck," I say to a smiling Igor, only his smile drops as he grips my hips tighter and grinds his cock against my ass.

"Don't ever use language like that in front of me, ever, мой ангел. This is your one and only warning."

I don't speak, I just nod. He loosens his grip but continues to get himself aroused on my naked ass. He has his suit trousers on, with a white shirt, it's unbuttoned and hanging around his body.

I stand up straight and lean my back to his front, but I'm still gripping the front of my towel. He slowly takes my hands, prying my fingers from the towel and it drops to the floor. I watch us in the mirror. I watch his beautiful face light up at the sight of me. I managed to shave in the bath, so I am all clean and shaven. He nuzzles my neck and his wandering hands reach for my breasts. He takes a breast in each hand and starts to rotate them. I wince from the pain. He looks up in the mirror and sees it on my face and stops immediately.

"I am so sorry, мой ангел. I got carried away, I forgot about your injuries." He moves away from me and I turn to face him.

"Please, Igor, don't be sorry. I'm just a little fragile, that's all."

"We need to let you heal properly first. I will not hurt you, in any way." He sounds sincere. Yet somehow I think if I crossed him, he wouldn't hesitate to hurt me, and going off Svetlana, I would say she's been hurt. I smile at him and stroke his cheek. He takes my hand and kisses my palm first on one hand then lifts the other and does the same.

"You have much healing to do, мой ангел. We must make sure you heal well first. Now come, you are late, get dressed, dinner is waiting."

He walks out with such swagger. I bet he commands attention from any room he enters, without even trying. I don't know what he wants me to wear, but I suspect nothing is going to happen between us until I've healed. I put on a little royal blue Gucci dress. It's crushed velvet on the front with a very low V-back almost to the top of my ass, I don't put on a bra and I pull out a lacy royal blue thong. I put on some matching royal blue Gucci shoes. Everything fits perfectly. I dress it up with a blue topaz choker and blue topaz teardrop earrings. My hair is up in a messy bun on the top of my head and I have just a touch of makeup on. I scrub up well, even if I do say so myself.

I eventually find the dining room. Igor is standing at a floor to ceiling window looking out. It's so dark outside I don't know what he can see from here, I don't even know where here is.

"Ah, here is мой ангел, finally. You are very late for dinner, please never be late again." He turns to face me, he has his full suit on now all fastened up and he's holding a tumbler of clear liquid, I would say being Russian it's probably vodka, isn't that what all Russians drink? I watch as he takes me in from head to toe.

"абсолютно чертовски красивый."

"Igor, I don't speak Russian. What did you just say?" I laugh saying this and he smiles at me.

"Absolutely fucking beautiful, is what I just said," he says, smiling as he saunters toward me with that swagger he has and a look on his face that says he wants me for dinner. I smile back at him. He stands in front of me, then leans down and kisses my lips gently. I inhale with a gasp. He stands up straight and steps back to look at me. He puts his glass down on a table.

"Turn around for me, мой ангел, I want to take you all in."

I very slowly turn around doing a full three-sixty until I'm facing him again. He's standing with his thumb at the corner of his mouth.

"Again," he says a bit sternly.

I do, but this time when I have my back fully to him, he stops me by putting his hands on my hips. He comes up close and starts to pepper kisses from the top of my back all the way down my spine to my ass. I shiver at his touch and I feel him smile against my skin. He then heads back up, this time licking me all the way to the top, then back down again with the kisses, but between each kiss he speaks.

"Чертовски." Kiss.

"Красивые." Kiss, all the way, repeating these two words.

I laugh. "Igor, what are you saying?"

He licks back up my back and then with the kisses back down.

"Fucking." Kiss.

"Beautiful." Kiss.

Ah okay, I get it now. I shiver at each touch. He stands tall and pulls me to his chest, wrapping his arms around me. I think this is so I can feel just how hard he is. He starts to grind into me with his cock and this time I bend slightly, and I start to rub my ass on him. Suddenly he slaps my ass, not hard, it's gentle, a playful slap.

"Stop being a cock tease, мой ангел, or I may just take you here and now. Would you like that?"

My heart is nearly beating out of my chest. Yes, I would. I nod, it's slight but I know he sees it. He presses the top of my back forward so I'm bent over like I was in the bathroom. He runs his finger all the way down my spine but he doesn't stop where the material of the dress ends. He carries on right to the crack of my ass.

"I really liked this dress on you, мой ангел, but I fear it will not last long."

I'm bent completely over now with my ass in the air. He still has one hand around my front splayed gently on my tummy and the other is wandering back up my spine feeling the ridges as he does. He bends over me, peppering back down my back with kisses again. Murmuring in Russian as he does, I just can't hear what he's saying. When he gets to the bottom where the material is, he takes it in his teeth and between his free hand and his teeth, he rips it right open so it hangs at my sides. I hear him inhale as he takes me in bent over in front of him. He kneels on the floor behind me and starts to lick and nip my ass cheeks, then kiss them, alternating between each one. He spreads my cheeks open with his hands and licks inside. He takes the material of the thong in his teeth and using his hands he rips the thin strip. He slips his hand between my thighs and through my pussy to the front and he removes the material, throwing it on the floor in front of me.

He stays on his knees, licking my ass while sliding a finger through my folds. I hear him move, he's rising from the floor, he grips both my hips. He stands, grinding his cock on my ass as his fingers move around to the front and start to find their way to my pussy again. I widen my stance slightly to give him better access. He bends and kisses my back

"чертовски идеально." He starts to stroke me.

"Igor, English." I laugh at him as I start to breathe heavily from him rubbing my clit.

"I said, fucking perfect."

He then moves us without letting me go. He stands us up straight and turns us to face the huge dining table. He's still pressed to my back as we move forward stuck together. He moves the chair that is in the way to the side making it scrape across the marble floor and he edges us forward and gently bends me over on the table.

"I want you to place both your arms flat out in front of you on the tabletop."

I do as he asks, and he slightly pulls my hips away from the table. This leaves me bent over with him at my ass. With one hand, he slides it back to my pussy in the front and very gently he starts to stroke me. He edges between my lips and finds exactly how wet I am for him. His hand disappears from me and I hear him moan making a point to let me know he's sucking his fingers making them pop from his mouth. It turns me on even more.

"Мой ангел, you taste sweeter than I could ever have imagined. I need more."

Suddenly he's turning me over to face him, I see the look of lust all over his face, with hooded eyes. He edges me onto the tabletop so I am now sitting on it. He removes the remainder of my dress, I'm now completely naked and he parts my legs to stand between them looking down on me. He suddenly takes both my legs and holds them up by the calves, he's watching my face the whole time. He then spreads them farther apart to form a V-shape and his eyes wander straight to my very exposed pussy, he bends down and very slowly with his tongue he licks from my ass upward to my clit. He watches me, watching him as he does this. I find it so erotic; him watching me, and I start to pant. I start to play with my nipple, the good one, flicking it and pinching it, he watches me while flicking my clit with his tongue. He has no hands free at this time. He licks back down and suddenly inserts his tongue in my pussy. I gasp as he wiggles it around. I move my hand down to my clit and start to rub. He watches my every move and I see the look on his face. He pulls his tongue out and leans forward and kisses me hard. I'm still playing with my clit as he does this. I throw my head back, panting.

"Stop," he says firmly, and I look back to him. "This is mine," he says, putting one leg on a shoulder to free his hand, and he knocks my hand away and starts to flick and pinch my clit hard. He then swipes his finger through the wetness and inserts it inside me. "Вы чувствуете, вкус и запах чертовски идеально."

I am panting with my hand heading back to my clit.

"English, Igor," I pant out as he puts my other leg on his other shoulder, freeing up that hand to bat mine away from my clit.

"I said, you feel, taste, and smell fucking perfect." He bends down and starts to suck my clit while inserting more fingers inside me. He sucks and teases with his tongue while pumping in and out of me. I'm starting to slide on top of the table. I use my hands to try to brace myself. I throw my head back, closing my eyes, I'm panting as he nears the spot.

"Watch what I do, мой ангел."

I open my eyes and I watch his beautiful face as I raise up slightly on my elbows so I can see his hand and tongue working at my pussy. We stare at each other, blue eyes to blue eyes, I find this so fucking hot watching him. I start to move in rhythm with his fingers, in and out. He suddenly pulls them out and puts them in his mouth and sucks and licks like you would a popsicle.

"Hmmm, so fucking perfect. I'm going to taste you properly."

With that, he stands back slightly, my legs still over his shoulder and he lifts my ass off the table so it's mainly my upper body resting on it now. He puts my pussy to his mouth, and he sucks and licks hard. We are just staring into each other's eyes, it's so fucking erotic, I then watch his mouth carefully, watching his tongue flicking. He then buries his face right in there and bites my clit, gently then flicking, so much so, I'm writhing on the slippery tabletop. He then inserts his tongue inside me and oh god, I think I'm going to combust. He lets go of one leg and he inserts two fingers in my asshole. I shudder and stop, his eyes shoot to mine and I nod slightly, he starts to pump them in and out while doing the same in my pussy with his tongue. I reach and flick my clit and before I know it, I explode on his face. I scream out with my release in pure fucking ecstasy.

"Oh, my, fucking god, Igor," I scream over and over.

"Watch," he shouts into my pussy.

I lift my head up and I watch him taking all my juice into his mouth as I explode even more onto his tongue. I feel like I may black out, this is by far the best orgasm I've ever had and it just keeps going on and on. He pulls back slightly, and I actually see my juices squirting in his face. Oh my fucking god, I never knew a woman could do that, but apparently, we can. It's hot as hell, having this beautiful Russian god wanting me as he does. He stops after licking me clean and he smiles at me, letting my legs down gently.

"сладкий гребаный вкус от моего ангела."

I laugh at him. "English, please Igor."

"The sweetest fucking taste from my angel," he says, smiling.

He moves me back up the table slightly so I don't ache from my legs hanging off the edge. I watch him with a big smile on my face. I follow his hands as he undoes the zip on his trousers and pushes them down. I watch as his beautiful cock springs free and I lick my lips. He plays with himself for a minute, moving his hand gently up and down his cock and over the tip playing with the skin as he does, I watch fascinated. I see pre-cum on the tip and I want to taste him. I sit up, lean forward and bending down I lick the top of his cock while holding it in my hand. I lick and suck while moving my hand up and down.

"Mmmmm," I growl while doing this. "Fucking delicious," I say to him.

"Lay back," he says, gently pushing my shoulders.

I do as he says, but I keep my head raised to watch him. He once again lifts my legs up onto his shoulders and he lines his cock up to my pussy, he plays with it again, but on me this time, up and down in the folds of my lips and rubbing it around my clit. He then lines up and very gently eases himself inside me. I thought he would have rammed it in, but he's treating me like I'm made of glass. He sighs and looks up to the ceiling,

"совершенства, мы идеально подходят, мы были сделаны друг для друга."

I laugh and he looks at me and stops. "English Igor, English, so I can understand you."

"Perfection, we fit perfectly, we were made for each other."

I beam at him. He starts to thrust, gently at first, rotating as he does then he builds and builds until he realizes I'm not going to break and I'm screaming at him.

"Harder Igor, faster, harder."

He does, with such vigor, he thrusts harder and deeper every time. I feel my orgasm starting and I reach down and play with my clit. He slaps my hand away.

"Mine and only for me to do," he shouts, breathless and sounding angry but it's not anger.

He starts to play with my clit as he's thrusting harder and harder. I explode once again and he follows right after me. He shouts out at the top of his lungs as he explodes inside me. He's also reached up my chest and grabbed a nipple, pulling it harder and harder and groping my breast hard. Luckily, it's not the damaged one because even if it was, I don't think he would stop. He thrusts harder and deeper like he's trying to climb inside my pussy as he empties himself into me. We are a sweaty, sticky mess. He falls on top of me, taking deep breaths, trying to calm himself down. He's still twitching inside me, and I can feel myself constricting his cock as he does. Wow, I have no idea what he shouted as he came, but I don't really care. I start to stroke his hair, the hair I imagined doing just this to when I first met him. Jesus, was that only yesterday?

"Wow, Igor, that was unreal. Perfection, as you said."

He lifts his head up to me and smiles. He still has hold of my breast and I see the moment he realizes and looks to the other one.

"It's okay, it's not the broken one." I smile at him.

My head has started to throb again. The hospital did say not to exert myself, does this count? He raises up above me and leans farther up and kisses me hard. He inserts his tongue which tastes of me and he duels with mine. I feel his cock twitching, coming back to life inside me, he's getting hard again and before I know it, I've grabbed his ass cheeks, digging my nails in, pulling him into me as far as he can go, and he's off once more.

I wake up in bed with a heavy arm over my back as I'm facedown, but I don't know how or when I got here. I try to move but the arm is weighing me down and I'm praying at this point it's Igor lying beside me. I need to pee. I start to edge out of the bed sideways, he wakes up and looks at me.

"Hey, you okay, мой ангел? You seem to have this habit of passing out on me. You worried me, it's why I stayed in here with you. I'm sorry if it was presumptuous of me but I didn't want you to be alone."

I smile at him and lean over and kiss his shoulder. "Thank you for caring about me. I don't remember how I got here." I look down and see I'm naked. "It was easier for you this time with me already being naked, huh?" I laugh and he smiles that beautiful smile at me.

I look at him for a second and I wonder how this beautiful man could be anything other than gentle, how could he be a Russian mobster or lord or whatever he is, I know I don't know for sure, but to have this wealth and authority, he has to be something, right? I get up and I limp to the bathroom to pee. Those shoes I had on last night did not help my toe-less foot, never mind the cuts that are still healing. I also see dried blood around the bandage on my tummy. Fuck, it must have opened up again and I didn't notice.

"Leave the door open, I need to make sure you don't black out again," he says as he watches me try to sexily sashay, into the bathroom, which I do on purpose, even with a limp. He sighs and I turn just as he's burying his head in the pillows.

When I get back in bed, he's lying there on his back with both hands under his head. He's thinking, I see the crease in his brow. I lean over him and peer down into his perfectly beautiful face. Those eyes and that nose and those lips. He is perfection. I stroke down his cheek to his mouth which he opens and takes a finger and sucks it.

"What are you thinking about, Igor? You look intense." I smile down at him. He smiles back, pushing my finger out of his mouth with his tongue.

"I was thinking how careless I was last night. I never have sex without a condom. The last thing I want is lots of baby Igors out there that I don't know about."

I lay back down. That's just what a girl wants to hear from her Russian god, I'm sure. I feel a pang of jealousy thinking of all the other girls he's had. Who the fuck am I and what have I done with the real Poppy? I never feel jealousy for any man, well maybe I was with Nick, but I am never this submissive with anyone. I don't think he's good for me, and I think once he's done with me, he will just toss me aside expecting me to work for him, just like Svetlana. He lied to me, telling me he was her uncle. I lay there getting angrier and angrier at him. He leans up and looks me in the face, but I don't smile, and I look away. He grabs my cheeks and twist my head around to him.

"What is wrong, what is the mood for? What did I say wrong?"

A typical male as well.

"Nothing," I say, and I turn my back to him, lying on my side.

"You are mad at me, no?"

I don't speak.

"Never ignore me when I speak to you." He pulls me back so I'm lying on my back.

I'm pissed. Who the hell does he think he is giving me orders.

"I'm not on the pill, I didn't have any with me. I need to see a doctor. One, for the morning-after pill and then to prescribe the pill for me, and two, I need to know why I'm suddenly blacking out when the hospital cleared me. Then three, stop telling me what to do."

He creases his brow again and looks worried and annoyed.

"I shall get my physician to come here and see you. I will explain on the phone about the pills so he can bring them with him. Yes, is that okay with you?" His accent has gotten thicker. Maybe yesterday he was playing at being an American.

I nod at him. The next thing I know he's between my legs again getting his breakfast.

A few hours later and I'm sitting waiting for the doctor. Igor left after breakfast for his meetings and said I could use anything in the apartment and to treat it as my home, but I was not to go out without him knowing. And so it starts. I'm a captive here, I know it. I'm going to ask him about the fake ID tonight over dinner if he comes home. Suddenly a man appears in the room, he's holding a case.

"Are you Miss Poppy?" he asks.

I nod.

"I'm Dr. Leonard, I am Mr. Ustrashkins' doctor." I frown at him, "Igor tells me you need the morning-after pill and also for me to prescribe you some pills going forward. Can you tell me about your other injuries, he said you had?"

I roll my eyes. I feel embarrassed again. I run through and show him what happened to me. He's happy with the way everything is healing, even where my toe was cut off. I showed him my nipple, which has healed back nicely now. I told him about the headaches and the blackouts which I have never suffered with before. He said it would be best if I could get a CT scan as the hospital didn't do one of those on me, so he was going to arrange this and clear it with Igor first.

I took my pills, then wandered around the apartment. It was huge. I went looking in each of the rooms in the long corridor and there were a lot of bedrooms, all decorated nicely. My bedroom is by far the biggest. There were three doors that were locked, I think one was his bedroom, but I don't know why he would have it locked, and the others I have no idea. It's not his office because that is off the entrance hallway. There are lots of other rooms not in the hallway, and again some of those were locked. He said to treat it as my home, yet there are rooms it seems I'm not permitted to enter.

I head to the elevator, as I was going to find the floor where I was the first night, there is a guard sitting there.

"You are not to leave without Mr. Ustrashkins' say-so, Miss Poppy."

Great. So, what do I do all day while he is out? I don't have a cell or a computer. I have nothing. I head back to the library and I pick a book to read. I must have fallen asleep while reading, I'm suddenly woken by kisses on my legs, heading up to my pussy. I have no shame. I pretend to stretch and in doing so I spread my legs, giving him easy access. He doesn't waste any time. He rips my thong from me and before I know it he's eating me again, then I'm flipped over the chair and he's inside me, only he's not being so gentle with me today, not that I mind, I love it rough.

He sent me to get cleaned up for him and to wear something nice to dinner. I'm not late this time, I don't think I want to find out the consequences of disobeying him, but then again it might be fun. We sit to have dinner after he devoured my mouth when I entered the room.

"You look beautiful, мой ангел. That yellow dress makes you look all summery and is perfect with your hair. It suits you."

I blush. We eat and I want to ask him about the rooms and what my boundaries are, but he brings it up first.

"Mavra, my guard, said you wanted to leave in the elevator but he wouldn't let you as per my orders?"

I look at him and nod.

"Yes, I was going to see what was on the other floors to the building, I'm intrigued. I was bored here on my own and didn't know what to do. I have no cell phone, no laptop or tablet, I have nothing. I have always been on the go. Can I ask you, why are some rooms locked, are they out of bounds to me and why am I not to leave?"

He puts his knife and fork down and steeples his hands in front of him, looking straight at me. He doesn't look happy.

"Мой ангел, I do have some rooms out of bounds to everyone. Yes, not just to you. I have private things in them, and some are for other uses. As for you not leaving. It is not safe for you to be out when you are injured and don't know where you are. You also have no ID on you. I am just protection you. Now will you tell me all you can about this Nick who tried to kill you, I need every detail so my men can try to find him. I also need to know your last name and your birthdate. I need to know more about you, Poppy, and where you have come from."

I must look a little worried. There is no way he is getting to Nick, that is my job, that is for me to do, I will have my own revenge on him. Maybe if I play it cool, I can get some tips on torture from Igor, if that's what he does, of course. Maybe he will show me how to get my revenge. I mirror him and put my knife and fork down, steepling my hands in front of me.

"Igor, thank you for wanting to protect me, but I am a big girl and I'm sure I will be safe enough out there. As for Nick, I only know his first name. I don't know anything else about him. But I don't want you to try to find him, I want to be the one who gets him and get my revenge. It has to be me, no one else. I would maybe ask for advice on how exactly to do this, you know, if say, for instance, you knew of any ways to do this or had any advice or ideas." I give him my best sultry smile and lick my lips. I watch as his eyes widen, watching me.

"You want to do that? You want to be the one to get revenge. Well, мой ангел, you do surprise me, I thought you would like someone else to do this. I think also, I may have a few ideas up my sleeve." He smiles.

"Now tell me about your family, your name, your birth, everything."

I smile back at him and lick my lips provocatively. He's up and on me before I know it. We end up in my bed. I still have questions, I suppose they will just have to wait.

"Igor," I say, running my fingertips up and down his back as I watch his beautiful face as he tries to sleep. He opens one eye.

"What is it, мой ангел?"

"Why have you not taken me to your bed? Why in here, in my room, why do I have a separate room if you clearly want me?"

He opens both eyes to look at me. "In time, мой ангел, when I am ready, I will take you to my bed. The only person I would ever take to my bed would be my wife. My bed is only for me and my wife."

I bolt upright. Is he fucking married? I scowl at him, trying to read him, but his face is so beautiful and so hard to read.

"Are you telling me you have a wife? Are you fucking kidding me right now?" I sit and pull my knees up to my chest and wrap my arms around them. I start to rock. Is he married? Is that why his room is locked, does he have a wife in there? What the fuck have I gotten myself into. Maybe I was a fool to think I could play along with this and get my ID, then help Svetlana. What am I going to do? I feel him sit up,

"Hey, мой ангел, what is wrong?" He starts stroking my arm. I turn and glare at him.

"Are you fucking married? Do you have a wife locked up in your room? Is that why the door's locked? Is that why we end up in here and not in there?" I shout at him and I see the anger slowly transforming his face.

He turns from the most beautiful man I've ever seen to the most dangerous man I think I have ever met, which rules Nick out. He climbs off the bed and heads around to my side. He grabs my arm and drags me from the bed.

"Hey, you're hurting me, Igor, stop, please stop."

He has a tight hold of my upper arm and if I don't walk with him, he will just drag me along the floor.

"IGOR," I scream at him and he stops. He looks at me, then at his hold on me, and he suddenly lets go as if he's been burnt. I fall to the floor. It was only his hold on my arm that was keeping me up. I look up at him and I see the horror on his face. In a second he's on the floor next to me and he pulls me onto his lap and cradles me to his chest.

He's chanting over and over. "Мне так жаль, пожалуйста, прости меня."

Of course I have no idea what he's saying. I'm somehow sitting in his lap on the floor, and I'm crying into his chest. He hurt my arm, he nearly pulled it out of its socket, but it's not the pain, I've been through worse, it's the murderous look on his face that terrified me.

He's still chanting while rocking me, I look up to him and I see the sorrow on his face. He peppers my face with kisses, still saying the same words.

"English, please Igor."

He takes my face in his hands and he wipes away the tears with his thumbs and kisses my nose then gently on the lips.

"I'm so sorry, please forgive me."

I sigh and close my eyes. He kisses each of my eyelids very gently then back to my mouth. He deepens the kiss, inserting his tongue in my mouth. He's not getting me that easily. I don't respond, but I know I have to be very careful with him, I've only known him a very short time and he's already shown me this side of himself.

"Come with me." He starts to move me aside, then gets up, helping me.

He takes my hand, and he leads me into the corridor and we stand outside one of the locked rooms. He disappears for a minute, telling me to wait. When he returns, he has a bunch of keys and unlocks the door in front of us. He opens it and guides me in, pushing gently on my lower back. I walk in cautiously. I have no idea what's in this room. I stand in the middle and I look around. There's no one in the room, in fact, the room is very sparse. There is a giant four-poster bed, some drawers, and that's it, really. To the side, I see two double doors similar to those in my room, which I assume are the bathroom and walk-in closet. What the fuck was all the fuss about this room? I turn on him.

"You hurt me like that for what. For this?" I throw my arms up in the air. "There's nothing in here. Is this your room? What was all that about a wife? This is clearly a man's room, so minimalistic, it's not even homey. I can't believe you fucking nearly pulled my arm out of its socket for this." I'm angry, I throw my arms up to indicate the room.

I see his look go from murderous again, to well, what? I watch the amusement on his face. He starts to laugh. He starts to laugh so hard he's in hysterics. I just stand with my hand on my hips. This is not funny.

He comes to me and he takes my head and kisses my forehead.

"Мой ангел, my angel, you are a very strong-willed woman and I fucking love it. What I don't love is your foul mouth, Poppy. That is what makes me angry." He stands back and looks down at me.

I'm still pissed, and I fold my arms over my chest. It's then I realize I'm naked as I look down my body. I didn't even think to cover up. What if his guards are around? He sees me coming to the realization that I'm naked.

"Do not worry, no one will see you. I will burn their eyeballs if they do." He shrugs like it's normal. It also helps he's stark naked too.

I run my eyes down his body, he's hard as usual. I take his cock and start to stroke him, then I go to my knees and I take him into my mouth until he's coming all over me, his cum running down my chest.

"This is my room as you gathered, the only thing I really use it for is the closet and to sleep on my own. This room is sacred to me, it will be the room I will make love to my wife in. No, I do not have a wife to answer your question. I have been looking for a strong woman for a long time. Most women I fuck are too scared of me and too submissive. I hate that. I am the king and I want a queen, not a servant. Once I have a wife, we will make this room ours. That is why I do not bring anyone in this room. It is untouched by any woman and you are the first to be in here, let alone giving me an orgasm in here. That is unheard of and now it is one I must repay."

I'm still on my knees in front of him, he kneels with me then slowly pushes me back and he fucks me. But this is a very different, slow fuck, he's watching me with such adoration on his face, I would say he is making love to me in his room, just not on his bed.

I'm falling hard for this dangerous Russian. God help me.

Five

Poppy
Present

I FOLLOW BLAINE FROM THE HOSPITAL GROUNDS. AUNT CASSY left him there when Uncle Trevor picked her up. I watched them say goodbye, he then stood there looking up to the sky and saying something. If she was dead, I'm sure I would have felt it, I always feel it when she's in pain, I'm sure the twin thing would have kicked in. I haven't felt anything for a few days. I don't know if she's been on life support and that is why or if she's recovering well. I need to find out for myself. First, I need to set my plan in motion. My revenge plan.

I follow him out onto the main street, wondering where he's going. He usually just heads home, but for some reason, he's gone in the opposite direction. He doesn't have a car. He walks everywhere, which suits me just fine. I don't let him see me. I will allow that when the time is right. I need to follow his pattern to set things up, but this isn't his pattern. He turns off onto Stanley Street. Why would he be going down there? There's nothing there, it's residential. I follow him but keep my distance. I stop as I see him go up some steps to a house. Who the fuck does he know here? Is he fucking someone else? I thought he was in love with Prim, his soul mate. I've never seen him come here before in the weeks I've been following him. Five minutes later, I walk past the house he disappeared into. I go slowly to see if I can see in the window, but I can't see anything, the windows are too high up. I make a note of the door number. I need to find out who lives here and why the fuck he would be visiting. He's screwing with my head.

I stay at the end of the street, facing where he would come out. It's getting late and there is no sign of him. I even checked on my cell to see if I could find out who lives at that address, but the hacks Igor showed me bring up a Mr. Lund. I searched that name, but there are several Mr. Lunds in the California area. I wait and wait, told you I was patient. He comes out, it's eight-thirty, he's been in there for a couple of hours. What the fuck would he be doing?

I follow him again and this time he heads for Prim's house. He stops at the mini-mart first, then he goes home. I stand outside of Prim's, looking up, I'm playing a dangerous game here. If he spots me, he will run for me. Maybe I like the thrill. I see him in the window, it's dark and I'm all in black so he doesn't see me. He stands there with his hands in his jeans pockets, he's deep in thought, he looks like he's aged from here. He looks a little gaunt, but he's still as gorgeous as ever. The one I thought I would get, but he had Prim's heart all along. He will die if my plan works. He killed my parents and he tried to kill me. He chose Prim over me. Precious Primrose, the one everyone loves 'cause they feel sorry for her. Well, I suppose I only have myself to blame for that. I sit on the wall behind me and I think back to when we were five, when it all started.

Poppy age 5

Why is it she gets all the attention from Mama and Pappy? Why is she so special? It was her own stupid fault she stuffed those things in her ears. I only said to do it as a joke, kind of. Fancy doing that though and getting them stuck all the way in. It's not like I didn't help her push them in, well only a couple of them. She was struggling, so I offered to help, I held her head and I stuffed them in deeper, in both ears. She cried out 'cause I hurt her. I bent over, feeling as though I was in pain and I cried out, it hurt, my ears hurt me bad. Mama and Pappy came running in to see what was wrong with us, and why Prim was crying. They rushed her to the hospital, and I had to stay with Aunt Cassy. I didn't mind doing that, I love Aunt Cassy, she spoils me, because it's just me on my own. I ended up sleeping at Aunt Cassy's because I heard her speaking to Mama on the telephone and they were going to do something to Primrose, I don't know what and I didn't care. We watched a movie and she made some popcorn just for the two of us.

The next day Aunt Cassy took me home, but it was late, I remember it being dark. I missed school as well. I didn't mind that though, but it was all because of Primrose, it was all her fault. Mama, Pappy, and Prim all came home a little later. Pappy was carrying her into the house. She looked so small in his big arms. Why wasn't it me in his arms? He took her straight up to her bedroom, and Mama and Pappy spent most of the time fussing over her. They didn't even speak to me apart from kissing my head at bedtime and to say goodnight. When I was in my bedroom, I could hear them going into Prim's room constantly seeing if she needed anything. I didn't know what was wrong with her. Aunt Cassy tucked me up in bed. It wasn't fair.

The next morning, I got myself ready, I'm a big girl and can do it all on my own. Prim was still in her bedroom. I stood at her open door for a little bit, just watching her. She wasn't asleep. What was wrong with her? Why wasn't she getting up and getting ready?

"Hey Prim, don't be so lazy. Get up, it's time for school. Mama will have breakfast ready now."

She didn't speak to me. She looked at me blankly then she burst out crying, loudly. I wasn't mean to her. I don't know what's wrong with her. She cried so loud that Pappy came running out of his room. He was half-dressed, his shirt his shirt was hanging down and not buttoned up. I laughed at him, but he scowled at me.

"What did you do to Prim?"

He was angry with me. She carried on crying, very loud. I've never heard her cry like that before. He looked at Prim, then shouted at me

"What did you do to her? Get down the stairs for your breakfast, Poppy. You have no right to be upsetting your sister like this."

I was shocked at the way he was shouting at me. Pappy didn't usually shout, that was usually Mama.

I moved away from Prim's room. First, I gave her a dirty look, then I slowly moved toward the stairs, hanging my head. I turned and saw Pappy sitting on Prim's bed with her in his arms. He was comforting her. Why? She cried for no reason. She looked fine to me. She's just playing it up for attention. When I got to the kitchen, Mama was making pancakes for us all. She had a tray out with some on it which I suppose was for Prim. She gets special treatment and can eat in her room. All because she stuffed stupid things in her ears. It's her own fault. Why does she get special treatment?

"Hey Poppy, what was your pappy shouting about?"

I don't speak. I climb onto the stool, ready for my pancakes. Mama puts a plate in front of me.

"Poppy, what was Pappy shouting about?" she repeats.

I shrug. "Prim crying, he thought I did it. I didn't, Mama, I didn't do anything," I say with a sad face.

The next thing I know, she's rushing up the stairs with the tray for Prim. I hate Princess Primrose. Maybe I should do something silly! Then maybe they will spend time with me. I look around the kitchen. I see a knife on the other side. Mama and Pappy always tell us no to touch knives because they can hurt us. If I could reach it and cut my hand, then they will have to come and see to me. Maybe Pappy will take me into his arms, maybe I can eat in my room too.

I jump down from the stool, I'm on my tiptoes, I reach over the side and I can just feel it with my fingertips. If I push, I won't be able to get it. I climb back onto the stool and I get the spoon Mama left me for my syrup. She knows I like to scoop it up. I take the spoon to the side and on my tippy toes again, I reach up and with one scoop of the spoon I bring the knife to the edge and watch it fall to the floor. I hear Pappy coming down the stairs, so I pick the knife up and I cut across my hand. I scream out, dropping the knife, and clench my hand. I see blood dripping onto the floor. My pappy comes running in.

"Pops, what is it? What's wrong?" He comes running over to me and sees the blood drops on the floor. I cry.

"What did you do?" He kneels in front of me and gently takes my hand to have a look. He gently opens it, I see blood, he looks closely.

"It's okay, it isn't deep. Let me get a cloth and a bandage and you will be all fixed. Come with me to the sink."

He lifts me up and runs my hand under the faucet. I watch as the blood disappears down the drain and see I only have a small cut on my hand. He dries it off and places the sticky bandage across it. He puts me back on the floor and tells me to finish my breakfast. He then gets his coffee and pancakes and sits at the island across from me. He doesn't speak to me again, just sits reading his paper. I just got a cut and that's it. What a waste that was. It hurt me too. I should have stabbed myself hard.

"Pappy?"

He doesn't answer me.

"Pappy?"

Nothing. He's too busy drinking his coffee and reading.

"PAPPY?" I shout.

He lowers the paper. "What, Pops?" He looks angry with me.

Why are they angry with me?

"What's wrong with Prim? Why did she cry? I didn't do anything to her, Pappy?"

He sighs.

"I know you didn't, she's just upset. You talked to her and she couldn't hear you."

I look at him confused. Of course, she heard me, she cried. "She heard me, that's why she cried."

He shakes his head. "Pops, Prim can't hear any of us anymore. She's lost her hearing."

I'm so confused.

"Well, can't you find it for her if she lost it?"

He gives me a small smile.

"It's not that easy, Poppy, I wish it was. When she stuffed the foam into her ears, she broke her ears inside, and they can't be fixed. So now Primrose doesn't hear anything at all. It's hard for her to understand what's happening, and when you spoke to her, she got upset because she didn't know what you were saying. We just have to be gentle with her for a while, while she gets used to it. Then we must teach all of us, how to talk to each other, all over again. Do you understand that, Poppy?"

I nod. "I think so. She doesn't know what we are saying to her? How are we going to talk if she can't hear us?"

"Well, she will learn to read our lips so she can see what we are saying, and then your mama says we all need to learn to talk using our hands. That's called sign language. We all need to learn, including you, Pops."

I roll my eyes. Great, school's hard enough, I can only just write my name, Prim can write better than me. She can write big lines with lots of words, words I can't quite read. She's smarter than me. I hate her.

—

Present

All these years and she never told anyone it was me that gave her the idea to stuff the foam pieces into her ears and that it was me that stuffed the last ones in as deep as I could. It was because of that, she became the favorite. I think they all would have been happy if I wasn't there. It's also why I pretended to be sick when they went to see Grandma. She always got special treatment from everyone, all because she couldn't hear. Who knows, it might have been me meeting the boy with the greenest eyes, aka Nick or Blaine. Who the fuck knows. But it might have been me he gave his heart to that day and not her. It's always fucking her. I hate her.

I look up when I hear a noise. It's him, he's standing on the top step. Stupid me, I was so deep in thought, I didn't keep my eye on the house. I freeze, I don't think he's seen me, or he would have been on me like a fly on shit. I try not to breathe, it's dark out, there's no way he's seen me. I've very slowly hung my head so my face wasn't visible, but now I need to see what he's doing. I don't hear any movement. My heart is beating so fast right now. The adrenaline is pumping through my body. Should I make a run for it? I very slowly lift my head up slightly so I can see him. He's just standing there, he looks lost. He's standing like he was in the window with his hands in his jeans pockets but looking straight ahead. I watch him from under my hoodie. Suddenly my phone vibrates in my hand and it lights up. Fuck, if I grab it, he will see. Too late, I hear him. I bolt. I run as fast as I can. I don't dare look back. I run and run. I hear him following,

"You fucking bitch, I'm gonna kill you."

Yep, he's after me. I run up and down a few streets, not looking back. I run down an alleyway, there's a fence at the end, I jump up and climb over. I'm so nimble on my feet, I hear the fence rattle. I glance around and see him struggle to get over it. I run through yards and over fences. I look around a couple of times and he's not there. I run a little more, until I'm sure I've lost him. I bend over, catching my breath. That was fucking close and what a fucking rush. I'm fitter than I have ever been in my life. It took a lot to get where I am today after he broke me. It was Igor that got me to this point. Without him who knows what would have happened.

A Year ago

I've fallen in love with Igor in such a short time. He treats me like a queen, but if I wrong him, I certainly know about it. He doesn't hit me, and he has never grabbed my arm like he did that time. No, instead, he likes to give me a good old hard fuck. The thing is, I like it hard and rough. He's learning this with me. I've been staying with him for six weeks now, I haven't seen Svetlana in that time, I'm still not allowed out of the apartment. He did bring me a cell and a laptop, but he warned me that he can track and trace every stroke I make on them both. It was just dropped in a conversation, just so I knew I couldn't have secrets from him.

"Igor, when can I go outside? It's driving me crazy being on lock-down, you are the only person I speak to, not that I mind that, but I need more conversations with people. I need fresh air and now I'm all healed, I need to start getting myself fit, I need to train."

He stands thinking for a minute, rubbing his chin, just staring at me.

"I have a gym here. You can use that, no? I also have a swimming pool. Come with me, I will show you."

I'm floored.

"You mean I have been here all this time and it's only now you're telling me this? Why, why did you not tell me before?"

He just shrugs and grabs my hand and leads me to one of the locked doors. He pulls out his bunch of keys and opens it. Behind the door is a stairwell, we head up with him still holding my hand, when we get to the top and he moves aside I see we are on the roof, but it's like a solarium, all covered with glass. There is a large swimming pool that spans the length of the building. There is a door I see leads to an outside seating area, then there is a door which I can see leads to a gym. I move over to the door and go inside. There is everything you need for a gym, in fact, it's better equipped than the last gym I joined. Everything looks new, maybe it's just not used much.

"Do you even use this?"

"Yes, all the time. I work out every morning and most nights."

Wait, what, how do I not know this? He must see the quizzical look on my face. He comes over to me and takes hold of me, wrapping his arms around my waist and resting his head on my shoulder.

"You мой ангел, are always asleep. You are like my little sleeping beauty. I get up very early, have a workout, and get ready for work. You are either just waking as I've finished or you are sleeping. Then again at night, if I don't stay in your room, I go for a swim after I have left your bed and do a small workout." He turns me to face him.

"No one has ever been up here. I have never had anyone I wanted to share my space with completely before. Yes, I have had some women stay in my apartment, but they are only temporary, so they see what I want them to see." He just shrugs again but kisses the tip of my nose.

"And what am I, Igor? Am I just temporary until you find your next мой ангел?"

He smiles at me and shakes his head. He laughs at my pronunciations of 'My Angel'.

"Now, do you want to use these facilities?"

Damn right I do. I strip down to my underwear and I dive in the pool. He stands and laughs at me. This is one of the rare days he hasn't gone in to work. He's standing in his gray sweats and white tee, which again is a rarity to see him in anything other than his suit. I'm swimming away from him when suddenly I'm being catapulted out of the water. He snuck up underneath me, scooping me up, throwing me back into the water. I come up for air, spluttering away, when I open my eyes, he is right in front of me, laughing. I splash him, the jerk.

"You nearly drowned me, you jerkoff."

His face suddenly goes serious.

"Oh no, I did not swear at you, there was no vulgarity from my mouth, so don't you even dare look at me like that, mister." I can make out the playfulness in his gorgeous blue eyes.

Then he smiles and his whole face lights up. He grabs me and pulls me into his chest. He slowly walks forwards with me holding on to him. I'm short, I don't think my feet will touch the bottom, so I wrap my legs around his waist. I cuddle into his chest, it's then I feel he is naked, I slip down very slightly, yep, completely naked. I wrap my arms around his body, placing my hands on his naked ass cheeks and I squeeze. He suddenly rips my bra from me, then does the same with my thong. Yet another one ruined. Well, he's the one that keeps them stocked up. We are now both completely naked, and he smiles down at me with that smile that any woman would find hard to resist. That smile could melt anyone's panties from them, it's a very sexy, lascivious smile. His blond curly hair is now straight with being wet and he looks like an angel.

He bows down and takes my mouth with his. I squeeze his ass cheeks harder. I start to fondle them, edging my hands down and under. I start to tickle his balls, then I have an idea. I bring one hand to the front and I caress his balls that way, but with the other, I leave it on his ass and I slowly move to his ass crack and start to play in there. I'm at his asshole. Just circling it, then with one of my fingers, I start to insert it. I do this while still playing with his balls. He's still kissing me, but he stops and takes in a deep breath. He's rigid in my arms. I start to lick his abs, then move to his nipples, one at a time, I suck and bite them gently but putting more pressure on each turn. He isn't moving, but his breathing is ragged. I insert another finger in his ass, then I move my hand from his balls to his cock. He is as hard as a fucking rock. I look up into his face.

His eyes are closed, he looks a little tense, but he's gently taking in what I'm doing. I stroke and pull on his cock. I insert my two fingers deeper, moving them in and out. He starts to thrust in rhythm with my strokes. He opens his hooded eyes and stares straight into mine. Blue eyes so intense, he looks confused, but he looks like he's enjoying it. He suddenly takes my mouth hard. His hands start to mirror mine. He inserts two fingers in my ass, then he inserts two from his other hand in my pussy. We thrust together, both of us in and out of each other, devouring each other as we do.

He suddenly breaks away, stopping what he's doing to me and stopping me from doing it to him. I watch his face as it looks conflicted. He turns me around and edges us toward the steps leading into the pool then bends me over. The next thing I know, he's thrusting his rock-hard cock in my ass. He's never done this with me before. It hurts at first and I freeze. He stops for a second. I take a deep breath then I start to move my ass around and around letting him know it's fine. He takes no time at all to start thrusting again. He grabs me under the chin yanking my head back and he tries to lean over to kiss me. I'm breathing heavily, I need more friction from him but also from me.

I take one hand and put it above my head, putting a finger in his mouth to suck, I then take the other hand and I start to play with my clit and insert a finger in my pussy. I'm panting away, I'm enjoying the feel of him in my ass and I can feel his cock with my finger in my pussy, I'm getting carried away, I'm almost at the peak when suddenly my hand is taken away from me,

"Mine and mine alone, not even yours to play with," he growls into my ear.

He's thrusting harder and harder in my ass and I'm meeting each of his thrusts hard by pushing back into him, our bodies slapping together, making the water around us splash. He reaches around my front and he starts to play with my clit, circling and pinching and rubbing, he then inserts three fingers in my pussy, he's circling around and around inside, in and out. I can feel him everywhere, but he suddenly hits the spot and I freeze, not wanting him to stop or move from that spot.

"Oh my fucking god," I scream and I explode all around his fingers.

He keeps pumping them in and out and it goes on forever. He screams out and starts jerking inside my ass at his own release, it never seems to stop and I'm still on my high at my peak. He suddenly pulls out and lifts me up facing him, he lifts me high enough out of the water to his face and he starts to lap at my juices still flowing out of me. I wrap my legs around his neck and he holds me up by the ass with his tongue deep inside me. I start to buck in his face, grabbing his head, forcing it deeper into me. I feel like a madwoman riding his tongue. He hits the spot again and again.

"Fuck, don't stop Igor, don't fucking stop," I scream at him, shuddering in his face.

He sucks and sucks, then as I come down, he licks me dry, then slowly lowers me so we are face-to-face. I roll my head back and moan.

"That was intense, Igor. That was the best fucking orgasm of my life."

He slaps my ass. "Watch that vulgar mouth, мой ангел, I don't mind when you're coming, it tells me how intense it is for you but not any other time."

I look at him and smile. I see all around his mouth and nose are glistening with my cum and I can't help it, I lick his face clean. He turns us around and sits on the steps. He is just out of the water with me on his lap. I lean in and kiss him hard. I taste us, I love it, he's so passionate. I edge forward and I take his cock, which is now rock-hard again, and I guide it to my pussy and insert it. I lean back with my head and body floating on the surface of the water and I let him slide my body up and down while inside me. I've fallen for this dangerous Russian god with his blue eyes and curly dirty blond hair and chiseled cheek's, I've fallen head over heels for him. At this point, I don't care if he keeps me locked up here with him. I'm happy, my revenge can wait, there's no rush, he will still be there no doubt. I'm going to learn what I can from this Russian god who wants me and only me. I'm going to learn all the torture methods they use in the mafia. I'm ninety-nine percent sure that's what he is, and I will learn how to get my revenge sweetly. This god who wants me, will teach me everything. He knows I'm not scared of him. I know he won't hurt me. I trust him, trust has always been hard for me, but I do, for whatever reason, I trust him and he's probably the most dangerous man I've ever met.

PART V

Blaine

Six

Blaine
Present

I'VE JUST COME OUT OF THE HOSPITAL WITH CASSY, I CAN'T describe the feelings inside me. I am so fucking relieved she finally woke up today. I wanted to cry as I sat there holding her hand. She's been in an induced coma for what feels like months. When Poppy stabbed her, it wasn't the stabbing, but the way she went down, banging her head first on the table and then on the sidewalk. I remember it all happening in slow motion as I tried to get to her. I saw Poppy, who somehow got across the street without me seeing her. I saw the look on her face and I knew what she was about to do. I watched her head toward Prim as I started to run, shouting for Prim to watch out, for all the fucking good that did because she wasn't watching me. She was just about to put the tray on the table when Poppy struck her.

I had cars beeping their horns at me as they slammed on their brakes trying to avoid hitting me. One car must have actually hit my leg and it wasn't until the paramedics were seeing to Prim that one of them asked me what had happened to me, and I looked at my leg. It looked twisted. How the fuck I ran on it, I have no idea. It's not the pain because I have that CIP thing and don't feel anything, but it must have just been the determination and the adrenaline rush that kept me going to reach Prim.

It all happened so quickly, but it felt like I was moving in slow motion, not being able to get to her. I watched as she went down with a thud. I saw her head jolt up as she hit the table, and then I watched as it bounced like a fucking ball on the sidewalk. I screamed and screamed, but I couldn't hear a thing. I felt at that moment like I was deaf. I knew how Prim must feel all the time.

I crouched down beside her and very carefully took my tee off and put it under her head. I remember a course we had taken on first aid. Prim wanted to be as good as she could to help when I injured myself, so we took the course together. I remember with a head injury you are not supposed to move them, but I needed to get her head off the ground. There was blood coming out of her mouth, I looked up and around seeing if anyone had called the paramedics. I saw her up the street. She was watching us. I looked back to Prim, there was no way I was leaving her, I saw blood by her side and it's then I realized Poppy had done something to make her go down. It wasn't just a push as I thought.

I looked back up to Poppy who was still watching, she signed to me, "Revenge will be sweet."

That fucking bitch was going to die once and for all. It's my revenge that will be sweet.

We were both rushed to the hospital. Prim never came around and I was terrified I was losing her. The paramedics said halfheartedly, she would be fine, they would get her to the hospital and they would sort her out. What did they fucking know? They probably say that to everyone. I watched as they patched her wound up on her side. They said it looked like she had been stabbed, but the hospital would have to see how deep it was and if it had perforated any organs. I was horrified. I kept hold of her hand and stroked the top of her head gently. They put a neck brace on just in case she had damaged her neck or spine. While one was attending to her, the other was trying to attend to my leg.

"Sir, you need to be X-rayed once we get to the hospital. I think from the way your leg is, you may have a fracture." I didn't acknowledge the paramedic, my eyes were glued to Prim, I was looking for any signs she was coming to, any fucking sign would do.

Once in the hospital, they rushed her to the ER and she was taken away. I tried to hobble along as they were wheeling her away, holding on to the gurney.

"Sir, we have to take her to be scanned and checked out. You need to go and be seen yourself." The nurse who was talking to me was trying to get me to move, but I didn't want to.

I had to let go of the gurney Prim was on. As it was being wheeled away, I just fell to the floor. I felt a person on each side of me and I was helped into a wheelchair. The problem with my condition which is Congenital Insensitivity to Pain, I still try to do the normal things like walk even though I may be broken. This then causes more damage.

They found that my kneecap was slightly twisted which is why my leg looked funny. The doctor said they would need to put me under so they could push it back. I told them there was no need for that and to just do it. The two doctors frowned at each other. I had to explain about CIP; they hadn't heard of it before, one of them pushed my kneecap back to where it should have been. I didn't even flinch. I was just looking for any signs of someone coming to tell me how Prim was.

"Doc, please can you go and find out how my fiancée is. It's killing me not knowing. That is pain I do feel here," I say, thumping my heart.

He left and I saw him speaking to a nurse. I watched them both carefully, watching their facial expressions and trying to read them, but I couldn't. The doctor nodded and walked back to me.

"What is it?" I asked, rushing my words out as he got near me.

"There is no news as yet, sir, I'm sorry. Let's get you rested in a bed so you don't put any weight on that knee, as soon as we hear anything either myself or Dr. Bond here will send someone in to tell you. I'm sorry, sir, I will leave you here with Nurse Stevens, she needs to get yours and your fiancée's details if you wouldn't mind assisting her?"

I nod, not knowing what else I can do.

It's been an hour since the doctor left and I gave the details to the nurse, and I haven't heard a thing. I've been looking at the time on my phone and it's going by so slowly. I called Cassy to let her know Prim and I were in the hospital. I only gave her a brief outline of what happened. I didn't, however, tell her who it was. If I get hold of Poppy, she will be dead, period. I don't want people to know she's back unless they see her.

Cassy rushes into my room, breathless.

"What is it, what's wrong?" I ask in a panic. "Have you seen Prim?"

She shakes her head no.

"I wanted to come and find you, I haven't seen her, but they said she's been put into an induced coma because she has a bleed on the brain. They operated to release the pressure but wanted her to stay asleep to give her a better chance. They said she had a knife wound in her side. What happened, Blaine?"

Fuck, what do they mean?

"What do they mean, a better chance? How bad is it, Cassy? Is she going to die?" I'm shaking, I don't feel it, but I think I have pain in my heart. I know I love her and would die for her. Is this what people feel? Is this real pain because I don't like it one bit.

"Blaine, they don't know. They couldn't tell me any more. They just said it's a waiting game. They said the wound wasn't deep, but it needed stitches. What happened?"

I tell her I was across the street when I saw her go down. I don't remember seeing anyone else. There were people around sitting at tables but I didn't see how she got stabbed.

The doctor who I saw earlier finally came back to check on me. He said he wanted me to stay for the night, that I had to keep all my weight off my leg to make sure the kneecap is okay. When I need to use the bathroom, I had to get the nurses to help me out of the bed and use crutches to keep that leg off the floor at all times. He gave me an update on Prim, they had to take her back to the operating room to release the pressure on her brain. I kind of know what she's going through. It's exactly what happened to me when Poppy hit my head. I was in the hospital for over a month. Prim told me everything about my head injury when I came around. I asked one of the nurses to put me in a wheelchair and wheel me to Prim's room. I threatened that if she didn't, I would just walk there regardless of my knee, I don't feel pain so it would make no difference to me. She could tell I was serious.

I'm sitting next to Prim's bed, holding her hand. She looks so peaceful just lying there. She has a bandage around her head. I talk to her for a while, I talk on the back of her hand so she can feel me talking, there's a nurse in the corner of the room who is monitoring her so I know she's not alone but I don't want to leave her.

"Primrose, baby, I know you can feel me talking to you. I remember hearing you when it was me lying there. I'm so sorry I couldn't protect you again. I feel like a complete fucking failure where you're concerned, I—" I break off as tears roll down my cheeks. I kiss her hand and hold it to my face. I just want her to move. No one has told me how bad this is.

"Nurse, how is she doing? No one has told me what her chances are."

She looks at me softly. Then gets up and comes over to me. "It's been touch and go, I won't lie to you. We just need to make sure we can stop the bleed and to release any pressure that builds up. It's not in the best of places as it's the front temple where she has a hematoma, as long as we keep releasing the pressure, then she stands a good chance. The best chance is if it stops. They think they have stopped it, if not they will need to release the pressure again soon. This frontal hematoma can stop oxygen from getting to the brain, and it can be fatal. It's why there is a team of us here to make sure that doesn't happen. Until we know the bleeding has stopped, it's touch and go. I'm sorry."

I can't help the tears falling down my face. The only time I've ever cried in my fucking life has been to do with Prim.

I'm released from the hospital eventually. But I very rarely left Prim's side. They let me stay with her, I'm not sure if it was the murderous look on my face when they asked me to leave the room or what, but the only time I left was when they were washing her.

Cassy has been great, visiting us both, but there is no news on Prim apart from the bleed has stopped which is one blessing. They say they are keeping her in an induced coma for a few more days. Cassy tells me this is exactly how it was with me when I had my hematoma. So now I get to feel everything Prim felt when it was me lying there, and poor Cassy has now gone through this twice.

I've been in touch with a guy that lives not far from here about hearing implants. I know we have to wait for Prim to be better, but I was told about them a little while back, that some deaf people have been able to hear again. Especially people who were not born deaf. I've been speaking to him, this guy, Mr. Lund. He's from a medical company but he isn't a doctor, I think he sells these things to the hospitals. I just wanted to find out about them before approaching Primrose. He had some leaflets he was going to mail to me, but I didn't want them mailed to Prim's house in case she saw them. I wanted to get as much info on them as I could before approaching a doctor about it. Mr. Lund said I could pick the leaflets up if I wanted to, that he didn't live far. I thought this was really nice of him. I'm going to see him after my visit with Prim.

I've been sitting talking to Prim, holding her hand to my mouth. They brought her out of the induced coma first thing this morning, they didn't tell me they were going to do it. It pissed me right off, the fact they did it without me being there. If she had woken up and I wasn't there for her, I would have gone mad. So far, she hasn't come around. I talk and talk about nothing in particular. A young nurse who came in to check on her asked me why I was talking to her when she couldn't hear me. I told her, not very politely, to get the fuck out. She looked terrified and scampered out of the room,

"What a fucking moron, how dare she. Fucking bitch, does she think just because you can't hear me that you don't feel me talking to you? How dare she."

"Baby, don't… be… mad."

I freeze and look at her face. Did she just say that? Her eyes are closed, she just looks the same.

"Baby, did you speak?" I sign on her palm, kissing it.

"Yes…. Thirsty," she mumbles.

I hit the call button for the nurse to come in. It seems to take fucking ages before one comes in.

"She needs water, she's awake."

Just then Cassy walks in. "Did I just hear right?" She rushes over and stands at the side of me.

One of the nurses goes around the other side and she checks her out. She opens her eyelids and shines a light in, and Prim winces.

"Don't… too… bright," she says slowly, taking a break between each word. I can see her lips are really dry and sticking together as she tries to speak.

"Will someone hurry up with that fucking water," I shout through the open door.

A minute later, a nurse walks in with a jug of water and pours some into her cup, I take it from her and place a straw to Prim's lips. I don't want it to spill all over her, so I take it easy. She takes a few sucks on the straw, it's difficult for her to swallow but we can't lift her head up. I raise the back of the bed up slightly to help her. I'm worried she's not opening her eyes.

"Nurse, why can't she open her eyes? She needs to see us talk to her, what's wrong with her? I want a doctor in here to assess her, now."

"It's okay, this can happen, sir, she's only just woken up, it might be minutes, hours, or days before they open. This can be one of the effects of a frontal hematoma."

"Blaine, I feel your vibrations… you're angry, what's wrong?"

I take her hand and kiss the palm. I sign on her hand, I'm worried she can't see yet. We've been learning to touch sign for a few months now, along with normal signing for me. We've come across a few people who have deaf-blindness or who have deaf-partial vision. We thought it would be a good idea, then she could also teach touch sign along with normal signing. The touch sign was Prim's idea, she's even thinking about learning Braille to teach that, she wants to help as many people as she can. That's my Prim with the biggest heart.

A doctor walks in to assess Prim, it's about fucking time. Cassy is keeping me calm. I have a very short fuse where Prim is concerned.

"Well, I don't think she has loss of sight. When I lift her eyelids up, she is susceptible to the light. It may just be a temporary setback. I will get the ophthalmologist to come and take a look, to give Primrose a good check over to be safe."

Great, now Prim might be blind as well as deaf, when will she catch a fucking break? She does nothing but good for people, always putting everyone else ahead of herself, yet she keeps getting dealt fucking shitty blows. Life is cruel. Maybe it's because of me, maybe it's because of what I've done. Who the fuck knows.

I leave with Cassy and we talk for a little bit outside the hospital. I feel the tears running down my face as we discuss the possibilities that Prim may lose her sight from this. I look up to the heavens and I pray to whoever is up there to give her a fucking break already. Hasn't she endured enough in her life. It's just not fair. In that moment, I feel a rage sweep over me. I run my hands over my face. I need Cassy to leave before I snap. I want to find Poppy. I want her dead. Almost everything Prim has gone through in her life is due to her. She's the bad fucking seed.

I say goodbye to Cassy as she gets into Trevor's car. I stand for a few more minutes, the rage bouncing around my head, trying to calm myself down before I head to Mr. Lund's.

Seven

Blaine

I'M WALKING ALONG SLOWLY THINKING ABOUT PRIM, THINKING about the shitty luck she has and questioning why her? Why couldn't any of this happen to Poppy? I'm heading to see Mr. Lund to find out what I can about these hearing implants. She needs this now more than ever. We don't know what's going to happen with her sight.

I've had that feeling of being watched again. I know it's her. She's got some fucking balls knowing what I can do to her. I don't turn. I don't want her to know I'm on to her, not yet anyway. I've felt it a few times lately, but when I have casually looked around, I haven't seen her.

It's not long before I'm at Mr. Lund's. I head up the steps and I'm slightly turned and I make out a figure down the street. A slight small figure, in black clothes with a hoodie up. Yep, it has to be her. I go inside and Mr. Lund, or John, is an older guy with graying hair, small build, with glasses. He is very enthusiastic about these new hearing implants. He shows me what they are; he has a prototype in his house. They are tiny little things that they attach inside the ear canal. I tell him how she became deaf and he thinks she would be a good candidate for a trial if she agrees. She will have to go through lots of tests to make sure. I need to speak to her about the implants, once she's healed from this trauma. I tell him what has happened to her and he says it would be good if he could get Dr. Splinsky to visit her while she's in the hospital. When she's up to it, they can run some of the tests there, which would be easier for her. I will talk to Prim before any of that. I think it might be too much for her right now. We will probably have to wait until she's home and fully recovered from this, who knows what trauma this has caused her. I just hope I can get her through it, like she did with me. Without her, I would have gone off the rails for sure. My mind was not in a good place, I just hope she stays as strong as she always does.

I leave, not realizing I had been in there for over two hours. I stand on the top step of his porch with my hands in my jeans pockets and I breathe out. I feel a little optimistic, Prim is awake, and Mr. Lund thinks these implants may work on her. It would be amazing if they did.

I head for home. I hate going there when I know Prim isn't there. I hate it when she has to go away for work, never mind her being in the fucking hospital for God knows how long. I haven't been anywhere with her yet on her travels. I don't have a passport, I still don't have any ID, I'm too afraid to get it, I don't want to be in the system, but I know I have to soon. We're going to be married at some point and I want to be able to travel with Prim, so I will need a passport. Prim doesn't go on about it but she's mentioned it a few times about me getting my ID sorted out. She says it should be easy to do as long as I was registered at birth. I'm sure I was, I lived with both my parents. I think we were a normal family until Papa left.

I'm ambling along slowly, I know she's following me, I feel her. I step into the mini-mart to grab some beer and some food. I head inside our home. I stand at the window and pretend to be somber, looking up to the sky. I don't act like I'm looking for anyone. I stay there for a few minutes, I then run up the stairs to our room where it's dark. I edge to the window, slowly I peer through and I can see her out there, that fucking bitch has the nerve to come near our home. I watch her for a few minutes, she's over on the other side of the road but, she's watching the house. She can't see me up here, it's too dark. I want to run out there and kill her, but I want to do it in my own time, I want her gone once and for all.

I head back down the stairs, I've had enough of her sitting out there, I open the front door, trying to be quiet, I want to scare her off. I just stand on the top step, looking straight ahead with my hands in my pockets. I don't look to where she is. I don't want to give away I know she's there. Looking straight ahead, I can just make her out in my peripheral vision, she's trying not to move. Just then, I see the light from her phone. It automatically makes me turn my head. Fuck, I was going to play this cool. I take flight down the steps in her direction, she bolts, as I knew she would. She was too far away from me, which is why I was only going to scare her. I give chase, why, I don't know. I think it's just instinct because I want to kill her so fucking bad.

"You fucking bitch, I'm gonna kill you," I shout after her.

She's fast, fuck, I know she had a head start but she's quick. I'm quicker and I start to gain on her, she's running down different streets trying to lose me. She jumps over a fence. Fuck that, I'm not going to chase anymore, I've done what I wanted to do. I approach the fence and start to rattle it. She looks around and I see the sneer on her face, thinking she got the better of me. Next time, bitch, I sneer back, but she's gone.

I head back home, I can't stop thinking about Prim, I need to call the hospital and just warn them not to let anyone other than Cassy and me in to see her. I'll tell them I think there's a possible threat on her life. I don't trust Poppy one bit, after all, I'm convinced she visited me in the hospital when I was out of it. Who's to say she's not going to do the same with Prim. Once home, I grab a can of beer from the fridge and set about making an omelet, it's my specialty since Prim taught me how to make them, plus I don't know how to make anything else.

It's early, real early, when I head to the hospital. I couldn't sleep last night, I was thinking about Poppy out there. I was scared of what she might do if she got to Prim. I know Poppy's watching my every move. I feel her there, but I'm a patient man and I will get her eventually. It's funny how she was the last person I thought I had killed, and I haven't hurt anyone else since. I haven't had the urge to hurt anyone else since. I don't know if that's because I found out I have a medical condition, so I know I'm not the fucking retard my mama told me I was all my life, or if it's the calming influence of Prim. I only have to look at her and I feel grounded. For once in my life, I feel I have a purpose. I'm going to get my ID eventually and I'm going to marry Prim, she will be mine forever.

I'm scared of what I will find at the hospital as I enter. Leaving Prim yesterday was hard, I'm fucking terrified she may lose her sight for good.

That would kill her, it's bad enough she can't hear but to not see either. She's an artist, I don't know if she would ever get over it. I remember her taking me to the attic that first time and unveiling all her artwork to me. I was astounded by her talent but also full of admiration for her. It didn't bother me she had all these drawings of me as she imagined me growing up, they were amazing. I was in awe of her talent. The fact she had me pictured just right blew me away, just like she did, she gave me the best blow job ever. It was quite erotic, her on her knees in front of me surrounded by drawings and paintings of me. I felt like she was worshiping me. It gave me a big head, in more ways than one.

Her whole life has to do with vision, in her art and her drawings for work, her architecture and hearing people by seeing. I'm really optimistic about the hearing implants, if I can talk her into going for them, but first we need to sort out her sight and see what the long-term effects are. I cautiously enter her room, worried about how she will be, no matter what, I will get her through this just like she did with me. It freaks me out that we both got the same injuries from the car blowing up when we were kids and that we've both suffered hematomas. She's facing the window so she doesn't see me enter the room. I walk over to the end of her bed, if she can see, I don't want to startle her, that will hurt her head. She has her eye's closed, I'm not sure if she's asleep or if her eyes are closed because she can't see.

I move around and stand between her bed and the window. If she can see, she will notice the difference in the light, she slowly opens her eyes, they are still swollen, as is her face, but she's still fucking beautiful. I see the smile on her face. I match it. I know she sees me, she fucking sees me. I grab her hand and bring it to my mouth and kiss it. One eye is open more than the other.

"Baby, can you see me?" I mouth to her, and she smiles and nods very slightly. I'm elated. "Baby, can you see out of both eyes?"

Her smile fades.

"I love you Prim, you know you're my world. We will get through whatever life throws at us. I'm so fucking relieved you're awake, baby, so relieved."

She smiles at me. "Blaine, I love you too."

I can't help the big ass smile on my face. I lean in and kiss her lips very gently. Just then a nurse walks in. I look at her, giving her the evil look for disturbing us, but she just ignores me. I think they are used to me and my moody looks. She wheels the cart to Prim's other side and starts to do the observations on her. I watch, as does Prim. I tap her hand and she looks back to me.

"Baby, what is your vision like?"

Still with one eye slightly closed.

"I can see you with my right eye, Blaine, it's blurry but I can see you. My left eye is, well, pretty bad, I can't really make anything out with that one." I kiss her hand again.

"Nurse, is the ophthalmologist coming in to see Primrose today? The doctor said yesterday he would get the ophthalmologist to come see her." The nurse finishes with the observations then looks at the notes in the file at the bottom of Prim's bed. She flicks through the notes.

"I don't see anything in here but let me go check on the system and see what is happening for you. I'll be right back." She turns to leave. "Oh, by the way, Miss Tomlinson, your vitals are all good this morning." She leaves.

Prim didn't see what the nurse said because she was looking at me. I tell her what she said. I grab the chair and sit at her side, we talk for a while, she gets tired and closes both her eye's but she's not asleep.

The nurse finally comes back and tells me that Prim's doctor has been delayed with an emergency and that the system is showing that Dr. Benedict, the ophthalmologist, is down to see Primrose tomorrow.

Great, we have to wait another fucking day to find out about her sight. It pisses me off, Prim must feel the tension in my voice as I tell the nurse what I think of this hospital, she squeezes my hand and I look at her. I tell her the doctors won't be coming to see her today, that it will be tomorrow now. It's fine with Prim, as usual, she's still very tired and spends most of the day just sleeping. I get on the bed with her and let her rest on me while she sleeps. I'm ecstatic that she is finally awake, but I know she still has a long road ahead of her. I don't want to leave her when visiting hours are over, but I have no choice. I stop at the desk and tell them to make sure no one goes in to see Prim unless it's me or her aunt.

I can't get to the hospital quick enough. I hated leaving her again last night, but I need to make sure she's safe. Those fucking doctors better come and see her today. I'm not taking the shit about them being busy. I want answers on Prim. I walk in and she's got her eyes closed. I move toward her. I'm scared each time I enter her room in case something bad has happened. I move to the window again so she can see the light difference and she opens her eyes. I smile and lean down to kiss her.

"How are you, baby? Can you see any better today?" I mouth to her.

"Just the same really, Blaine. Not much change."

I smile and tell her it will get better. It feels like hours pass before finally a doctor comes through the door, followed by another doctor and a horde of other people in white coats. Fuck, what's this? A game of how many people can fit in one room.

"Thank fuck for that, I didn't think you were ever going to come and see how she was doing," I say, really pissed off at the doctor. I shake Prim gently, and she opens her good eye, and smiles at me.

"Doctor's here to see you," I mouth and nod with my head in their direction. She slowly turns her head to look.

"Hello. Miss Tomlinson. I. Am. Dr. Westley. How. Are. You. Feeling. This. Morning?" he mouths to her and shouts as if that's going to do anything. Some people make me laugh, why do they feel they need to shout at a deaf person? It's not like they can hear, no matter the volume, then some like this doctor, not only shouts, but speaks to her like she's from another country and has to pronounce every word on its own like she doesn't understand him. She looks to my hand on hers. I look and see I'm squeezing her hand, I'm annoyed, and she knows it. She smiles at me then turns to the doctor.

"I have a bad head, Dr. Westley, and I can't see out of my left eye and my right eye is blurry, but other than that, I'm good," she says and smiles at them all. He looks a little taken aback by the fact she can speak pretty normally to them, even if she is a little nasally, but she is clear in how she speaks. He smiles at her.

"Do. You. Mind. If. I. Check…"

I've had enough of him already, so I interrupt him. "Doc, for fuck's sake, she can read your lips just fucking fine, you don't need to shout at her or pronounce each fucking word individually."

He looks a little horrified at the way I spoke to him and just nods.

"Sorry, Miss Tomlinson, do you mind If I check you over? I just want to unwrap the bandage on your head and then I have Dr. Russkett here who is the ophthalmologist and he would like to check your eyes. We also have some student doctors here to watch if that is okay with you?"

She nods at him to let him know she agrees. The nurse, from earlier, comes forward and very gently starts to unravel the bandage around Prim's head. I see Prim wince a couple of times, I know she must be in pain, the problem with Prim is she plays everything down. I still have hold of her hand and I stroke my thumb on the top of it to let her know I've got her. She's sitting up with her eyes closed as the nurse unravels the bandage and I'm glad she isn't looking at me as it's removed. I think the look on my face would have caused her more concern. I'm shocked when I see her head. It's all shaved, she has no hair around her crown at all. Her scalp is very red and she has two big scars parallel to each other that are stapled. That must have been where they had to cut for each surgery to relieve the pressure and try to stem the bleed.

She looks to me. She does that to gauge my reaction to most things. I smile at her and mouth "Beautiful", I lean in and kiss her forehead. I don't know what her reaction will be once she sees she has no hair, I think some women would go mental but somehow, I doubt Prim will, she's not like that.

The doc comes close and examines her head, he's gentle but I see her wince.

"Is it tender, baby?" I ask her and she blinks at me, that's a yes. "It's only to be expected, they had to take you to surgery twice because you had a bleed, it's a frontal hematoma and the little sucker wouldn't stop bleeding, just like mine didn't." I laugh and she smiles, her left eye still mostly closed.

"This looks like it's healing nicely. We should be able to leave the bandages off now and just put a dressing on it." He says this but not to Prim, I raise an eyebrow at him and motion with my head to tell Prim, not me. He looks her in the face and says it again.

"Dr. Russkett here is now going to look at your eyes, it should just be a temporary setback because of the frontal hematoma, but we need to check just in case, and who better than an eye expert." He steps back and the other doc steps forward.

I see the look on the female students' faces, they are all in lust with this guy. They look like they're wetting their panties. Great, just what I fucking need at a time like this. I watch him, he puts on his gloves and he takes Prim's other hand in his, I growl, I actually fucking growl at him. Prim looks at me. She could feel the growl through her hand in mine. She smiles, she knows what I'm like. The doc looks over to me and I give him a fucking evil scowl. He doesn't let go. I see a very slight smirk on his face, as if he's goading me. If it wasn't that he was going to help Prim, I'd have knocked him out cold for touching her.

"Miss Tomlinson, I'm just going to shine a light into each of your eyes. Try not to flinch, it may hurt your head. I know how tender that is. When you say you can't see out of your left eye, is there anything at all when you try to open it? Do you see outlines or shadows?" He's right in her face so she can watch what he says. He speaks with an accent, but I don't know where from.

I must be holding her hand too tight. She starts to wriggle it, trying to get feeling back. I loosen my grip and she looks at me. I mouth 'Sorry' yet again. She tries to open her left eye while looking at my face. She closes the right eye as she does. I can see the struggle, but I don't want to touch her.

"Turn to the doc so he can see you," I say to her face, but she doesn't see what I say. I tap her hand to get her attention.

She opens her right eye and I repeat what I just said. She turns to the doc. I can see she closes the right eye again and tries to open the left one.

"I can barely open it. It's like I don't have control of my eyelid. I'm trying really hard." The doc leans in and lifts her left eyelid for her.

"I can't make you out, but I can see an outline of your head and I see shadows." She opens her right eye and he shines the light into both of them one at a time. He has her moving her eyes from left to right and up and down, he has some eye instruments he uses to see right into her pupils.

"You are having trouble with the left eye, but it looks normal to me at this point after a frontal hematoma. I don't see any scarring in the pupil, I've examined patients after, who are unable to open either eye. Your right eye you can control much better than your left and I think you will get your full vision back in that eye very soon. The left eye is going to take a little longer. It may be that you need to train it again, get the muscles you use to control your eyelids moving. Hopefully with some exercise, but if not, we may need to perform surgery to help. It's in the early stages yet to discuss that. I will come back in a couple of days to see how you are doing. If there is no change, I would like to have you visit my clinic here in the hospital so I can do further examinations on you. Once you are able to get out of bed, that is." He smiles a big cheesy grin at her.

I'd like to knock his teeth out, the smarmy bastard. He's just told us everything we already knew, really. He's all smiles and swoony, with his bright white teeth. Looking over at the student doctors is making me angry. He says goodbye and they all leave. Thank fuck for that.

I feel Prim squeezing my arm and I look to her. She's smiling at me.

"What's with the scowls, if looks could kill he would be dead. I thought he was a nice doctor. At least he's given me a little hope that I will see again."

She melts my heart. I lean down and kiss her gently on the lips.

"I love you, Prim. You know I get all protective of you. He was a bit too smarmy for my liking. You should have seen the way those student doctors were all swooning over him."

"I saw how they all acted with Dr. Russkett, who can blame them with his chiseled features, blond curly hair, those blue eyes, and that accent is to die for. Miss Tomlinson is his first patient with us, he's standing in while Dr. Benedict the resident hospital ophthalmologist had to take a sudden leave of absence, we were very lucky to get him last minute, but you can guarantee all the students will now start to volunteer to be on his rounds." It's the nurse coming back in the room with the dressings for Prim's head. She looks all dreamy.

"Well, he better lay off my Primrose with his big vibrant blinding smiles," is all I say.

I sit down and let her fuss over Prim. She's worn out and is asleep, I want to go out for a bit of fresh air while she's out of it. Cassy will be here later, so no doubt Prim will be exhausted from all the visits. My routine normally is to stay with her all day until they kick me out in the evening. Now she's awake, I can sit with her on the bed and cuddle her, giving her and me the comfort we both need.

I look out of the window to see if Poppy is lurking anywhere. It's just after one now, so I'll grab something to eat downstairs in the restaurant after I've had some fresh air. I can only see the front of the hospital from this window and Poppy could be anywhere. It's killing me not being able to just go for her after what she's done. But I'll let her know that I know she's around like last night, but I won't do anything just yet. I know she's got some plan cooked up for her revenge on me. I just need to watch my back.

I stand at the front of the hospital just outside the doors and look up, then around. There's a garden area to the side which I have never paid attention to before, I see her there, sitting on a bench watching me. I bet she's been there every day and I haven't noticed her before. I turn toward her and start to walk. She jumps up and stands, staring at me. I can see her wondering what I'm going to do. I saunter slowly toward her with my hands in my pockets, in no rush, I smirk at her. She's not quite sure what to make of me, I can see the confusion on her face. I just walk, she doesn't let me get close. She turns and she's gone, sprinting away first, then breaking into a run around the back of the hospital. I just want her to know, I know she's around.

I head back inside and go and eat in the restaurant. I see the slimy doctor through the window of the restaurant. He's just in normal clothes, not his white coat,. He looks like he's in a rush and he looks angry. I watch him head out of the hospital. I watch him go, wondering why he's in a rush. He heads to the parking lot and gets into a car. He pulls out of the lot in a fucking Lotus sports car. I know my cars and that is one hell of a car. How does an eye doctor afford a car like that, it has to be a million dollars plus? Like I said, smarmy bastard. Wouldn't surprise me if he was some sort of trust fund brat. I need to watch him around my Prim.

The rest of the day goes a little quicker with Prim now awake and talking, Cassy and the girls arrived, I decided to leave them to it. They were going to wear her out anyway. The girls were so thrilled to finally see her awake. I think it's a little too soon for them to be visiting, but they keep Prim entertained with all their teenage talk on boys. I just rolled my eyes and left.

Eight

Blaine

I T's been a week now since Prim woke up. Her right eye is back to full strength, but she's still struggling with her left eye. Her head is healing nicely, and she's had the staples removed from both the wounds. She was shocked when I got the mirror for her to see her head, but she didn't have a meltdown. She just said it's only hair, it will grow back. She got out of bed a couple of days ago. They tried to get her out not long after she woke, but she was dizzy and had to get back in bed. She wanted me to try to get her out, knowing I could just lift her, which I did, and put her in a wheelchair. She wanted some fresh air, so I took her to the gardens, I saw Poppy right away, she's been there each day. It's gotten to the stage when I'm leaving the hospital, I just salute her with my hand as I leave. As soon as she saw I was wheeling Prim, she was gone before Prim could see her.

I pushed her around the hospital which she loved, I also saw there was an exit out the back which must be where Poppy disappears through when she runs. I've taken Prim outside each day now and she loves it. I've even helped her with walking and she's doing great in the hospital, but I won't let her walk outside yet and doctor's orders were in a wheelchair only. We have an appointment to see Dr. Smarmy this afternoon. She hasn't seen him again since that first visit. I think the nurse said he hasn't been in. Maybe it was something to do with him rushing out of the place last week when I saw him. I haven't seen him since either. She's getting better every day and I can't wait for her to come home.

We're sitting waiting on Dr. Smarmy. Prim's a little scared in case this is it with her left eye, I know she doesn't say much about it but I know Prim.

I just know whatever the outcome, we will be fine with this, we have each other. The door opens, I don't turn to greet him.

"Good afternoon to you both, sorry to have kept you waiting. It's been a busy day." He leans over and shakes Prim's hand and then extends his hand to me. I'm not that rude, so I give it a quick shake.

"Okay, Miss Tomlinson, may I take a look at your eyes? I will just do the usual, shine a light and have you move your eye and then see what tests we need to get done from there. I know I wanted to see you sooner, but I haven't been in since I last saw you."

She smiles and nods. He was looking straight at her face while talking, making sure she could see what he was saying. He gets up and does what he did last time he saw her. Then he does an actual eye examination, seeing how well she can see with her eyes.

"As we expected the left eye is still not fully healed, it's improved since last week, so there is that. The right eye is good, and you seem to have most of your vision back from that, although it is such that you may need to wear glasses to help you see clearer and sharper as you don't have twenty-twenty vision. I would like to do some routine tests on your left eye, see if we can see what's going on behind there as it's nowhere near anything like the right eye. I want to make sure there is no permanent damage so I will need to schedule you for the test."

"Does it look like it might be permanently damaged? I think we would both rather you be honest and upfront about it. Is it normal for one eye to not be as good as the other in your experience? What are the chances of full vision with the left eye again?" I sit up tall and ask him, but I make sure Prim is facing me so she sees what I am asking.

"I have seen this a lot and, in most cases, both eyes go back to normal. It's difficult to say what the outcome will be until we do more tests. If it looks like permanent damage, meaning if it stays as it is, then as Miss Tomlinson is not blind in her left eye and she has some vision, it may be that we can do corrective surgery. We will know more from the tests. Now, unfortunately, I won't be in this week to do these tests myself so I can schedule them with Dr. Patel, or you can wait until I am back. It's your choice, Miss Tomlinson."

"The sooner the better, doesn't matter who does the testing as long as the tests get done." I jump in before Prim can speak. She watches me talking, then looks into my eyes and nods.

"Yes, the sooner the better please, Dr. Russkett. I don't want to wait. I think they will be discharging me soon so if you could schedule the appointments while I'm still in here that would be better for me."

He nods. "I will do it now for you, just one second." He does some things on his computer and I hold Prim's hand, giving it a squeeze. I notice his eyes flick to our hands.

What the fuck is that about?

"Unfortunately, all the appointments are taken for the next two weeks here in the hospital. I have my own practice if you would like to go there. It's local, I will be able to fit you in as soon as you are discharged. It's up to you. It's just unfortunate that I am only covering here when I can, and Dr. Patel is covering when I am not able to."

I look at Prim, fuck, I wanted to see the other doctor, I don't trust this slimy bastard one bit, but if it's going to take that long what choice do we have?

"Yes please, Dr. Russkett, if you can see me when I'm discharged that would be great. Can you message me with your details, and I can message you when I am discharged, and we can arrange to come and see you?"

"Yes, of course, I have your details on file here. I will message you with my details. As soon as you are released, let me know." He stands up, basically to dismiss us and we leave his office with me pushing Prim out in her wheelchair.

I'm not sure what to make of that. It seems odd there are no appointments, yet he can see us privately. I'm really not sure about this guy. I don't know where his accent is from and I just get a bad feeling about him. I don't think it's anything to do with jealousy, it's just my instincts. There is something not right with him. I don't say anything to Prim about it, the last thing I want is for her to start worrying. I head back to Prim's room, I know she's tired, I can see it in her face. I place her back in bed. I know she can get in and out of bed and she's getting more mobile each day, but I love taking care of her. I get on the bed with her and have her snuggled up to me.

"Baby." I turn her face very gently toward me. "What if I go home tonight and get Cassy to help us find another eye doctor to see you? It just doesn't feel right to me."

She frowns at me. "What doesn't feel right? Are you a little jealous of him, Blaine, he seems very nice to me."

I scowl at her. "I am not jealous of him, Prim, no. I just don't get a good feeling from him. He has an accent I haven't come across before and have no idea where it's from? I just don't know Prim, I don't like him."

She frowns at me because she has no idea what I'm talking about. I kiss the top of her head, it's getting prickly now with the hair starting to grow back, and she falls asleep in my arms while I think about what it is I don't like about that doctor. I just don't know why I feel uneasy with him. He comes across as arrogant and cocky, too sure of himself. He has this aura about him, like an authoritative aura that we should all bow down and kiss his feet or something. He's all high and mighty.

Prim has spent another week in the hospital. They still didn't want to discharge her because she was still a little wobbly on her feet. They've had her going to physical therapy in the hospital to help get her moving again, they won't let anyone go home if they can't go up and down the stairs, and she's struggled a little with that. They said again it's a normal side effect, but that with her being deaf and the hematoma, that it may just be taking longer to get her balance back on track. She can walk around good, but the stairs are a challenge for her. I even take her up and down the stairs to practice, and I see what they mean. She just doesn't coordinate her legs very well. They have assured us she will get it.

Her left eye has improved and is almost the same as her right eye now. I don't see why she needs the tests. I asked her doctor if she still needed them or for us just to see an optician for glasses. He seemed to think it wouldn't hurt to have the tests but that he didn't personally think it necessary at this point and maybe just glasses would be good to correct her vision.

I've seen Poppy a lot, she's been letting me see her for some reason. I don't think she's been to the house but who fucking knows with her. We had all the locks changed after Poppy attacked Prim there and we got a new updated security system where it alerts us on our cells if anyone goes near the house and I haven't had any alerts so far. I know she's up to something and there is no way I am letting Prim out of my sight when she gets home.

"Good news, Miss Tomlinson, you can go home today. I'm happy with all your progress and your balance and sight are almost perfect. Maybe see about getting some glasses to sharpen your vision, but other than that, you are good to go. You're all healed from the surgery and from the knife wound on your side. You were very lucky in both cases."

Thank fuck for that. She looks at me and we smile at each other. I take her in my arms, I'm so relieved she's coming home where I can keep an eye on her twenty-four seven, I don't give a shit if she likes it or not. I'm not leaving her side. Cassy can do the fucking shopping for us.

I pack up her stuff and on hospital orders, I have to wheel her to the front doors. Cassy is waiting for us with the car to take us both home. I glance over to where Poppy usually is and she's there watching. She now knows Prim is going home. Fuck, I was hoping she wasn't around to see her leaving, but then she would have realized by tomorrow anyway.

We get settled in back home. Cassy had been shopping, so we have everything we need. Prim still gets tired quickly, which is understandable, so for today, under protest from Prim, which I won, I take her to our room to rest.

"I promise tomorrow we can veg out on the couch watching movies all day. Please, just get some rest for now. I'll make you a nice omelet, I know you've missed my specialty, and I will come up here with you and stay here. We can put the TV on and watch a movie in bed. How does that sound?" I ask, wiggling my eyebrows at her.

"Perfect, my knight in shining armor as usual. Always saving me, I love you, Blaine, thank you for looking after me." That hits me right in the chest. All I've thought about is what a fucking failure I am to her. How I never manage to protect her, and she says I'm always saving her.

"No need to ever thank me." I kiss her gently on the lips and leave before she questions my mood change.

It's been a few days and all we've done is veg out on the couch and watch movies on Netflix. Prim usually falls asleep on me on the couch, which I love. I can then turn the TV to football, I understand the rules now, Prim taught me, turns out she's a huge 49ers fan. I've even learned a lot of the teams and I root for her team. I haven't been out of the house once. I've looked out the window from upstairs to see if Poppy is around, but I haven't seen her, thank God.

Prim loves all the old eighties films and she has me watching all the girly films. We are currently watching *Some Kind of Wonderful*, which is good. She suddenly turns to look at me, she wants to ask me something, I can tell by the look on her face.

"Did you see what happened to me that day, Blaine? How did I get stabbed? Who was it? Where were you? All I remember is you sat outside at the table and I was inside getting the coffees, I headed out and you weren't there. I started to put the tray on the table and that's it. That is all I can remember. What happened? I've been trying so hard to remember."

I've been waiting for this and I'm surprised she hasn't asked me until now. I vowed to myself I would never lie to her again. I have to tell her who I think it was and who I think I saw. She has to know. What she does with it after that is up to her. When the police came to question her after she woke up, she couldn't tell them anything and I told them I didn't see anything, that I was at a shop across the street when I saw her go down. I lied to them. I rub my hand over my face.

"I didn't want to upset you, Prim, but you need to know. I'm sure it was Poppy."

Her eyes go wide in shock and she gulps in air. Suddenly she starts to shake. Fuck, what's wrong with her? She's gulping for air, she can't speak, her eyes are looking at me for help.

"Prim, baby, what is it?" I'm kneeling on the floor in front of her, looking up at her face so she can see me speak. She's gasping for air. Fuck, what is it? I sit on the couch and pull her to me, rubbing her back. I lift her face to look at me.

"Slow breaths, baby, I think you're having a panic attack. Look at my mouth, breathe in and out slowly like this, copy me." I show her and she copies what I'm doing. She's starting to calm down and her breathing is getting better. She inhales deeply and exhales slowly.

"This is why I didn't want to fucking tell you, but I will never lie to you. I'm just going to get you some water and some tablets. Hold on, keep doing what you're doing, breathing in and out slowly. That's it, baby."

I run to the kitchen and get her some water and some painkillers. I know it helps with her headaches and she's bound to have one after this. I knew I should have kept my big fucking mouth shut. I hate seeing her like this. I hurry back to the room. She's okay, she's lying on the couch with her head on the armrest. She hasn't seen me come back in and I stand for a second watching her. She looks so fragile right now. It fucking rips at my heart. I may not feel physical pain but I fucking feel something when she's hurting. I kneel in front of her and she sits up. I can see the tears running down her cheeks. She takes the tablets and water. I sit on the floor, facing her, with my back against the table so she can see what I say.

"This is why I didn't want to tell you. I knew you would ask me at some point, but I wanted you to be ready. I'm so sorry, Prim. I fucking hate you have a sister like her. I never had any siblings, but If this is how they treat each other then I'm fucking glad I didn't. I know my family, well, me and Mama were not close, but I always had it in my head most families were close. I don't know why." I shrug. I pull my legs up and I lean my head on them, not looking at her. She taps my arm.

"Most families are close, yes, siblings argue and fight, but to be honest, Blaine, it scares me she's like this. That's twice she's left me for dead. I don't know what I ever did to her to make her want me dead." She's crying, the tears now streaming down her face. I kneel and I pull her gently into my chest and I just hold her, soothing her, I know she feels the vibrations through my chest. She cries for a while, then she starts to get a little agitated, which I know is anger. She pushes me away and looks at me.

"Why didn't you stop her? Where were you?"

Yep, she's getting angry now. I explain it all to her and why I was across the road. I don't tell her the last part where Poppy signed about revenge to me. I don't want her to worry she's going to come back. I also don't tell her that she's been hanging around. I just hope she was only doing that to see how Prim was, I hope she felt remorse and needed to make sure she was okay and that she hadn't killed her. I don't want Prim to know, she will go into another panic. All I know is I need to sort this out once and for all and get rid of Poppy permanently. I fucking hate myself that I failed, me, a fucking failure just like Mama always used to say. I failed Prim. I let her down. I swore I would protect her always and I failed. How could I not have killed Poppy, I don't understand how she is still alive. I fucking buried her. She should have died from that alone. What a fucking failure. I put my head on her lap and I cry. I cry for Prim and all the suffering she's gone through and I cry because I failed.

She strokes my hair, then taps me so I look at her.

"What's wrong, why are you crying?"

"Because I'm a failure, Prim, I failed to protect you. Not once, but twice from your own fucking sister. I couldn't protect you. Maybe me coming back into your life was wrong and selfish, so fucking selfish. If I hadn't wanted to find you so bad, none of this would have happened. It's all my fault. It's because of me she attacked you, twice. I fucking hate myself for it. I love you with everything I am, and you know I have since I was ten years old, but I'm bad for you, Prim."

She pulls me into her chest and cradles my head, she's now trying to soothe me. How did I turn this around so it was her comforting me? She's the one that nearly died at her sister's hand, twice. Just then her phone buzzes. It's on the table, so she hasn't felt it. I turn and pick it up and hand it to her.

"I think you have a message. It just buzzed."

She checks it and then turns it around to me, showing me the message on the screen. It's that fucking Dr. Smarmy asking when she's coming in to see him. I frown at the message and look at her.

"I thought you messaged and told him you were fine and only needed glasses."

She nods. "I did, but he messaged me back and said he would still like me to go in and see him, and he could sort out my prescription for some glasses. I didn't reply to him, and I've forgotten about him. I could still go and see him. My doctor said it wouldn't hurt to have the test done." She shrugs and I'm mad, real fucking mad that he's messaging her. Who the fuck does he think he is?

"Baby, why do you look so mad? He's a nice doctor. Maybe you can take me to see him for the tests."

I take the phone from her and start to type back to him telling him to fuck off, she suddenly snatches it out of my hand and reads what I typed, I didn't get a chance to press send.

"Don't, Blaine, what the hell. He's a doctor, stop being so possessive and jealous. How dare you use my phone to tell him to fuck off, that is so wrong, on so many accounts." She winces because she's shouting, and I know her head must hurt.

"If I want to go and see him, I will. I'll get Aunt Cassy to take me. I don't want you coming anyway. God knows what you'd do to him." Now she's really angry again. She gets up and storms up the stairs. That fucking slimy doc, I don't trust him.

Nine

Blaine

IT'S BEEN A COUPLE OF DAYS SINCE PRIM FOUND OUT IT WAS POPPY that attacked her and that smarmy doctor messaged her. We're good, but we haven't spoken about either since. I've asked Cassy to come over and sit with Prim for a few hours. I said it would be nice for Prim to see other faces for a while instead of mine all day and I know she would love to see them. I want to see what I can find on the eye doctor. I want to go and see where his practice is. Make sure he is who he says he is. I got the address from Prim's phone when she was sleeping. I know I shouldn't snoop, but it was the only way I knew where to go. I haven't told her I'm going out yet and that Cassy is coming. I think she's going to bring the girls over with her. I'll make up an excuse about not wanting to be in on all the girl talk and about getting some fresh air.

I've just made breakfast for us. I'm getting better at this domesticated shit. We sit at the island. Prim insists on trying to be normal. She is so stubborn.

"Baby, I know we haven't spoken about it since, but are you going to tell Cassy or the police it was Poppy?"

Her eyes widen slightly and she sets her fork down.

"No." That's all she says.

No, what? I look at her, furrowing my brow in confusion.

"No, I'm not going to tell anyone. You must have your reasons for not telling the police, I'm not sure what, but I'm not telling anyone. If I tell Aunt Cassy, it will destroy her again. I saw how she was last time Poppy attacked me. She blamed herself for not helping Poppy more, for being a shitty aunt to her, even though she wasn't. If I tell her, she will want the police to know. Why didn't you tell the police, Blaine? Were you protecting her?"

I set down my fork and I stare at her.

"Why would you think I was protecting her? What fucking reason would I have for protecting her? She almost killed you, twice, Prim. I hate her, I never want her to come near you again. I don't know what I would do if she did. I was trying to protect you, the police would have questioned you about her, and you would have known, and I didn't want you to know then, look at the reaction you had the other day. It's you I'm trying to protect, not that fucking bitch." I'm angry, angry because she even thinks I'm protecting that bitch. Her look softens, she reaches over and squeezes my hand, then holds it.

"I'm sorry, Blaine, I shouldn't have said that, I don't know why I said that. I realize it's me you want to protect, but she can't be allowed to keep doing this to me. What if next time she succeeds, Blaine, what if she comes back and tries again because she's failed twice?" She looks scared and worried. I get up and walk around the island to her, I swing her to face me and I take her head very gently and cradle her to my chest.

"I won't let her try again, baby. I will fucking kill her before she has a chance to."

She looks up at me, the look is the 'what did you just say' look. I shrug and gently hold her face with both my hands and lean down and kiss her gently on the lips. She pulls me closer to her and tries to deepen the kiss, but there is no way she's ready for anything sexual just yet. As much as I want to fuck her, no, make love to her, I won't until I know she's okay. I kiss her back, getting more passionate but still holding her face because I don't want my hands to start wandering, my cock is rock-hard, I fucking love her so much. Her hands start to wander to my ass and she squeezes and tries to pull me into her, I resist, I stand firm, not letting her move me. I break the kiss and rest my forehead gently on hers. I pull back slightly and let her see my mouth.

"Baby, no, it's fucking killing me, but no, not yet, you're not ready yet." I see anger sweep across her face, it turns to hurt. I know exactly what she's thinking.

"Of course I want you, don't give me that look. See for yourself." I nod my head in the direction of my cock. I see her smile at the sight of him stuck out, tenting my gray sweats. She licks her lips, I lift her chin up gently to look at me.

"No Prim, you are not going there. Baby, your head is too fragile, and any kind of pressure could cause you damage. I will not, no, I fucking refuse for you to have any more pain. When you are ready, I'm telling you now you will not leave our bed for a week. I promise." I'm smiling at her and kiss the tip of her nose, then her forehead, and I cradle it against my chest again. I feel her hand start to creep around to my front, she just about sweeps her hand over my cock but I jump back from her reach, making sure I don't hurt her.

"Can I just help you with that?" she asks, pointing to my tented sweats.

"I promise it won't hurt me. I don't want you getting frustrated and I would love to help you out."

I shake my head and laugh at her, I sign 'NO' sternly, and I walk around to my side of the island, a little uncomfortable and making a show of it for her by exaggerating my strides. It works and she's laughing at me. I love that, and she isn't wincing at laughing, which is an improvement. I pretend to straddle the stool awkwardly, again making her laugh. We finish our breakfast.

I settle her on the couch for a bit.

"Baby, I'm gonna take a shower. I won't be long."

She nods and settles in to watch one of her reality shows. It's one of those housewives of somewhere or other that she likes to watch. All those women screaming and fighting each other gets on my nerves, I leave her to it most of the time when she puts them on. I head to our room and I strip. My cock is still semi-hard, I walk to the bathroom and start to stroke him. I think of Prim and her fucking amazing mouth and he's sprung to full length in no time. I turn the shower on and walk in, stretching and pulling him. I lean against the shower wall and close my eyes and imagine it's Prim stroking him. I picture her, on her knees in front of me in this very spot. I picture her licking her lips, looking up at me, and smiling just as she moves forward and starts licking my cock, swirling her tongue around the tip and playing with my balls. I mirror the image of her tongue on my cock using my finger and it's fucking bliss. I picture her taking him in right to the back of her throat and me starting to thrust, holding the top of her head.

I have my head back on the shower wall with my eyes closed as I start to thrust into my hand, imagining it's Prim's mouth. I see her smiling up at me as she's doing it and seeing the adoration I have for her. I pump away with my fist, gripping tighter and tighter as I pull. My other hand wanders to my balls and I start to fondle them just like she does, then move my hand farther under to my ass, I slip a finger into it, she loves to do this and I thrust harder and harder. I'm getting so breathless, I'm deafening myself in the stall from my heavy breaths and grunting, it's not long before I'm squirting cum everywhere.

I'm shouting loud, "Fuck, fuck, yes, FUCK."

Thrusting and thrusting. I don't want it to stop. I slide down the wall and sit on the floor of the shower. The water is running over me and the room is full of steam when I open my eyes. I see cum running down the glass shower partition opposite me. I feel a little guilty for doing it, knowing Prim missed out, but it won't be long before she's back doing this to me.

She likes to watch when I do this to myself, yet I fucking hate it if she tries to pleasure herself in front of me. That's my fucking job. This only happens if we've argued, which isn't often, I start to pleasure myself when we argue 'cause it breaks the ice and I love her licking her lips watching, trying her darndest not to join in, but it's never lasted, not once. She always had to take over. But the two times she's laid on her bed when I've been pissed, and she's blatantly spread her legs and started to play with her pussy, right in front of me, I've become like a maniac. I've screamed 'NO' and taken over telling her it's mine and mine alone to pleasure, not even hers. It ends up with us having the hardest and most passionate fucks.

I finish my shower and put my jeans on, but don't fasten them. I have my T-shirt over my shoulder, I'll put it on before I go out. As I head down the stairs, I hear a noise in the kitchen, I can see Prim sitting on the couch from where I am. Fuck, who's in the house? I stealthily descend the final steps, I'm barefoot and I know where every creak is, so I avoid them. I hear the fridge door closing. I creep toward the kitchen, just then, Pixie comes out and sees me. She screams and drops the cup in her hand. The cup smashes and hot coffee spills everywhere, Cassy comes running out of the kitchen to see what's going on, Trixie comes out of the living room at the same time and they all stand staring at me.

"What, I didn't even know you were here. Fuck, you scared the shit out of me."

Cassy scowls at me for my language. Pixie and Trixie stand staring at me. They both have the same look on their faces. It's a dreamy, lust-filled look, both tilting their heads to one side in unison. The look is one I've seen countless times. It's then I remember I have no shirt on and my fucking jeans are undone, showing my happy trail.

"Wow," they both say together. They turn to each other and giggle, then straight back at me. Cassy frowns at me, nodding to my body. I fasten my jeans, slowly, then take my tee and start to put it on.

"Aww, do you have to?" Pixie says, smiling.

"Enough, Pixie, that's your cousin's fiancé. Stop drooling, it's inappropriate."

I laugh and wink at the girls, then just stand there.

"Erm, Blaine, I think you need to move, you have hot coffee all over your feet. It may blister if you don't wipe it off." They all know I have this condition where I don't feel pain. Cassy quickly dashes into the kitchen and comes out with a damp cloth.

"You two, get the brush and sweep this up before he cuts his feet on the shards of pottery. Blaine, don't you move."

I stay where I am as they all move into action. They clean it all up and Cassy wipes at my feet, she checks there are no cuts. Trixie brings me my sneakers to put on just in case there are some more shards they missed. All the while Prim is totally oblivious to any of this, I watch her still watching the TV.

"Did Prim let you in? I've told her not to answer the door when I'm not around?"

"No, I had to use my key. I messaged Prim to tell her I was at the door. I did ring the bell a couple of times, but no one came. You know I don't use my key when I know you are both home. I thought it strange she didn't see the light flash, or read my message, unless she fell asleep." It has me thinking about her eyesight. I wonder if she can see the lights flashing. We don't really know the extent of any damage that's been done.

"Let me try the bell and make sure the lights working in the living room, will you stand and watch it for me?" I open the front door and press the bell.

"It's flashing in the living room and in the hall," Cassy and Pixie shout. Everyone is standing behind Prim and she has no idea what's going on. She still didn't see the light flashing. I pull out my phone and I stand just behind her and I put the light on and start making it flash. She doesn't notice. I text her phone and I see it flash on the table in front of her, she doesn't see it. I walk over and stand in front of her. She looks up and smiles.

"Hey baby, have you seen Cassy and the girls, they went to the kitchen." I still have the light on my phone flashing. She doesn't even look at it.

"Prim, baby, what do you see on my phone?"

She furrows her brow, looking confused at my question.

"Nothing, why? What have you done to it?"

Oh fuck, when they'd shone the light in her eyes, she was sensitive to it. I thought one of the tests they did was a flashing spot, but maybe they didn't do that.

"You don't see my light flashing?"

She looks confused again and shakes her head.

"Cassy, will you ring the bell again, please?"

She goes to the front door and Prim is looking at me very confused. The bell goes and I turn and see the light flashing.

"Do you see the bell light flashing, Prim?"

She shakes her head no.

We need to get her eyes tested for real. Fuck, that will mean going to see that douchebag. She looks scared now.

"What's wrong with me, Blaine? Why don't I see the lights flashing? I see everything else clearly now. I don't like it."

I kneel in front of her and hold her hands. "It's okay, we'll get you sorted. Don't worry, baby. It's just taking time, that's all." I kiss her lips then sit next to her.

Cassy comes in with a tray of coffee, followed by the girls. I'm not sure I should leave her now. Maybe I will hang around. It doesn't take long before all four of them are shouting and laughing and signing to each other. That's my cue to leave them to it.

"If you girls are all going to talk girly shit and discuss the Kardashians, then I'm out of here. Baby, I'll go for a walk and get some fresh air and stop at the mini-mart to get some stuff for us. Is there anything in particular you need or want?"

"No thank you, Blaine, you be careful out there. See you soon, don't be too long."

I know what she's referring to when she says be careful. She thinks Poppy might be around. I give her a kiss and say goodbye to the others. Cassy walks me to the door.

"I'll stay until you get back, I won't leave her alone. To be honest, I can see it's doing her good, especially having the girls here. I'm just worried about her sight. Is it getting worse or is it that we just didn't notice until now?" I think back to the test the douchebag did, I don't remember him flashing a light or anything like that. Surely that's what they do. I remember when I had an eye test last year after my accident, they did that to me.

"On an eye test, do they ask you about flashing lights? I remember they did with mine last year, but that was my first and only eye test."

"Yes, they do, at every eye exam I had to look at a flashing red or green or white dot. I have to tell them the color each time. Did they not do that with Prim?"

I shake my head. "There was something odd about that eye doctor, I don't know what, but he didn't do that, which thinking about it now was weird. He didn't do much of anything, mainly just lifted her eyelids, shone his light in her eyes, and got her to move them. That's basically it, in fact, her normal doctor did that much, but then he's not an eye specialist. Right, let me get going, I shouldn't be too long. I think we'll find a new eye specialist and get her to see him this week. I was going to talk to you as well about her hearing. I've been talking to someone about hearing implants and they think she might be a good candidate for them. Have any of you ever looked into that before? I haven't broached the subject with Prim yet, I want to get her better from this first."

"No, we haven't. The doctors told us she will never hear again, but that was many years ago now. Technology advances so quick. I did see something about implants, but I haven't looked into it with it all being new technology."

"Just a second. Let me get the leaflet for you to read and see what you think. See if you think it would be worth discussing with Prim and pursuing. Mr. Lund, the guy who sells these to hospitals, thinks she will benefit because they work mostly on people who went deaf, not those who were born deaf." I can see the surprise on her face, probably the fact I've been looking into it. I run up the stairs and grab one of the leaflets and then pass it to her.

"Don't let Prim see it just yet. I want to discuss this with her first. Let me get going then, I won't be too long. See you in a bit." I head out and head to the main street where I can get the bus to head to the douchebag's office.

Ten

Blaine

TWO BUSES LATER AND I'M IN THE AREA WHERE THE OFFICE IS, according to Google. It's not the best part of town which surprises me. I thought it would have been in a more affluent part. This can't be right, it's taking me to a residential part of the city, and not a very nice part. I sound like a fucking snob. I was brought up in a fucking shed and now because I've lived with Prim all this time, this to me is a shit hole. I curse myself for being like this. If I hadn't been living with Prim, I would have thought this area was a dream to live in. Real houses with real people around. How could this be the right place? He drove a sports car probably worth more than all the houses on this one street.

I head down a couple more streets, following google. Finally I think I'm in the right place. I'm now in downtown San Fran, I've been here a couple of times with Prim, her bank is not far from here and her office is close by. This must be it, maybe I misread the bus I got on, I still struggle with my reading sometimes, that must be it, I must have gotten on the wrong bus. I walk down another road with tall office buildings, and then I start to see the names of different specialist doctors. I stop at a building, this is the address he sent to Prim. I don't see his name but I suddenly see a name, Dr. Benedict, Ophthalmologist, I recognize that name. He's the doctor that is the resident at the hospital that Dr. Russkett is covering for. His practice is in this tall office building and looking at some of the other names listed, they are all different doctors' offices. I just don't see slimy doc's name listed anywhere.

I head to the reception area and a young woman directs me to the fifteenth floor to Dr. Benedict's office. I may as well see if he's here and see if he will see Prim. The young woman doesn't ask who I am or if I have an appointment, I take it she just directs people to what floor they need. I head up in the elevator, once the doors open, I step out, and to my left is a set of doors with a plaque saying Dr. Weaks—Neurosurgeon and to my right is a set of doors with a plaque saying Dr. Benedict—Ophthalmologist. I head to the doors. I go to pull one open, but they're locked. I ring the bell on the side and wait. No one comes. I try the number that's etched in the smoked glass panel at the side of the doors, giving opening hours, etc. I hear a phone ring inside but then it goes to an answering service. I hang up. The times on the door say he should be open now. I remember the nurse saying he suddenly took a leave of absence which is why Russkett was standing in. I peer through the writing on the glass which is clear, and I don't see anyone. In fact, I can't see much of anything.

I turn to leave and jump, he's standing there, the douchebag is just stood watching me, I didn't hear the elevators open, and I certainly didn't hear him. He's dressed in a suit, no white doctor's coat. He's standing with his legs slightly apart, one hand in his trouser pocket and the other with his thumb at the side of his mouth, and he's watching me. He has piercing blue eyes and dark blond wavy hair. If I was into guys, I would definitely do him. He's like a male Prim. What the fuck am I thinking?

"Can I help you Mr.…."

Yeah, douchebag doesn't know my name, he never asked, and I never told him. I revert back to my old self, lying about my name.

"Turner, it's Nick Turner."

He scowls at me.

"Funny, I remember Miss Tomlinson calling you Blaine?" He smirks at me. He caught me.

"That's my middle name, only used by those close to me," I lie and he knows it.

He gives off such an aura about him, it's one of authority, like he's in charge, the boss and everyone does as he says. What the fuck, well I don't do as he says. He takes his hand out of his pocket and rubs his clean-shaven chin, he's waiting for me to speak. I mirror his stance, but with both my hands in my front jeans pockets. He's virtually the same stature as me, well built, tall and I would say has the physique to match mine. We just stare at each other. I'm wondering what the fuck he's doing here when it's not his office.

"Did you want to see me about something? Miss Tomlinson messaged me to say everything was fine and she didn't need any more tests."

He's a cocky bastard.

"The last I saw it was you messaging my fiancée for her to come and see you. Why are you hassling her? She told you she was fine."

He puts his hand back in his trouser pocket and he tilts his head slightly to the side, he's sizing me up.

"I want to make sure she's seeing the best doctor for her sight. I believe she is still having problems."

How the fuck could he know that. She's been fine until today. I need to play this cool. I have no idea what his agenda is, but I would put my life on it that he's not a doctor. The clothes look expensive like his car, his watch looks like very expensive. Why is he being standoffish and why hasn't he just opened the office and asked me inside, if he's really using this office, which I doubt. I need to leave and make sure Prim doesn't go anywhere near him. I think this man standing here is a very dangerous man, and I don't know what he's playing at.

"No, she's fine, her vision is almost back to normal, she just needs some glasses for her reading. I came to tell you that and let you know there is no need to contact her again, only to my surprise this isn't your office, yet this is the address you sent to Prim. This is the missing doctor's office who works at the hospital. Anyway, thanks for your help, but we don't need you anymore."

Time for me to leave, the vibes from this guy are rotten, I start toward him to head to the elevator. He doesn't move as I approach. I scowl at him. The prick just smirks at me. He's goading me, I make to move past him. Just then I see a figure emerge from the open elevator doors. It's fucking Poppy. What the fuck is she doing here? I stop dead. What the fuck. Well, I didn't see that coming.

"Hello again, BLAINE, my old buddy. How's it hanging there," she says, emphasizing my name with such a cocky sneer on her face as she steps next to the slimy guy.

I watch as he takes his hand from his trouser pocket and pulls Poppy into his side, before bending to kiss her on the lips. I just watch, trying to comprehend what I'm seeing. Fuck, I walked straight into this. I would never have guessed, not in a million years. Well played Poppy, well played. I don't speak. I think I'm a little shocked, I'm trying to process this whole situation. He was a fucking plant at the hospital to get info on Prim, it has to be. These two are a couple, that's plain to see.

"The lady said hello, aren't you going to answer her?" he asks, smirking at me.

"I don't see a fucking lady, so nothing to say."

He steps closer to me. It only takes one stride, and he's in my face, almost nose to nose. I think I might be a touch taller, but there's really nothing in it. I take my hands out of my pockets and I ball them into fists at my sides, ready to fight if I need to. I've never been scared of anything in my life, but I'd say what I am feeling now is fear of him. He's bad news, I've thought about him since seeing him rush out that day and drive away in his expensive car, trying to work out if I knew where he was from with his accent. I remembered when I did my ankle in, I watched all kinds of crime series and I watched a documentary series about the different mafia families. I remember being fascinated by these people and how powerful they were and how they seemed to rule the world. Well, if I was a betting man, I would put a thousand bucks down on him being one of them. He reminded me of the mafia men I watched. The documentary was on the Italian, Russian, Serbian, and Mexican mafias, or Bratvas as some were called, and Chinese Triads and I would bet my thousand bucks he's Russian or Serbian mafia, just from his aura alone. If he is who I think he is then they are bad news all around. I saw how they killed people and what they do. You don't mess with them according to this documentary. Not something I would ever want to be mixed up with.

I sneer at him. If he wants to have a go, let him. I'm a fucking killer myself, albeit women, but I'd have a damn good fucking go at this douchebag if I had to.

"You better apologize to her now."

"For what, DOCTOR?" I say, pronouncing the word so he knows I'm on to him. "Is that even your name, Dr. Russkett? Or are you like me, only using your real name for people close to you?" I sneer at him again with spittle coming out of my mouth.

He removes his arm from around Poppy's shoulders and slowly reaches into the inside of his jacket, he never takes his eyes off mine. I step back slightly. What if he's reaching for a gun? I watch as he starts to slowly pull his hand out of his jacket. He smiles a cocky smile at the look on my face and what must be relief as he pulls out a handkerchief to wipe his face. I'm playing with fire here, I know it, he's not even bothered about the venom in my voice, most men and women cower at that, but not this asswipe.

"Enough of this already. Let's just take him so we can be done with this and then we can finish her once and for all." Poppy walks up to me as she's talking and she's smirking at me while saying it.

"You fucking bitch, don't you think you've done enough to Prim? You've failed to kill her twice now. I ought to just fucking wring your neck here and now." I sidestep him, I'm now in her face, bending down to be eye to eye with her.

"What happened, Pops, you couldn't have my cock, so you thought you'd get someone else's cock and let them do your dirty work for you? You're an evil bitch, Poppy." I spit in her face. She at least flinches at my venom.

"His cock's way better than yours could ever be, BLAINE, you son of a bitch. I'm not the only failure here am I though, when it comes to trying to kill someone?"

I don't even blink at her words. He's standing slightly to the side leaning against the wall watching us with his hands back in his pockets. I know if I tried to do anything to her, he would pounce. I would say he's packing if he's who I think he is, there is no way he wouldn't be. Suddenly my head is jarred. I look to her; she fucking slapped me.

"You fucking bitch, you'll pay for that." I go to grab her neck when douchebag whistles just as I put my hand to her throat and start to squeeze.

From the still open elevator doors come two huge guys, his men, I presume. Both wearing jeans and black leather jackets, and black leather gloves. He speaks to them in his native tongue, so I have no idea what he just said. The elevator door now closes and Poppy's got both her hands on mine, trying to pry my hand from her throat. I squeeze as hard as I can, trying to do as much damage as I can before they reach me. I can see blood on my hand, I take it she scratched me. Great, how do I explain that to Prim? I squeeze hard and see her eyes start to bulge as they become bloodshot, the two men come for me, one takes my free arm before I have a chance to lash out at him, the other uses both hands to pry my hand from her throat and they both take one each of my arms and hold me.

She comes toward me and she signs in my face, "Revenge is going to be fucking sweet. So, so fucking sweet." This time she punches me straight in the mouth, hard, because my head jolts slightly, I lick the metallic taste of blood from my lips.

"Tastes sweeter than your pappy's blood." I sneer at her.

The douchebag moves over toward her and wraps his arms around her shoulders and kisses the top of her head. He looks down to her neck, I can see the marks from my hold on her, I'd say she's going to be bruised.

"Are you okay, мой ангел?"

She looks up to him and nods.

"You are so right, my love, he will be all yours to do as you wish." He leans down and kisses her on the lips.

Fuck, I can see these two together are dangerous, I don't think I'm going to get out of this one alive, she's going to kill me, she's going to get her revenge.

PART VI

Poppy

Eleven

Poppy
Present

AFTER HE CHASED ME FROM OUTSIDE PRIM'S LAST NIGHT, I need to be a bit more careful. I didn't see that coming, my stupid fucking phone lighting up gave me away. I outran him. I knew I could, he's no match for me anymore. I'm sitting on the bench on the hospital grounds. I haven't seen him arrive yet, which is unusual, he's normally here by now. What if he came here early? Or what if something did happen to Prim yesterday, and I just didn't feel it? I'm sitting, keeping my eye on anyone entering the front, I look at the message I just received on my phone and type back. When I look back up, he's there. He's looking straight at me. Fuck, he's walking toward me, I get up quickly ready to run. There's an exit at the back of the hospital, I already have it planned out. I watch him, he's smirking, as if laughing at me. He's not rushing, he's just looking cocky walking slowly toward me. I don't let him get close. I turn and head for the back of the hospital. I start to jog, just casually at first, then without looking back to see where he is, I run full force around the back and through the exit. I don't stop. I don't look back, I just run the route I had planned out.

I ease up and look back, he's nowhere to be seen. I don't know if he chased me again or thought better of it after last night. He knew I was there. How did he know? When did he arrive? Or had he just arrived? I was too busy messaging on my damn phone and not paying attention. I need to keep my mind focused, he's going to get me if I keep losing concentration.

I head to our house. I know Igor is out at the moment and I don't want to tell him about my run-ins with Blaine just yet, he'll get mad at me for blowing it, not that it matters. Our plan is coming together nicely now. I just need to know what's happened with Prim. Blaine seemed okay when he came toward me, he didn't look upset or anything.

I've been at the hospital for a week now, since that day he saw me there. He's seen me each day, because I've let him. The cocky bastard thinks he's so clever because he salutes me, but he never comes for me. I find it really odd he's not trying to get me. I reckon he's doing what I'm doing and biding my time. Maybe he thinks one of these times he will get me, when I least expect it, he's got it wrong, I'll get him when he least expects it. I finally told Igor about my encounters with Blaine, he said it was a good idea to let him know I was there and he hadn't frightened me off, show him I am someone to be reckoned with, let Blaine know I'm permanently here and not going anywhere anytime soon.

I'm sitting on the bench again just flicking through my phone, I look up just as I see him wheel Prim out in a wheelchair. Fuck, she looks good and I feel a sense of relief mixed with anxiety from actually seeing her. I get up off the bench as he turns and heads in my direction. I turn my back and dash around the back of the hospital to the exit. I hope she didn't see me. I hope I got up and turned quickly enough. What's he playing at? I wonder if he's even told her it was me that got to her again. In all honesty, I knew where I was stabbing her, Igor showed me, I knew it was only shallow and wouldn't do any damage as such, but I wanted to let Blaine know I was dangerous, and he better watch out. What I didn't expect was for Prim to fall forward and smash her head on the table and then the ground. I thought she would have just felt a pain and reached around to see what it was. It was him coming at me from across the street. He made me panic a little and I guess I knocked Prim, sending her flying without realizing.

I know it must have been bad for the amount of time she's been in the hospital, that's when Igor came up with his next genius plan, being a doctor, so he could find out exactly what has been going on. He's so smart, he's taught me so much, not only about myself and how I am such a powerful woman, but he's trained me in all the ways to survive and get what I want.

———

A Year Earlier

I've spent a long time locked in Igor's apartment. I haven't tried to leave again after he showed me his bedroom and his gym and pool, I've been happy being with him. He's showed me all the locked rooms, apart from one, he said that room was never for me to see, he's even showed me his office, he's had me sitting naked on a chair in front of him a few times while he's worked away. He's told me that all the rooms that are locked, no one has ever been in them, but that he knew I was special and he didn't intend to ever let me go.

I like what he's doing to me, he's empowering me. He likes that I answer him back whenever I've thought he was out of order, that I don't kneel to his every command, well not unless it's to take his cock into my mouth, that is. I kneel with pleasure at that command. It's like he worships me, this dangerous god worships ME, a nobody, that is what empowers me. Why would he choose me when I'm sure he could have anyone he wanted with his looks.

I remembered Svetlana telling me she was once his, as with many other girls. I've been wanting to ask him why me, but I have to ask him when the mood's right. He's been gone at one of his meetings, he's always at endless meetings, sometimes he comes home in such a good mood, but other times I steer clear of him just from the look on his face. There have been a few times he's walked into the apartment in just his tight boxers, I now know why, but that first time was a shock to me in more ways than one.

"Why are you only in your underwear? You left here in a suit." I stand with my hands on my hips, waiting for his reply. If he's been fucking anyone else then I'm out of here. He sneers at me and goes to walk past me, I stand in his way.

"Fucking answer me, have you been fucking someone else, is that why? Did you get your suit dirty with cum or did it smell of sex?" I'm so angry, as is he by the look on his face.

He gets up in my face and slams his forehead to mine, not a headbutt, as such, but it certainly felt like it. Looking me straight in the eye, he says, "Get the fuck out of my way or you'll be sorry."

I glare back at him, trying to hold my own with his forehead digging into mine, trying to push me out of the way. He doesn't use his hands, just his head.

"Move, NOW, мой ангел, before I do something I'll later regret," he shouts at me.

I stand tall and push back with my head. He brings a hand up and wraps it around the front of my neck and pushes me away, he's far stronger than I am and it's hot as hell. He lets go, and it's only then I see blood on his arms and hands. Okay, not what I thought then. I move slightly to the side and he barges past me, knocking my shoulder and sending me flying onto my ass.

"You fucking asshole, there was no need for that," I yell after him and he turns to see me on the floor. I see the look of remorse on his face.

He stops, stands there for a few seconds with his back to me then turns and heads back. I scoot backwards, not knowing what he's going to do. My hands are sweaty on the marble floor and are sliding, I can't get the grip I need to back up, I use my legs to try to get away from him. He stands over me, I stop trying to move and I look up his gorgeous body to his face. He's not as angry, he looks pained. He bends down, putting an arm under my knees and one around my back, and he lifts me up as though I weigh nothing, scooping me against his chest. I look up at his face, I can see a couple of spots of blood, I didn't notice them before.

"Мой ангел, I am so sorry. I did not mean to knock you to the floor. Please forgive me. I am not used to answering to anyone. I never have. Please forgive me, мой ангел."

Wow, that's a sudden change. He snapped out of being the monster that walked in, to suddenly showing such remorse because he thinks he's hurt me. I smile up at his face. I stroke down his cheek and wipe one of the spots of blood from it. I show him the blood on my finger. He just stares at it. Not saying a word.

"Come with me to the shower, I need to clean up."

He walks us to my room and straight into the bathroom where he places me on the vanity unit next to the double sinks. I watch him start the shower then take his boxers off, watching me the whole time. He moves over to me and spreads my legs, standing between them. He wraps his arms around my waist and rests his head on my chest. I wrap my arms around his head and I run my fingers through his hair. We stay like this for a minute until he decides he wants me naked. He strips me, but keeps me on the vanity unit, he opens my legs wider then kneels in front of me, and before I know it his tongue's in my pussy.

"Нmmm, you are a tonic to me, мой ангел," he says, pulling back to look at my face.

I have my hands behind me holding me up. I grab his head and push it back, wanting him to finish. He laughs in my pussy then gets to work on my clit, inserting his fingers in me. I'm screaming my release with my cum squirting all over his face. He stands up and doesn't give me time to come down from my orgasm before he pulls me forward and slams his rock-hard cock right in. He starts to rotate, then he's at it like a fucking maniac, letting out all his pent-up frustrations right into me.

I fucking love it.

My head is now back on the mirror, it's going to break with him slamming into me so hard, he's gripping my hips, digging his fingers into me and pulling my body as much as he can onto his cock. The whole unit is moving with the force he's shoving it into me, bottles fall, some crashing to the floor. He's grunting loud and his breathing is getting so erratic, I think he may have a heart attack if he carries on. His face is getting so red, I reach up and I pinch both his nipples, rubbing and squeezing them, he looks at me with such lust and then he screams out with his release. His face contorting, his eyes screwed up as he thrusts and thrusts into me.

"Look at me," I shout at him and his eyes fly open.

I take my middle finger, suck it then I play with my clit as he's still releasing into me. He bats my hand away growling and takes over. I scream out with my second release and we pant and stare into each other's eyes as we slowly come down. He leans forward and kisses my lips.

"I fucking love you. You are the tonic I need to anchor me on the bad days. Don't ever leave me, мой ангел."

I freeze, still panting hard from the exertion, but I stare into his eyes. He just said he loved me. Was that just in the heat of the moment, in the throes of passion or did he mean it? I don't speak. Instead I push him away from me, watching his cock pop out of my pussy. He's still semi-hard, he's a fucking machine. I jump off the vanity unit and head to the shower. I feel like I may pass out. The room is full of steam, I've just had two fucking amazing orgasms and he just said he loved me. I slide down the shower wall and sit on the floor. I feel myself burning up from the heat in here. I sit up and reach for the shower dials to turn the heat down. I pull my knees up to my chest and wrap my arms around them, resting my head on my knees, and I cry. I fucking cry like a baby.

I don't know why I'm crying. Maybe it's hormones. Before I know it, he's pulling me onto his lap, sitting on the shower floor. He rocks me and strokes my back.

"Shhh, мой ангел, what is wrong? Why are you crying? I am sorry if I hurt you. Please look at me and tell me what is wrong."

I look up at his face, the most beautiful face, I can't believe he wants me, I must look like a mess, no doubt my face is all blotchy, I'm soaked, and my hair is stuck to my face. He moves some strands out of the way and peers into my eyes. I have never felt loved by anyone. Yet I feel so loved and cherished by him, like I'm his world. I have only ever had casual boyfriends growing up, my one boyfriend I thought loved me only wanted my money and then used me as a whore for his clients. He had everyone fuck me that came to buy drugs from him. I was an added extra perk for them, to make them keep coming back to him for drugs. I never felt loved by my parents, it was all about Prim. It was like I was an afterthought. Yet looking at this beautiful face, the one who is looking at me with such concern and admiration, the one that makes me feel alive and wanted, I know I love him back.

"Мой ангел, what did I do wrong?" He looks hurt and conflicted.

I stroke down his cheek to his lips and I lean up and kiss them. "You did nothing wrong, Igor, you didn't hurt me, no, I just wish you would trust me sometimes. I saw the blood on you, what happened to your suit, how did you get blood on you?"

He looks at me, I can see the turmoil in his eyes, since living with him I've gotten really good at reading him. I remember at first, I couldn't read him at all.

"I see how worried you are, Igor. I can see the conflict in your eyes. You don't have to tell me if you don't trust me. It's okay, I understand." I lean my head back on his chest. I don't want to see the hurt there and I don't want him to see the hurt on my face.

"Мой ангел, look at me."

I look up into his eyes and he leans in and kisses me gently.

"It is very hard for me to trust anyone. I only trusted one person in my life and that ended badly. I rely on me alone, I am the king around these parts, I own the streets and no one crosses me. You must know by now I am Russian Bratva, mafia, and this is my turf. What I do is not nice, I am not nice, мой ангел. If I tell you things and we don't work out, then there is only one option for me. I never want that option. Do you understand what I am saying?"

I think so, if we don't work out and I knew his business, he would kill me. I nod at him and lower my eyes.

"Мой ангел, that does not mean it will not work out, I never intend on letting you go, but we have to take it slow. You are, how do they say? A firecracker, and I love that about you. No one has ever dared answer me back the way you do, you are different. Just know I have not been with another woman since you came into my life. I don't intend to go with another woman as long as you are in my life. When I come home like this, it usually takes me a long time to calm down, but with you, it is almost instant. You calm me like no other. I promise you now, I will never go with another woman for as long as we are together. I never, ever break a promise. My word is an oath. Do you understand me, my angel?"

I nod, I do and I will make him trust me. "I like it when you call me that in Russian. Don't stop," is all I say.

I lean up and kiss him again but don't deepen it. I don't want this just to be about sex, although the sex is amazing, I want this to be about feelings, us feeling, I need his trust. He has to trust me before we take this any further, and that means letting me in on some of what he does and teaching me. We shower and then have dinner.

It's happened only a handful of times since that first time, him coming home in just his tight boxers, we end up having the most amazing fucks, then shower, sometimes he is covered in blood, others just a little. Each of those times he has told me he loves me, never any other time, just the times he has done a kill. I say that because well, why else would he be in the state he's in and it's the only explanation for the blood and his moods.

Every night he is home we have dinner. It's always waiting for us as we enter the dining room. He has staff everywhere. Sometimes it un-nerves me having other people around that I don't know and very rarely see. I have never cooked once while being here and I don't even know the names of the staff apart from Mavra, the guard, I've spoken to him a cou-ple of times. Then there is Andrey and Ivan, who are his personal guards and are with him all the time. Now those two are big, mean-looking guys.

I'm still too afraid to tell him I love him, that one time I did tell some-one, it was a disaster, but he's told me he loves me a few times now, was that genuine? Or was that because of the situation? Until he tells me when he's not been in those situations, I won't tell him how madly in love I am with him. I sometimes think to hell with my revenge on Nick, but then I only have to look at my missing toe or the scars on me and I hate him all over again and the anger bubbles deep within me and I know I need to get him back.

"Igor," I say sweetly, we have just made love, not fucked and I know he gets all soppy after a real tense lovemaking session.

"What is it, мой ангел?"

"Please don't get angry with me. When I was locked in that room on the other floor, the day you brought me here, I had a conversation with Svetlana. Promise me you will not harm her?" I feel him tense up, shit this is maybe not the time. Maybe there will never be a time. I start to get up off my bed but he pulls me back.

"Continue," he says, irritated and sternly.

Well fuck him, he knows that doesn't work on me. When he gets stern and commanding, I close down on him. I start to get up again, but he grabs my arm and squeezes tight.

"Ow, that fucking hurts. Get off me."

So now it's going to turn nasty with me storming off as usual. He lets go immediately, it's instinct with him, but as soon as I tell him it hurts, or he sees the pain on my face, he lets go right away. He tries to grab my hand as I climb off the bed, but I pull it away from his reach.

"No, Igor, go to hell. I wanted a conversation with you but as usual, you get all demanding and authoritative on me, it doesn't work. Now I'm going to make some coffee, kindly leave MY room before I return." I storm out of the room, forgetting I'm naked.

"POPPY, get your naked ass back in this room and cover up, unless you want to be responsible for any of my staff losing their fucking eyes," he shouts through the door.

Another thing I fucking hate is that I can't walk around naked if I want to. It just doesn't feel like a place I live, and I'm starting to hate it. I walk back in slowly, sashaying my hips and I grab my robe from the stool. I turn my back on him and walk out, only putting the robe on once I'm in the hallway.

"Вы будете чертовски смерти меня, женщина, и многие из моих сотрудников" he shouts through the door at me.

"Fucking English, Igor, you know I don't understand you," I shout back at him.

"I said, you will be the fucking death of me, woman, and many of my staff, now get your ass back in here so we can talk like civilized people." I hear him chuckle to himself and it makes me mad.

"I want coffee, do you want one?" I shout back, trying to soften the hostility between us.

"Yes please, strong and black."

I make him wait before I return to the bedroom. I didn't see any of the staff around which was good, but still, I had to fasten my robe. The last thing I want is for any of them to lose their eyes, I wouldn't put it past Igor to do that. I walk back into my room expecting him to still be in my bed but it's empty. I put the cups down and walk into my bathroom to see if he's there. Nothing. He left when he knew I was bringing coffee? I go out into the hallway and I listen. Nothing.

"Igor," I shout and listen, nothing.

I walk toward the living room. I walk around looking everywhere. I see Mavra and ask if Igor left but he just shakes his head at me. I don't think he understands a lot of what I say. I head back to my room, just before I reach it, I notice a white towel outside the door to his room. As I get closer, I see the door is open. I walk up to it and stand at the door and peer in. The cocky bastard is lying in his bed, with his hands behind his head, and he's got the biggest smile on his face as he watches me.

"What are you doing in there? I just brought coffee for you, it's in my room."

He continues smiling at me.

"You told me to get out of YOUR room so I did, now can you bring my coffee here, please? Into OUR room."

I huff and turn to leave.

"Also, bring your coffee."

What is he playing at now? I walk into his room a few minutes later with the coffees and I put them both on the bedside table next to him. Just as I turn to leave, he grabs me by the arm and then launches me on top of him on the bed.

"What are you doing, Igor? You said no one has ever been in this bed with you." I smile because I know what he's doing. He's trying to prove to me that it's just me and no one else. He smiles back at me, pulling me up so my face is above his.

"I want you in my bed, мой ангел, with me, I want this to be your room." He's trying to be serious, but he's smiling, and I would say he's glowing.

I shrug. "But I quite like my room now, and besides, you're never in here anyway, you sleep with me all the time, so I don't see what difference it makes." I stare at his face and watch as the smile drops from it. He takes me seriously all the fucking time. I don't smile and just wait for his reaction. I goad him and wind him up all the time and he falls for it. He may be king out there on the streets, but he's an equal in here with me.

He furrows his brow and I can tell he's thinking. He suddenly shrugs and throws me off him onto the empty side next to him.

"No, this is OUR room from now on. I want to take you out shopping so we can pick all new furniture and anything you want to go in here. Apart from this bed, this bed stays, it will be our bed where the only two people ever to use it will be us, me and you. I love you. That is final." He picks the coffee cups up all matter of fact, and hands me mine as I sit up. He sits drinking his and I stare at him. I mean really stare, taking him in, I love him, I love what he represents and how he treats me, I love his moods, his looks, just him.

"I love you, Igor."

Twelve

Poppy
A Year Earlier

ELLING IGOR I LOVED HIM WAS THE HARDEST THING I'VE ever done. I trust him, maybe I'm foolish and naïve because I don't know what he actually does. Yes, I've heard stories about the mafia, but I don't know for sure. I've also not known him long and Svetlana told me he's had many women. I'm going to ask him about that when he's home tonight.

I'm sitting on a lounger up on the roof garden. I suddenly hear lots of loud popping noises, like a car backfiring, but it's going on for too long. Could it be gunfire? I run to the outer railing and peer over to where I think the sounds are coming from. It's so high up here, I don't know how many floors this building has because I've never been out of it. There is an alley below and I can make out three big black cars, but I can't make out what type they are, and I can't make out the people. They look like ants. I hear more popping and see flashes, it's definitely guns. Fuck, what's going on? What if it's Igor down there? I head inside and run down the stairs to the elevator. No one is here, Mavra isn't around. That's really strange. I look at myself in the doors of the elevator. I'm in a skimpy bikini, there's no way I can go down dressed like this. I run to the bedroom and throw on my jeans and a tee over my bikini and put on some sneakers.

I run back to the elevator and push the down button. The doors open only after a few seconds. Mavra comes out of the elevator but he doesn't look right. He staggers and falls forward. I just about stop him from hitting the floor, he's a big stocky guy. He's holding his side.

"Mavra, what is it? What's happened?" I go into a panic as I see blood pouring from his side. I run for a towel and come back and press it on his side.

"Igor is down there, lots of guns, lots of men, girls dead." He passes out.

I have to leave him. I need to find Igor. I press for the doors to open and get inside. Fuck, I don't know where he is or where anyone is. I press the button for the ground floor. I see we are in the penthouse but that there are forty-two floors to this building, and he said he owns this. I'm pacing the tiny box wanting it to go faster, it stops, and the doors open. I start to head out, there are four men with guns, they could be Igor's men, but then what do I know? I don't speak, then behind them is Svetlana and three other girls, they don't look much older than her, they all look young. I look at the panel and see we stopped on the ninth floor, not the ground floor.

"Svetlana, oh thank god, what's happening?" I see the look on her face, it's one of shock.

"There are some rivals of Igor's, they came to kill us all. Igor's men have killed most of them. These men are taking us into the basement to hide." I don't like the way she is looking at me, like she's in disbelief, I squint at her.

"How are you still here? How are you still alive?" I look at her, shocked and a little perturbed by her comment.

"What do you mean alive, why wouldn't I be?" She just shrugs and one of the guys speaks to her in Russian. She speaks back and mentions my name and Igor's. I don't know what they are saying. I look to one of the men.

"Where is Igor? Is he okay? Please tell me where he is."

He looks at me confused then speaks, but in Russian. Svetlana speaks.

"He said Igor is at the back of the building trying to stop the men entering."

I put my hand to my mouth. I saw lots of gunfire. What if he's hurt? I press the button repeatedly for the ground floor as if that would make it go any faster. I hear Svetlana speaking but don't pay attention because I have no idea what's being said. It seems to take forever. I turn to Svetlana, I'm agitated and annoyed as her words sink in.

"What did you mean, how am I still here and alive?"

She doesn't speak. I glare at her, ready to go for her when the doors open and I hear gunshots. I check the panel to make sure this is the ground floor. I leave, but one of the men follows me. I heard Svetlana say something. She must have told him to go with me. I don't need him. Just then there are shots coming my way. I'm suddenly swung round so I'm behind the man with the gun and I dive to the floor on instinct. There is no way I am fucking dying now when I survived being buried alive. The next thing I know, I'm being pinned down on the floor. I manage to lift my head and turn it enough to see the man who followed me out of the elevator, with the big gun, is now laying across my body. I can barely move, he's huge and so heavy. I think he's dead. I hear more gunshots. I keep my head down until they stop. I raise it slightly to see what's going on. There are men in black everywhere, but I don't know if they are Igor's men or not. They do look like the guy who is currently laying on top of me, crushing me. It sends me into a bit of a panic. It brings back flashes of being in that grave. I put my head down trying to calm myself, so no one sees me, I play dead until it's over. There's nothing I can do with this big body on me, I'm too small to try to get him off me.

A few minutes pass before I'm brave enough to look up, I see bodies ahead of me but from this angle, they look as though they are dressed differently than the others. I don't know who is who, I'm terrified lying here, I want to see Igor. I need to see him, make sure he's okay. I put my head back down when I hear footsteps on the marble floor.

"Мой ангел, fuck, мой ангел, FUCK," he shouts, it's Igor. I'd recognize his voice anywhere.

I try to move to get the dead guy off me, only he isn't dead. I feel him being lifted off me, I turn over and smile up at Igor but my face drops when I see he's covered in blood and the angry look on his face.

"I thought you were fucking dead. What the fuck are you even doing here, Poppy? Ебать, ебать, ебать," he screams into the air.

I know that word means fuck. He is livid with me. I've just added to his burden. I hear police sirens. He quickly gives out orders and before I know what's happening, I'm pulled up off the floor and put over his shoulder as he marches to the elevators. I lift my head up and see a team of men clearing up the bodies and cleaning up the mess, it's like watching worker ants. He slides me down his body.

"Are you okay, мой ангел? Are you hurt anywhere, you have blood on your back, did you get hurt?" I shake my head and he pulls me tightly into his chest and cradles my head, chanting something in Russian that I can't quite hear. I pull away and look up at his face.

"I'm sorry if I scared you, Igor, I was on the roof and heard gunshots. I wanted to get to you and make sure you were safe. Mavra is injured in the apartment, he needs medical attention, I don't think it's bad. I panicked when I saw him. All I could think of was to get to you. Are you hurt? You have blood all over you."

He shakes his head and kisses my lips gently as he cradles my face in both his hands. I cry as I rest my head back on his chest. I think I'm in shock, I start to shake, and he holds me tight to comfort me. We arrive at the penthouse, I turn as the elevator door pings open. I didn't realize Andrey and Ivan were with us along with the other man who was on top of me.

"Hey, are you okay? You saved my life, thank you." I can see he's holding his arm and there's a lot of blood. He got shot saving me. I cry harder as Igor picks me up and carries me to our bedroom. I didn't see Mavra, I had my head buried in Igor's chest. I can't stop shaking and crying. I look up to him as he places me on the vanity unit in the bathroom.

"What if you had been shot, Igor? What if it was you lying dead on the floor down there? Igor, I ˮ

He's on me, kissing me hard before I finish. This is different, this is desperation, I can feel he needs this as much as I do. It's the what-ifs. We're the same in this situation. He takes me on the counter but it's not the usual fuck when he's come in with blood on him, this is much slower, more of an appreciation fuck, almost lovemaking but not quite, it's desperation but somewhere in between. We cling to each other, afraid to let go.

We both climax at the same time, but it's slightly subdued because it's how we both feel. It's the what if we'd lost each other. We shower and just as I'm about to dry my hair I hear a knock on the bedroom door.

"Igor, the door, someone is knocking."

We are both still in the bathroom. He didn't hear the knock. He heads to the door. I hear voices and then I hear Igor's angry voice.

"Ебать," Igor shouts and then starts ranting in Russian. He comes back in to see me.

"I need to go back down and speak to the police. Will you be okay here while I go and sort this shit out?" I nod and stroke his cheek. He leans in and kisses me. He's put on his sweats and a tee, it's unlike him to go out of this apartment in anything other than a suit which tells me he won't be long.

"Igor, I love you, baby," I shout just as he's about to leave the bathroom.

He turns and looks at me intensely. "I love you, мой ангел, more than you could ever know. I'm going to fucking marry you after all this." With that, he's gone and I'm left open-mouthed, standing in the bathroom about to dry my hair. Is he just saying that because of the situation? I need to speak to him about Svetlana and get him to open up about what he does before I agree to marry him. I don't know If I can cope with this all my life, wondering if he's going to come home at night.

I wake up to Igor pulling me to his body In our bed. He's spooning me, wanting me close. I hadn't realized I'd fallen asleep. I dried my hair then laid on top of the bed thinking about what he said. I turn in his arms and face him.

"Is everything okay with the police?" he nods looking deep into my eyes. I'm not sure this is the time but I need to know "Were you serious earlier or was it just a heat of the moment thing, like the shock with what had happened?"

He smiles and kisses the tip of my nose then pulls back.

"The police are sorted and everything is cleaned up. Yes."

That's it, just yes? I pull back and raise my eyebrows at him.

"I was deadly serious, мой ангел. When I saw you on the floor down there, I nearly grabbed a gun to shoot everyone standing, including myself.

I thought you were dead. Just the thought of that nearly made me lose my mind. It was only because I saw you move that I didn't do it. If I had lost you, I knew in that moment I didn't want to live without you. I knew it there and then that I wanted to make you mine. You have no idea what I feel for you and just saying I love you doesn't even cover those feelings. I have never felt like this for anyone, мой ангел."

I need to know the rest, the unanswered questions I have.

"Then what about Svetlana and the other girls you've had since her. I know you brought her over from Russia because you fell for her and paid her parents and promised to look after her. What about the other Russian girls since then? Do you fall easily for them? Is that what you are doing with me? Will this all blow over?"

He frowns at me.

"Did you just hear what I actually said to you? Let me spell it out. I. Have. NEVER. Felt. Like. This. For. Anyone. EVER. No, I do not fall easily. I have never given my heart to anyone, I have never wanted to give it to anyone until you, Poppy. Yes, I brought Svetlana over from Russia and lots of other girls. But I did it for a reason. I always have a reason." His accent gets thicker the more annoyed he gets, and I can see him getting annoyed with me. I stroke his cheek and lean in to kiss each of his eyelids. He exhales deeply, then opens his eyes. "Can we talk about this tomorrow, мой ангел. It has been a bad day and I want to just hold you and sleep?" He looks exhausted, I nod and kiss him. I watch as he falls asleep in my arms. I lay looking at him for a while, wondering If I belong in his world. I know nothing about it except what I witnessed today. I need to know more before I can make the decision.

He's gone when I wake up. It's late morning though and I didn't hear him leave the room. I'm upset because I wanted to get the answers I need, but I know he's busy. I will wait for him to come home. I use the gym and take a swim when I head back down to the apartment I'm surprised to see Igor in his sweats and Tee making some lunch for us.

"Come, lets eat in the bedroom, мой ангел," He grabs my hand with his free hand and we enter our room. He places the try down on the already laid out table then moves over to shut the door. "We do not discuss anything about us or our business outside of this room. This is the only safe room I have that is one-hundred-percent secure. I secured it all myself, I also have a device for bugs which I carry around with me. I have found bugs in my apartment before now. People have lost their lives because of it." It doesn't really surprise me, what he is saying. "Now we can have the talk you wanted last night. Sit, мой ангел, let's eat and talk." I couldn't love him anymore right now.

"Did you cut your day short so we could talk, Igor?" He starts to eat and looks at me.

"Of course, мой ангел. I know you have a lot on your mind and you need to talk. Here I am. Now what do you want to know?"

"Tell me, I want to know everything, Igor. I want to know all about you and what you can tell me of what you do, I want you to trust me. If you've given me your heart, I want to give you mine, but you need to trust me. I will stand by you. I will help with your business in any way you want, and I want you to teach me how to fight and defend myself properly. I want you to train me, you, no one else, just you. I want to learn from you and then I want you to help me. I want to get my revenge on Nick. Some days I ask myself if it's worth it, why bother? Then I remember lying in that grave on top of another body trying to gasp for air. I remember sucking in the hair from the skull and that smell, and when I remember those things, I see my scars and missing toe and I can't wait to get my revenge. I had a panic attack when your guard was on top of me, I had flashbacks of being buried, so yes I do want to get him. Will you do that for me, Igor, will you help me?"

He nods and smiles.

"Then I will gladly give you my heart and be your wife with one stipulation." I smile at him. I can see the worry on his face.

"Name it and it's yours."

"You need to propose properly. Not like that half-assed one you did in the bathroom, although you did make me speechless."

We both laugh.

"Okay, but you will not know when." We eat the rest of lunch, I can't help the big smile on my face.

"I will teach you everything to protect yourself and also torture and revenge. I need to know you are cut out for this because it can be brutal." He places his elbows on the table top and steeples his fingers to his mouth. He watches me.

"Once we start, there's no going back and we will set a plan in motion and we will get the bastard who did that to you. You also need to tell me what you know about him and your sister. You never speak about her. As for Svetlana and the other girls. I am part of the Russian Bratva, as you know. There are many branches, and divisions, of the Bratva and we each run our own sector and we each have a godfather, just like the Italian mafia. My father was the godfather until he was killed here in LA. He taught me everything I know and so the gauntlet was passed down to me because it stays in the family and I was his only living son. My brother Dimitri was killed when I was only seventeen and he was twenty-one."

I think he has just told me he's a godfather, holy fuck. I can't believe he is actually opening up to me like this, he's going to tell me everything. I stand up and lean across the table, I stop him talking and I give him a kiss.

"You have my heart, Igor. It is yours forever. Let's sit on the bed and be comfortable for story time." I smile and take his hand leading him to the bed where we lay facing each other. I lean in and kiss him again and nod for him to continue.

"Before I continue, you have to know, мой ангел, if you ever betray me then I have to take your life. I need to tell you that before we go any further. It will kill me to do it and I may not survive myself after giving you my heart but you need to know where you stand and what you are getting into."

My eyes spring open wide. "Okay, I understand that, but it has to go both ways, Igor. If you betray me in any way and that means especially with another woman, then I will take your life."

He smiles and leans in to kiss me.

"That's my girl, and I would have expected nothing less from you. It is one of the reasons I love you so much. The fact you even risked your life coming to find me tells me everything I need to know." I smile back and nod.

"My brother Dimitri was my idol, I looked up to him and it nearly destroyed me losing him at a young age. He was on a job that went wrong. He trusted people he shouldn't have, and they turned on him and killed him. They were playing him, from then on my father said we trust no one, not even our closest friends. He said the only ones we can ever trust are the ones we give our hearts to fully. That is why I do not trust anyone or tell anyone my business." He smiles at me, but it doesn't reach his eyes. He looks sad talking about Dimitri.

"Now, I did drop it in before but not sure you caught it but I am the godfather, I am privileged as to what happens in other divisions. All the godfathers get together and we discuss what is going on. We are not enemies as everyone believes, but we stay out of each other's business, we don't tell each other how to run things, we do as we want. So, my rules on something may be different from theirs but that is my choice and they respect that. We never fight each other, well, not never, but very rarely unless one division goes rogue. We have one person who oversees all of the divisions, that person is the overall Russian Pakhan, the boss, no one crosses him and if he has to intervene, you will know about it. He can cut a family down with no hesitation and appoint a new family, it's only ever been done twice. No one knows who the ultimate Pakhan is, there are always rumors flying around but he is never revealed. If a division goes rogue, you can guarantee he will find out. The word goes around if someone is doing something wrong." I'm in awe, but I'm terrified. I've fallen hard and agreed to marry a Russian Godfather. I really don't know if I will be cut out for his life. He must see the worry on my face. He pulls me to him and cradles my head to his chest.

"I know you will have lots of questions and in time I will let you in on what I do but now is not the time for that. I will show you a lot, мой ангел, just a little at a time."

"I found out that Svetlana, who comes from where I come from in Russia, she was being abused by her father. He was a bastard. He is now dead, but she does not know that. Let's just say I will not tolerate sexual abuse. My girls here are not prostitutes, or whored out, yes, they work for me but that is all they do. I did have sex with Svetlana, yes, she stayed with me for a while up here and we got close. No, before you ask, I was never in love with her, I think I was more intrigued by her, not any of the others. She is the only one I brought over that I had a relationship with. The other girls I brought over, again from abusive families, I never had relationships with them. I don't give a fuck what any of them say."

I can see this is hard for him to tell me, every now and then I give him a small kiss on the lips to let him know it's okay to carry on.

"You are truly my Russian god, Igor, you saved those girls from who knows what."

He scoffs at my analogy of him.

"Russian god, huh, I'll take that from you, мой ангел. I know you're going to ask and yes there have been others that have stayed here, lived here even, but only for a short time, the longest I think was probably four weeks or so, nothing longer. None of them ever went into any of the locked rooms, and never in here, not even Svetlana. They don't last very long because I get tired of the constant whining about being locked up. I don't lock anyone up, I protect them from what's out there. I have never been serious with anyone. I thought I was with Svetlana, she was the only exception, she lived with me for a long time, just over a year I think it was. I then realized I was just infatuated with her, nothing more, she never had my heart, no one has ever, and I give you my oath, ever had my heart."

I think he sees the look on my face as I'm counting the weeks in my head.

"What are you thinking, мой ангел?" He strokes his finger down my cheek and along my arm.

"I was trying to work out how long I had been here. I thi—"

"Six weeks, three days, and two hours. Do you need the minutes also?"

I laugh at him.

"In all honesty, Igor, telling me this will not stop me whining. I have loved being here with you and sometimes it's felt like you are holding me against my will, because you will not let me leave. Don't get me wrong, I have loved it, but when you are gone most of the day and don't return until late at night it gets kinda lonely. I want to go out, I want to be able to shop, or go to the coffee shop, or just walk in the park. You cannot keep me locked up here. I know you said we would go shopping for stuff for in here, but that isn't enough. While I'm on a roll, this does not feel like home to me. Yes, it's beautiful and spacious, but the fact I can't walk around naked if I want to really bums me out. I'm worried when there are people around, lord knows I don't want them to lose their eyes over me being naked."

We both laugh.

"It feels more like a hotel than a home. I would like to cook for you sometimes instead of always having meals prepared for us. I'm a pretty good cook, I'll have you know, and I bake." I give him a big smile.

He's suddenly turned serious. I reach over and lift his mouth up at each side to make him smile. He laughs at me.

"Okay, I hear you, мой ангел, I will start to train you first thing in the morning. That means you get your pretty little ass out of bed at five a.m., then we start with some workouts to build your muscle mass up and then on to combat and self-defense, before we even go near the other stuff. I agree you should be able to come and go, it's just me being so protective of you. I know how bad it is out there. I know if any rivals of mine think I have a weakness, they could try to use it and that would mean you getting hurt. Would you object if one of my men goes with you but stays back out of your way?"

I think about it. I know he wants to protect me and to be honest, with that first day in the park and Svetlana luring me here I see how easy it is to be duped.

"Okay, but only for a while. Until I can look after myself and am fit enough to run and fight. Is that a good enough compromise with you?"

This is how it should be, talk and compromise. He nods.

"Agreed, so then the people in the apartment. I need to keep someone by the elevator at all times. That covers the stairwell also because it is next to the elevator. I will not compromise on that. Mavra will be back soon, I told him to take a couple of weeks off to rest up. The bullet did not do any harm internally. It got stuck in his stomach, I told him he needs to lose weight, that it was the fat that stopped the bullet, but he argued it was his muscles."

We both laugh. Thank god he's going to be okay.

"Andrey and Ivan have their own rooms, and when they are not with me, they are either out or in their rooms. Their rooms are above us. They access them via the stairwell once they step out of the elevator. I have a whole section up there for the staff I need on hand. That is why the roof area is very small. The only staff usually around during the day is Polina who cooks for us and Daria who cleans. It is a big place to maintain and I am always out during the day, not that you would find me cleaning it anyway. So, we need to decide what to do. What do you think?"

I ponder for a minute, let's do what normal people do.

"Well we could have the cleaner, Daria, come in, say two times a week, on set days so we know when she is around, she doesn't need to live here, most people who have cleaners, they usually come and clean once a week. I'm here and can do a lot of the daily stuff like laundry, then we could have Polina come in a couple of times a week and cook, again on set days or if we are both busy, then call her to come in. If I am going to be training with you, then at first I will be too tired I suspect, maybe it's good she comes in, but I don't want them living here. I don't know what the floors below us are but maybe they could have a room down there."

He nods.

"Okay, I agree, but I will give them a room on another floor. Andrey and Ivan, I'm afraid will be staying."

I nod in agreement.

"Мой ангел, can I please make love to my future wife, it is killing me laying here with you. I then have a few things to take care of in my office? We can continue tomorrow, but we need to be up early to start your training."

I smile, nodding madly. He's on me before I can say anything else.

Thirteen

Poppy
A Year Earlier

THE DAY STARTED OFF SO SHIT. HE WOKE ME UP AT FIVE AS promised. It was still dark outside. What the hell. I forgot what it was like when working nights. That life seemed so long ago now. I didn't move, I lay pondering my old life and how I was helping all those girls. I think back to some of them and I remember there were quite a few eastern European girls that had been brought over with the promise of a new life with a job and lots of wealth, only to be duped and used as sex slaves. I used to think what a terrible life they had, and I only saw the ones brave enough to make a run for it. I heard the stories of girls ending up dead or tortured to set an example to the others because they tried to run. To think I used to help those girls and yet I've now ended up maybe either being part of that problem or if what Igor said about rescuing them from Russia, maybe I could set up a foundation to help girls like that. It's certainly something to think about.

The comforter is being pulled off me. I open an eye and see my Russian god standing in front of me and he looks delicious. Maybe if I take his cock into my mouth, he will forget about the training. I start to move toward him and reach for his shorts. I try to pull them down, but he takes hold of my wrist.

"Uh no, мой ангел, get this ass out of bed, we have a lot to do."

He slaps my ass, it stings, and I scowl at him then bury my head back in the pillow. He suddenly pulls the pillow from under me and he lifts me up out of bed and takes me into the bathroom where he unceremoniously places me under a showerhead and turns it on. I'm standing there naked and the water is freezing. Yep, that woke me up. I march out of the shower, pushing him hard in the chest. I am so angry. He laughs at me. I notice there are workout clothes on the dresser in the bedroom. Where the fuck does he get this stuff from on such short notice?

He takes my hand and leads me up to the gym on the roof. He works me hard and he shows no mercy. It's my first time, surely he would go easy on me, but oh no, he says no pain, no gain. Stupid Russian mafia godfather god.

The rest of the day I am useless. He worked me hard and I've not been able to walk properly or lift my arms. I feel weak. I'm in bed flaked out when he comes home. He climbs on the bed naked and ready to go, kissing the back of my neck all the way down to my ass, then bites my ass cheeks. I bat him off me.

"Not on your life, mister. I can barely move after your workout this morning. There is no way I can have sex unless I just lay there like a corpse."

He laughs into my neck, then I don't remember anything else.

I'm woken by him sticking his cock between my ass cheeks and playing with my hole.

"Hmmm, I like that," I say into my pillow.

He pulls me over onto my side so he can spoon me. Only it's not just for a cuddle. He lifts my top leg up high, exposing all my pussy to him. He starts to play with my clit using his cock, stroking up and down and around. He positions himself, straddling my other leg that's flat on the bed, with my other leg held high and as far back as it will go, and then he suddenly rams deep inside me. He stops for a second to make sure I'm good, he starts to rotate then he's in and out, slamming his balls on the top of my thigh. With his free hand he starts to play with my clit, pinching it then rubbing.

Fucking hell, this is hot.

I grab my leg to hold it as high as I can, which frees up his other hand. He swaps hands and now has a finger in my ass as well as playing with my clit and slamming into me. I feel revived and I start to try to thrust to each of his slams into me. I want him deeper. I want it all. Before I know it, I'm screaming out my release into the pillow. I'm shuddering all over, fucking hell, the angle he's at hit the spot perfectly. He's still slamming in, I can feel the erratic movements as he gets closer and closer, he freezes as his cum squirts into my pussy and seeps out the sides. He gyrates round and round with his release, his breathing is erratic, I feel down below to his cock and I scoop his cum with my fingers then I lift my hand and bring it to my mouth, licking it like a popsicle.

"Hmmm, baby, I love tasting you for breakfast." I lick, then go back for more.

He's still rotating and releasing inside me. I keep scooping and licking. He pulls out and pushes me onto my back and then straddles my face, putting his cock to my lips. I automatically open up and I lick his cock all over. I love the look on his face as he watches me.

"Well, that was a much better way to wake up than yesterday. Maybe you need to do that each morning to get my ass ready and out of bed." I smile at him and he leans down to kiss me.

"Okay, now get your ass up and training we do, no?"

I love his accent. I smile, then we both get up and train.

It's been three weeks nonstop, he's killing me, but I know this is what I need. I'm so much fitter than I was. I do thirty minutes in the pool after each session with him, I even start to run around the roof garden.

"Baby, I need to start running properly, meaning in the park. I haven't pushed to go out yet, but I'm ready."

He looks at me, scowls then nods.

"Okay, I agree, now can we also go out and pick things for our room, мой ангел? I feel like you don't want to and that makes me wonder if you are happy?"

He's right, I haven't wanted to, not because I don't want to, but because I still don't feel like it's home. Maybe if we decorate it together and pick out things together then it will feel more like home. He had all my things moved from my room to the closet in our room. I have so much stuff—clothes, shoes, purses—they're all designer. I have never been one for designer things and I don't really care for them now, I only accept them because I don't have my own money yet. Which reminds me.

"Igor, when are you going to sort out my fake ID so I can get my bank sorted out. I hate living off you, I have my own money. I want to be able to go out and spend my money." I give him my pitying look.

"You do not need money, мой ангел, I take care of you and everything you need."

I roll my eyes and sit down like a bratty teenager sulking. He kneels down in front of me.

"Why do you defy me on this? I like buying you things. I like to look after you."

He just doesn't get it.

"I'm an independent woman, Igor, I love that you want to provide for me, but it makes me feel uncomfortable. Besides, YOU, do not pick out anything for me, you have a shopper that does that for you, so although you pay for it, you do not pick it and it's just stuff. We don't even go out anywhere for me to get dressed up in half the things in that closet. Sometimes it's like you don't want anyone to know about me, like I'm this big secret."

He sits back on his heels, he's angry, I can tell from the look, he watches me, I stare him out. I'm not budging on this, he promised me right at the start he would get me a fake ID.

"It's not just about the money, Igor. I need ID, I need my identity back and the only way I can do that is by getting a fake ID to then get my real ID. Don't be angry just because you know I'm right." He scoffs at me and runs his hand over his face.

"Okay, okay, I will have a new ID for you tomorrow."

Just like that, he can do it that quick, now I'm angry.

"If you can make it happen so quickly then why the fuck have you left it for so long? I've been feeling like a nobody all this time when you could have sorted that a long time ago." Now I'm really mad, I get up from the couch and I storm to our room where I get my jeans and sneakers on and I rush out past him without saying a word. I stand at the elevator waiting for it to arrive. I glare at Mavra.

"Don't you dare try and fucking stop me," I say to him. I see his eyes move past me, and I know why. I can feel him. The doors open and I step inside to the back of the elevator. I don't turn around to look at him. The doors close and I breathe out a sigh of relief that he didn't stop me. I'm just about to turn around and face the doors when my body is pushed up against the elevator wall by a body, by my god's big body.

"You are fucking hot when you're mad at me." He breathes into my neck, then he suddenly takes both my hands and puts them above my head against the wall. He presses harder into me and I feel how hard his cock is at my ass as he grinds it against me. I push back with my ass into his cock, letting him know I can give as good as he gives. Suddenly he moves and the elevator comes to a stuttering halt. There's a bell ringing, I try to turn but he stops me.

"Don't turn around," he grits out into my neck.

He then pulls back slightly, and I hear him take his T-shirt off. I turn my head and I see he's throwing it over the camera in the corner. I smile to myself. I know what's coming next, for both of us. He reaches round to the front of my waist and he unfastens my jeans, he yanks them down hard so they are at my ankles. He bends down and taps each ankle for me to lift. I obey him, I love it when he's so domineering. He then puts a finger in my panties, and he rips them off me, leaving me naked from the waist down. I turn my head around and he devours my lips, sticking his tongue in and licking all over my mouth. He lets go of my hands and he lifts me up by the waist, I'm now face-planting the wall at this point.

"Wrap your legs around my waist."

How the fuck do I do that? I try anyway, and it works. Now he has complete access to my pussy, I don't remember him taking his sweats off, but his rock-hard cock is certainly free. He slams it inside, I'm pressed up against the wall, I turn my head to the side so my cheek is getting squashed and not my nose. I reach up over my head and I grab his head for leverage. It's a bit awkward, to say the least, he pulls us slightly away from the wall so now it's my chest resting on it. I have hold of his head and my legs are wrapped backward around his waist. He starts thrusting harder and harder, I'm panting like a madwoman, he has a firm grip on my waist, so no free hands, I let go with one of my hands and I reach down and under and I can just about manage to squeeze his balls.

He groans out loud, I'm almost screaming at the thrusts, it's so intense this way, I'm putting my trust in him that I don't fall, I'm so breathless. I squeeze his balls tight. I know he loves that, the next thing I know he's thrusting me straight into the wall over and over, it hurts my tits but it's so fucking erotic. He shouts out with his release. He thrusts and thrusts and twists harder and harder. I know I'm going to be bruised from this, on my chest, my hips and God knows where else. I suddenly scream out as he hits the spot over and over.

"I wish those fucking bells would stop ringing," I shout as I scream out.

We both come down from the awkward but hot as fuck, fuck. Where did he learn to do that? Oh no, wrong thought to have. I cry. I cry like a fucking baby yet again.

"Мой ангел, I am so sorry, I didn't mean to hurt you. You drove me wild, I could not help it." He did hurt me, but that's not what's bothering me. He gently lowers me to the floor and sits, cradling me on his lap.

"Where did you learn to do that, Igor? Is this one of the regular things you used to do? Sex in the elevator. You knew to cover the camera and you knew the position you wanted me in."

He stops stroking my back and pushes me slightly so he can see my face.

"Are you fucking serious, Poppy?" He's livid, he rarely calls me by my name.

I shrug without answering.

"We have an amazing fuck and that's all you can think of? NO, I have never had sex in an elevator in my life. NO, I have never had sex in that position in my life. I just improvised, just like I always do with you. I want to try different ways, see what we like. Maybe I saw it in a porn film when I was younger and it stuck. Who the fuck knows? Most things I try with you are new, мой ангел. Do you not like to experiment?" He's softened his voice. The anger has left and it's now hurt that I hear. I look at him and I see the confusion and hurt on his face.

"I love you, Igor, I'm sorry, the thought just popped into my head. I love that you try new things with me. I love the new positions, each one is

different and hits differently. I didn't mean to sound like a complete bitch."
I lean up and kiss him.

It starts to get heated again with his fingers finding my pussy until I realize the bell has stopped and we can hear voices, albeit Russian ones. We move quickly. I put my jeans back on and he tucks himself in, making sure he tucks my ripped panties in his pocket and grabs his tee, just as the elevator moves and the doors open. We're on a floor I haven't been on before. I look at the panel and it's the ninth floor again. This is where Svetlana was.

"Igor, can I please see Svetlana?"

He looks horrified and angry.

"NO," he shouts at me. I wince from the venom. What the fuck is that about?

"Hold on, don't speak to me like that. I just wanted to ask her about something she said to me the day of the shooting."

I stand there with my foot stopping the elevator door from closing, I have my hands on my hips and I'm scowling at him as he glares at me. He scowls back, huffs, says something in Russian that has the word fuck in it, then takes my hand. He marches me down the corridor, it's like a hotel with lots of rooms with numbers on them.

"Is this a hotel, Igor? Do people stay in all these rooms?"

He doesn't answer me, he just pulls me forward by the hand. I yank it out of his hold, and I stop. He turns to see what I'm doing. I can see some people farther down the hallway and a couple of them are young girls who have stopped to watch us. I fold my arms over my chest, and I glare at him. He walks back up to me and he takes my face in his hands. He kisses my lips gently then his mouth goes to my ear.

"One thing, мой ангел, never, ever show insubordination in front of the girls. I have a reputation to uphold and I cannot have them thinking I am soft. No one ever gets away with speaking to me like you do. No one ever survives speaking to me as you do. Please do not make this difficult, it is something else we need to discuss and compromise on. I will never hurt you intentionally, мой ангел, but the girls cannot see you speaking to me like this. I also need you to be authoritative with them, they need to know you are going to be their queen."

He pulls back to look at my face, he's still holding my head with both hands and he leans in and kisses the tip of my nose. He smiles at me and raises his eyebrows. I nod very slightly to let him know I acknowledge him and smile back at him. He takes my hand gently and we turn and start walking back down the hallway. He brings my hand to his mouth and kisses the back of it then he puts his arm around my waist pulling me into his side. This is him showing them who I am to him. That they must not disobey him. I feel his body go rigid the closer we get to the end. We've passed a few girls who are milling around in and out of each other's rooms. They all greet him with a slight bow of the head, not looking him in the eye. He just gives a slight nod.

"Девушки" is all he says.

I look at him because he knows I don't understand him.

He smiles then whispers in my ear "I just said 'Girls' as a way of greeting."

I nod to let him know I heard him, and I smile. We walk through the door at the end without knocking, it's unlocked. The room is huge, it's like a big suite. There are a few girls, some undressed, who smile at him, nod and avert their eyes. All of them except Svetlana. She looks to him then to me and I see the scowl on her face. We approach her and Igor speaks to her. She nods and gets up and enters a room to the side. We follow her. This is a bedroom which I just presume is hers, there's no one in here.

"I just told Svetlana we wanted to speak to her alone."

I look at him, I'm not sure I want him here, I don't want him to do anything to Svetlana.

"Igor, may I have a minute alone with Svetlana, please? I won't be too long."

He scowls at me. "Anything you have to say to her can be said in front of me." He's a little annoyed. I rub his chest and nod a little then turn to Svetlana.

"Hi Svetlana, glad to see you are safe after what happened the other week."

She stands, on the defensive with me, with her arms folded over her chest. I step closer to her. I have to show Igor I can do this and I don't want to be a tyrant. I want to win over the girls, as me, as Poppy, not their boss.

"Come sit down with me." I guide her to a couch near a window. We sit and she still looks standoffish to me.

"I just want to know what you meant that day in the elevator, I asked you twice what you meant but you ignored me. What did you mean that you were surprised I was still here and still alive?"

She looks straight over to Igor.

"Svetlana, you're talking to me, not Igor. I wanted to come, and he wanted to stay, so please answer my questions." I'm going to lose my patience if she doesn't talk. It's been playing on my mind a lot. She doesn't look back to me when I speak, instead she talks to Igor and it's angry talk, I can tell.

"Svetlana, you will answer Poppy's questions. You will also speak in English when she is present. Do not disrespect either of us." He's angry with her. She looks back to me.

"I only meant I hadn't seen you around and thought you were gone."

"No, that is not what you meant at all. Please don't lie to me."

Her eyes widen at my tone and she looks to Igor again. I get up and walk over to him.

"Please, can you let me talk to her alone? She is scared to say anything in front of you. I need an honest answer."

He thinks about it then nods. He takes both my forearms and rubs them, then leans in and gives me a kiss. He leaves us, shutting the door behind him. I turn to Svetlana.

"Okay, now please tell me the truth."

She bites her thumbnail, looking at me.

"It's just I didn't see you for a few weeks, you know after we spoke and we were going to escape together, so I thought you had either left or he had killed you. One girl told me she saw Igor, Andrey, and Ivan out on the wasteland near the Port of LA. That is Igor's land, I know it is where they get rid of bodies. I have been with them when they have done it before. They usually put bodies in a vat of acid in the basement here and leave them for a day or two, then they get rid of whatever remains on the wasteland or they tip it into the ocean. There isn't usually much left, the acid is strong and dissolves practically everything, even the teeth." Wow, she does know a lot, more than I do, seeing as though Igor told me he doesn't trust anyone, yet she knows all this information, that even I don't know. Something isn't right here.

"So why did you look surprised when you saw me, you thought he had killed me and put me in the acid? Why would you even think that?"

She looks scared as she looks to the door. She leans in.

"The girls I usually find for him never last long. They get used and then he does away with them. The majority end up in the acid. When he found me getting too close to what he does, he had me packed up and sent down here. He doesn't trust anyone. If you tell him what I just said, he may do away with the two of us." She plays with a thread from her T-shirt.

"Svetlana, I am not going anywhere, anytime soon, and I will make sure you don't. I will never lie to him and he will ask me what we talked about. I am telling you now, I will tell him, but I will make sure nothing bad happens. You have my word."

She looks at me in shock, then she laughs. She laughs out loud. I scowl at her.

"You think you have that much power, you are a fool, he will do what he wants to do, regardless of what you or anyone else says. Poppy, I thought you were smarter than that, falling for his charm like you have. He is a very charming man and with just one smile he can have any woman he wants, young or old, yet I've seen him out with much older, well-to-do ladies. You are a nothing, you are just one of many. I kind of pity you, Poppy. You should run while you still can. He will come for me when you are gone, why do you think he keeps me around, when I say he will come for me, I mean it literally, he always comes for me when I have his cock in my mouth."

"After each new one, he gets rid of them and comes straight for me. He cannot live without me. He brought me here from Russia because he fell in love with me, I love him as much as he loves me, he is my love. He just likes variety and I am okay with that because I know he always comes back to me."

I stare at her, shocked. I don't know this woman. I don't know if she is lying to make me leave or if she is telling the truth, I don't know if Igor is telling the truth. What exactly has he told me so far? Nothing, really.

"Did you ever get to meet Dimitri?" I ask her, I want to know if she knows who that is, I know she won't have met him if he died years ago, she's still young. I see her face change. She's trying to think who that is.

"No, I do not believe I did. Is he important?"

I don't say anything.

"What did your papa do to you in Russia, Svetlana?"

Her eyes go wide and I see a tear spill out of the corner of one. She wipes it away.

"He told you?"

I smile at her, then I get up and head for the door.

"Don't ever lie to me, Svetlana. If you lie to me again, I will let Igor do as he pleases with you. Oh, don't get the wrong idea. I don't mean let you suck his cock, I mean torture you before putting you in the acid and I will watch. Never. Lie. To. Me. Again. You will regret it."

I see the look of remorse on her face as she looks down, breaking eye contact to play with the thread. I walk out, leaving the door open. Igor is standing by the window with his hands in his pockets. The room is now empty. The other girls must have left, or he told them to leave. I watch him for a second. I walk up to him and put my arms around his waist.

"Hey, you okay?" I ask.

He turns in my arms and puts his around me. He leans down and kisses my lips gently.

"You ready to go now, мой ангел?" he says and we both turn around as we hear a gasp.

It's Svetlana standing in her doorway. She's watching us. I see the hurt on her face. I don't smile to make it worse, I don't want to be her enemy, but she's also put doubts in my mind. She backs up and shuts the door. I look to Igor quizzically. He shrugs and takes my hand and we walk out back toward the elevators. She gasped when he called me his angel. Did he used to call her that? Was she more to him than he's let on? Why keep her around?

"You didn't answer me earlier when I asked was this a hotel?"

He looks down at me.

"This floor is not. The ground floor has a swimming pool, gymnasium, and some shops. Floors one through eight are hotel rooms with meeting rooms. Then floors ten through thirty-eight are office spaces, floors thirty-nine through forty-two are my space."

"What about the basement?"

He stops dead, tilting his head slightly as he turns to look at me. I can see him thinking. He then starts to walk, taking my hand again, but he doesn't speak.

Fourteen

Poppy
A year earlier

IT'S BEEN A WEEK SINCE I WENT TO SEE SVETLANA AND HE HASN'T asked me what we talked about, nor has he mentioned the basement. He's started to train me in self-defense and combat. We work out each morning at five. I've gotten used to getting up early and going to bed early, most of the time it's before Igor gets home. The day I talked with Svetlana, we went back up to the apartment and got changed. He then took me out and we picked all new stuff for the bedroom. It's not minimal anymore, and he agreed with all my choices. I loved going out. He had Andrey and Ivan with us, of course, we went all over and he took me out for dinner to a really posh restaurant which I was not dressed to go to, but he didn't care. It was okay for him he was in a suit like he always is when he leaves the apartment. I was in jeans, but I did have on heels and a nice shirt. It still wasn't dressy enough to be where we were.

I haven't been out again since, but I'm going out for a run today. I've been in a funny mood since my encounter with Svetlana, and a couple of times Igor has asked me what was wrong. I just played it down, telling him I couldn't wait to get Nick. The more time passes, the more impatient I get. I head out on my own for the first time in months. I know one of his men will be following close behind somewhere, but I don't care. I walk to the park doing stretches as I go. Once in the park, I start off with an easy jog then get faster as I push myself. Igor very kindly bought me a fitness tracker, so when I've had finished, I can't believe I've run over six miles. That shows how much fitter I'm getting.

There's a Starbucks over from the park and I really want a cold iced latte, but I don't have any money. I look around and I see the man who's been following me. I walk up to him.

"Do you have ten dollars I can borrow, please?"

He looks shocked that I'm speaking to him and he looks around. I look at where he's looking, and I see him. He's sitting on a bench on his own, just watching us. What the fuck, does he not trust me and how did he know where I was? I march over to him and stand in front of him with my hands on my hips.

"What are you doing, Igor? Why the fuck are you sitting here watching me? Do you not trust me? Did he let you know where I was?" I say angrily, pointing to his guard.

"Hello to you too, my angel."

Oh fuck, he's pissed at me now.

"I wanted to watch you running, is that so bad. You did excellent. Your stamina and strength are coming along. Now, what were you saying to Steve?"

I scoff at *Steve*, that's the first common name I've heard him call anyone. They are usually all Russian. He scowls at me. I laugh.

"I was laughing because Steve, that's not very Russian. Anyway, I asked him to lend me ten dollars so I could go and get a nice cold iced latte from Starbucks over there. Seeing as you are here you can buy it for me."

He smiles at me, gets up and takes my hand and walks me over to Starbucks where he then buys me my coffee. We walk back home, but we hardly speak. Once in the apartment, I shower, then go to the kitchen to look for something to eat. I stop dead when I see Igor in there cooking. I lean against the island and watch him. He's taken his jacket and tie off and his shirt sleeves are rolled up and his buttons undone.

"I'm making you my specialty, мой ангел, then we will eat in our bedroom and we will talk." He turns to look at me, raising his eyebrows, daring me to argue.

I shrug. "Okay, what's your specialty? It smells like toast."

He turns and smiles at me. "It is bacon, sausage links, scrambled eggs, and toast with coffee."

"We're having breakfast in bed at, erm, six in the evening," I say, looking at the clock.

"It's the only thing I can make," he says with his back to me.

I move around and I put my arms around his waist. "Thank you, baby. I love that you're making it for me."

I finish the coffee while he plates up the food and puts it on trays. We head to the bedroom. I know when we come in here to talk, it's private. He scans the room with his little pocket device he has, then joins me on the bed. We eat in silence, but we keep feeding each other and leaning in for stolen kisses.

"Okay, now I want you to tell me what has been bothering you since you spoke to Svetlana. Before you do, here." He hands me an envelope and inside is a driver's license with a picture of me on it and all my details, it's even a San Francisco one. I pounce on him, kissing him all over his face.

"Thank you, thank you, thank you. Now I feel like I'm someone again."

We laugh and I stay on top of him for a little while, he strokes my back.

"Okay, мой ангел, now start talking."

I tell him everything about my talk with Svetlana and about the things she said. I also told him he was not to do anything to her because I gave her my word. I could see the anger building on his face as I was telling him.

"Do you believe her?"

"The truth?"

He nods. "Always, never, ever lie to me, мой ангел."

"Ditto. I don't know, I was so angry, because I did believe her as she was telling me, and I wanted to run out and punch you in the face. But the more I watched her, I realized she was making a lot of it up. I knew from her body language, she was lying to try and make me jealous, to get me to leave. She wasn't lying about the acid, but about you always going back to her. I could just tell. Even so, it still made me angry with you. Then when I asked you about the basement and you ignored me completely, that really pissed me off. You said you wouldn't lie to me."

He looks deep in thought.

"I haven't lied to you, мой ангел, I just didn't say anything so I wouldn't lie. Come with me."

He takes my hand and we leave the room and head to the one room he hasn't shown me inside of yet. He pulls out his keys and unlocks the door, only this door has three locks and a retina scan on it before it will open. He doesn't open it straight away, instead he turns to me.

"Again, no one has been in here. Only Andrey and Ivan have ever stepped foot inside. I want to show you because this is me, this is the mafia, this is who I am. I put off showing you this room, well, because not that I didn't think you could cope with it, but I didn't want to scare you off."

He gives me a nervous smile as he turns and opens the door and steps back so I can walk in first. He flicks on the light. The room is so bright with all the fluorescent lights on, my mouth drops open from the sight before me.

"Talk about a red room of pain. This is certainly a room of pain." I turn to him. He has no idea what I'm referring to and I laugh.

"I'm a bit disappointed really, I was hoping for the red room of pain."

Again, he looks confused. I turn and reach up to kiss him.

"So, you are laughing at my room because it is not what you expected, and it is not red? But you are not shocked by what is in here?"

I shrug at him and laugh. I turn back and wander farther inside. It's a room of pain alright, but it's a torture chamber and not a sexual one. There are so many guns, knives, gadgets that look like they could be painful, tools like pliers, ropes, in fact, there is so much stuff in here. It's all neat and tidy, pinned to walls and there are what look like big bank safes along the back wall. I turn to him and raise an eyebrow.

"What are the safes for? Don't tell me there are bodies in there."

He laughs at me and shakes his head. "No, мой ангел, that is where I have explosive devices, they are safer in a safe, less impact if they were to go off."

What the fuck, I glare at him.

"You mean you have like dynamite or C4 in there, in the apartment I sleep in, in fact, just down the hallway. What the fuck, Igor."

He's in hysterics, laughing at me. He walks up to me and takes my face in his hands and he kisses me hard.

"You astound me, мой ангел, there is all these torture devices around you with every type of gun and knives and you don't bat an eyelid.

You're upset because it is not this red room of pain. Now I know you are ready to see the basement. Come with me."

He takes my hand and we leave the room. He locks it all back up. I don't know why it doesn't bother me. Maybe because I know he isn't a good guy, he's a fucking mafia godfather for God's sake. Of course, he's going to have shit like that. It just scares me having the explosives nearby.

"By the way, the red room of pain is also a torture chamber," I say and he stops and looks at me, raising an eyebrow.

"You have seen a room like that before?"

I laugh. "No, it's in a book I read. The guy takes the girl to his secret bedroom. It turns out to be a red room of pain. It's full of whips and chains, a bed with all sorts of sex devices to have fun sex on, and drawers and drawers of butt plugs and little pussy balls and god knows what else but it was all for her pleasure. He was a dominant. He liked to sexually torture women, only with consent, of course." I shrug at him and he stops us before we reach the elevator.

He picks me up and walks back to the bedroom with me. He throws me on the bed, and he strips.

"The basement can fucking wait. I need you now, you are the hottest woman I have ever met. You are upset because my room did not have all those things for your pleasure, we can start to experiment with that now if you want to. Will you marry me, мой ангел?"

I laugh at him just as he dives on top of me and he tortures me in the best way ever, with his fingers, mouth, and cock.

It's almost nine when he takes me to the basement.

"I need to know you are ready for this. What you will see in here may terrify you. It is not a nice place. Some of it is dark with lots of rooms, think of a very old prison, like in medieval times, it resembles that. I then have rooms where I take people I need to get information from, rooms where I have lots of instruments to extract that information. It is not nice. Are you ready to see it?"

I look up to him and I nod. I want to see it. I want ideas on getting Nick back. If that means bringing him here or we take the instruments as Igor calls them to him, makes no difference. I need to learn this stuff. It's been a few months now since he buried me, and I know I'm getting into the best physical shape I have ever been in. Igor is working me hard, in every way, most of my problem is mental. I sometimes have nightmares of suffocating in that grave with my head buried in a skull. I wake up gasping for air.

"Are you going to teach me some of your techniques to get my revenge, Igor? You are going to leave that part to me, aren't you? It has to be me, you understand, yes? You can help, but it has to be me that gets that motherfucker back."

He scowls at me for swearing. He hates when I swear, except while he's ramming his cock in me, then he loves it.

We reach the basement. He uses a key card in the elevator to gain access to the basement level. Below the ground floor is the parking garage, then there is another floor below that, and unless you have that key card, you cannot gain access to it. The doors open and it's not so bad, we walk out into a well-lit corridor, it's all painted white, it looks very clinical. I was expecting dungeons the way he was talking. At the end of the corridor which isn't very long, there are double doors. I look in the opposite direction and that's the same. He lets go of my hand and he takes out a key card to swipe it and then puts his face close to another retinal scanner. Wow, he's very James Bond. The doors open.

"Is it the same that way?" I point in the opposite direction.

"Somewhat, I will show you everything." He takes my hand and we walk down another corridor. This one is like the last, painted all white. We stop at the first door and he opens it and there is a man inside, who I haven't met before, and Igor speaks to him. I have no idea what they talk about. He pulls me to him and lets me look in the room. There is another man inside, and I notice they both have guns on them. They are watching monitors all mounted on the wall in front of them. It's like something out of a film or NASA.

"This is my control room. We can see what goes on everywhere in this building right from here. It also monitors everything that happens down here." He leans forward and he uses what looks like a joystick and the monitors change. He zooms in on a room. I try to look closely, it's a very white room like the corridors outside, very sterile looking. The more he zooms in, I can see what looks like a naked man curled up in a ball in a corner. There is no furniture or anything in this room. I notice what looks like a drain in the middle of it and leaning in, I can see the walls and floor have red splatter on them, blood.

Just then a big bulky guy appears, he's in tight black shorts, but nothing else. The muscles on him are huge, he has tattoos all over his body, neck, and head, his head is shaved on both sides with just a mohawk down the middle. I would not like to meet him down a dark alley. He walks to the naked guy and Igor zooms in. I can see the naked guy is all battered and bruised, it is definitely blood, I can see it everywhere now, he looks covered in it.

The giant gets hold of the other guy's hair and lifts him off the ground. The guy's eyes look all bloodied and bruised and it looks like they may be shut so he can't see anything. I lean in to get a better look. Igor flicks a switch and we have volume, the giant is saying something to him, again I have no idea what, the naked guy doesn't move or speak. He's being held up in the air by just his hair. I don't know how it doesn't rip from his skull. Igor zooms in on his face, I gasp at the sight. I was right, he can't see because it looks like his eyes have been burned out. They look like black holes. The giant has what looks like a fire poker in his hand, but it's probably got some other technical name. He takes it and starts to put it up the naked guy's nose. I turn my head away, instinct I think, it didn't freak me out, Igor notices.

"Are you okay, мой ангел? Should I turn this off?"

I shake my head. I want to see what happens. I feel all strange when I turn back and watch. It's hard to explain but it's not sickening me, it's like I'm impatient to see what happens next. I want to see what happens. He sticks the poker thing up his nostril very slowly. I lean in as I watch the blood trickle out of his nose. The naked man starts to make a noise, but I notice he isn't speaking. I look to Igor quizzically.

"He has no tongue. It would have been removed because he either told them what they wanted to know, or he hasn't told them anything, but it is time to move on. We don't spend weeks torturing, just days, depending on the severity of the issue. We don't like to waste too much energy on one person."

I turn my head back just as I see the giant jamming the poker up the man's nose until it pops out of his head. The man's body goes into spasms for a few minutes and then stops. The big guy then starts to twist and pull the poker thing back out, slowly. As it slides out from his nose, it comes with what I think might be brain matter. I can tell the poker thing has a sharp end to it and it looks like a hook unless that's bone. It's disgusting, but what a way to go. I strangely find it fascinating, I must be sick in the head. I feel like it's some kind of achievement to take a life, and we can safely say the naked guy is dead.

"Are you okay, мой ангел?"

I nod, a little too much, I feel like a kid in a candy shop, but I'm a little in shock at actually seeing someone die, but it didn't frighten me one bit. I know I've left Prim to die, but she didn't die, to me that was different, because I didn't intentionally try to kill her, just hurt her. I beat her, sure, but I didn't think for one minute about actually killing her, not in my head anyway. Although Nick said I left her for dead, that wasn't my intention. Liking things like this makes me similar to Nick. He's a killer. This is going to turn me into one. Do I want this life? I don't know. What I do know is I need to pay him back regardless, but does that mean kill him? Do I want to be a murderer? I need time on my own to think about this. One thing is for sure, if I don't want this life with Igor, I think the only choice will be my death now he has shown me this stuff.

Igor takes me in his arms, and we walk out of the room. I'm curious.

"What did he do? Why were you trying to get info from him? Is this a regular thing, like is there always someone being tortured down here? What did you do to his eyes, they looked like black holes, did you burn them? They looked scorched."

He looks at me in awe.

"I love you're so inquisitive, мой ангел, the fact you watched and were not nauseous from it. I've seen grown men be sick watching someone have their brains pulled out through their nose before now. But not you." He leans down and kisses my forehead.

"You astound me, мой ангел. His eyes got burned with hot bars so as not to kill him right away. When someone doesn't want to speak, we torture them for a while. We have different torture methods, eye scorching, waterboarding, or pulling out their nails or teeth, those are just some things we do. Then we give them so many hours and warn them if they do not speak, then we will remove their tongue. We do not mess around and that is what we do. Then we finish them off in a few different ways. He was an informant for a rival we have. You saw the shoot out last week, he had a lot to do with that. No, we don't constantly have people down here, but I would say we do more than we don't. We have more here at the moment than usual because of the drop on us last week. I need to find out who made the hit on us and why."

We walk along and pass a few more doors on the right of us and just a brick wall on the left of us, then we go through some more double doors that are locked, and again Igor uses the retina scan. Through these doors, it's completely different. It's much darker and the floor slopes down. We pass more doors on the right side but these have little windows in them which are mostly shuttered.

"What's in these rooms? May I look?" I nod to the door we are approaching.

He looks down at me and smiles. He walks to the door and slides back the shutter over the little window and peers in. He shakes his head.

"Not this one, let me see the next one."

I don't move.

"Why not this one? What don't you want me to see? Is watching someone have their brains pulled out through their nose not bad enough? What could be worse than that?"

He frowns at me.

"Not. This. One," he says firmly.

I stand with my arms crossed over my chest and I glare at him, daring him to make me move on, I'm stubborn. He moves back toward me and gestures for me to look inside with a nod of his head in the direction of the door. I'm now a little cautious. It must be something bad if he didn't want me to see. I have to stand on my tiptoes to peer in the window.

"Just before you do, it is only temporary. She will not be harmed."

Now I'm worried. I move closer to the door, grabbing the little window ridge to help raise me up on my tiptoes to peer in the window. It's dark inside, I let my eyes adjust and see movement. Just then Svetlana's face appears right at the little window, she sneers at me and I fall back, she made me jump.

"You said you would protect me," she screams at me.

I turn to Igor. "What the fuck, Igor. I asked you not to do anything to her. I promised I would protect her. How am I going to be your fucking QUEEN and gain their respect if I can't keep a promise?"

He scowls at me as I stand with my arms crossed over my chest, again scowling at him. I'm livid. Just what I fucking need. She starts to bang on the door. I look back at her and I mouth 'Sorry.' I turn on him.

"Well? How? Why is she in there?"

I see him take in a breath. "Come with me and I will tell you."

I turn to Svetlana and give her a sad face and shrug. What else can I do? Igor is in charge here, what he says goes. I start to walk but I stay away from him so there's space between us, as we head further down the corridor.

"She should not have said those things to you that were untrue. She is not being hurt and she will be released tomorrow. This is a small punishment."

Wait, what?

"How did you know what she said to me when I only just told you about it, like a couple of hours ago."

He stops and takes my arm gently, swinging me to face him.

"I told you, I know everything that goes on in this building. Everything. I knew what she said to you and she has been locked up down here since, for her lies. I know you promised her I would not do anything. I haven't, but you have to understand, yes I want you as my queen and I understand you need to gain respect, but it cannot be seen that a woman is ruling me. My reputation would diminish within seconds. I am sorry, Poppy, you need to know this. My word is final, no one else's. Can you live with that, мой ангел, is that something we can do together?"

I really need time to think about all this again to see if this is the life I want. Is it already too late? Now he's showing me all this, is it too late for me. If I decide I don't want this, will I end up in the acid? I just shrug, turn, and carry on walking.

He walks next to me. He takes my hand that is folded over my chest. He brings it to his lips and kisses it. I look to him and he smiles a nervous smile at me. We enter yet another set of double doors. It gives me the creeps through here. It's dark with very dim lighting. I feel like we are in the dregs of the earth, we have been on a decline for a while. There are more locked doors here, but these are horrible doors, they are steel doors with a little window with Perspex covering them and bars on the inside. The walls here are bare brick and it feels damp and cold. Now this reminds me of medieval dungeons. There are rooms with open doors, these are empty but these are surely torture rooms. Some have old wooden chairs with shackles attached to the legs. Some have surgical beds and tables of different instruments on them.

I wander into one of the open rooms and I stand there. It's very dim, but I can see the room may have been used recently. The bed is dirty with blood dripping from it, and it looks like it has been soiled. I can see blood on the floor around the bed. Some of the instruments are next to a sink and are all bloody. It smells foul in here. I cover my nose with my hand. It's then I notice something fleshy on the floor. I move closer to try to get a look at it. Igor shines his phone light on it so I can see. It looks like a tongue, and there are two fingers next to it. I stand up straight, backing away and I bump into Igor. I want to back out of the room. He puts his phone in his pocket and takes me in his arms. I'm not upset by what I saw, but this must be where they tortured that naked guy.

"Why take him up to the white rooms from here?" I look up at his face.

"Even though he couldn't see, I always think they should be finished off in those bright rooms. I am a monster, мой ангел, but I have a soul and a heart. I just feel if they pass away in a light room, they will pass to the other side easily. I believe that in the light, white room, they pass to goodness even though they are bad, but in a dark dim room they pass to badness." He shrugs.

"My king has a good heart. Even to his enemies, he wants them to pass over to the good side." I lean up and kiss him.

"Why put Svetlana in one of the dark, horrible rooms? Why not in one of the white rooms?"

"She has been in those rooms before and obviously they have not done her any good. She needs to learn the more she disobeys me, the worse the punishment. I have never hurt her, I don't want to hurt her, but she is pushing her luck. Now you have told me yourself to release her, I will let her be released tonight and I will let her know it is only because of you. I know if you are to be with me you need to have authority and gain the respect of the girls."

I smile up at him.

"How far have we gone down? I feel like we are in the earth itself here, Igor. It's very different here."

He nods. "Yes, this is not a nice place and this room here is even worse."

He takes me to the room near the end and we walk through the doors. It's a bigger open space but it smells terrible in here, I start to cough, and he hands me a mask to put on. It's very dim, damp, and dirty in this room. I let my eyes adjust and I can see three huge metal boxes with steps leading up to them.

"These are acid vats. That is why it smells so bad in here and why you are coughing. The fumes can get to you, especially if you get too close. I do not want you in here unless you are going to use a vat."

I look to him in shock. He smiles.

"Why would I use one, you don't actually mean unless I'm put into one, do you?" I ask him nervously with a worried look on my face.

He laughs at me. "Never, and I would kill anyone that laid a finger on you and they would not pass to the good side. I just meant unless you were getting rid of someone yourself."

Oh, okay. We head out and through some more doors that he used the retina scan on. This is now a corridor much the same as the middle section, like where Svetlana was. I can hear noises when passing a couple of the doors.

"How many people do you have locked up down here?" I watch his face, he's thinking.

"I am not too sure. Maybe about twelve people. Some of them have only just been brought in. We had an informer who was more than happy to give me some names of who started the shoot out last week. I don't have many more to obliterate before they are all wiped out." He shrugs.

"May I?" I ask as I stop outside of a door where I can hear noises.

He scowls and then gently nods his head and I move the shutter to the side and stand on my tiptoes to peer inside. It's dark, but not as dark as Svetlana's room. I'm not sure where the noise is coming from or what it is, just then as my eyes adjust I can see a naked woman tied up by rope on her wrists so her hands are above her head, she's moaning. I look down her body and I see two naked men on the ground in front of her. One gets up and moves to the side, I think to retrieve something and I can see her feet are not touching the floor and her legs are parted wide with shackles on both ankles so she can't move her legs. I turn to Igor, confused as to what is going on. It looks and sounds more like a sexual thing than a torture.

"Is this sexual, Igor? I thought this was just for torturing and killing down here?" I'm a little scared right now. Is this what he does down here? He rubs his chin and nods. What the fuck is the nod? I frown at him.

"Yes it is sexual, it is sexual torture that is used on males and females. We hang them there for a few hours and then they are tortured by implements inserted into them. Never sex, but let's just say they are constantly being aroused over and over until they can't stand it any longer or until they are damaged." He looks into the room and steps back.

"Ah okay, these two are arousing the female by using instruments in her vagina. They inflict pain and pleasure until she orgasms over and over. Some would say that it is not a torture but, believe me when they have hung there for hours and been aroused for hours, it is a torture. On males they have very, very thin implements that have lots of tiny spikes inserted inside their erect penis, these are rotated over and over giving them orgasms. It causes both pleasure and pain, with the spikes tearing at the inner penis. More and more are inserted until he screams as his cock is splitting with the width from so many being inserted. Now on the female, they put clamps on her clit that they keep rotating, twisting it, and they insert thicker, longer spiked implements inside her vagina and do the same thing with her. She will have more orgasms than the male, and she has to have thicker, longer implements, as you can imagine, the vagina can spread so wide. They insert so many until her vagina actual tears. We have found this to be a very successful form of torture on those that are hard to crack in the more traditional ways."

He reaches over to me and pushes my chin up very gently to close my mouth. I'm stunned this is a torture, I have never heard of anything like this, not that I've ever heard of much in the way of torturing. I was obviously standing with my mouth open, listening to him. I look back into the room. I let my eyes adjust and I see the look on her face as she starts to moan again. One second she looks like she's enjoying it and the next she looks in pain. She screams out with what must be her orgasm. She pants and pants and is muttering things that are inaudible to me, but she sounds Russian, I don't think she is old either. One of the men must hear me gasp as I see him holding the thing Igor spoke about. He moves slightly to the side so I can see what he's doing. The one man I can see is turning something while the other is now back to inserting the implement. She screams out as it goes in. I squeeze my legs together in sympathy for her. I move away and close the shutter.

"Are you okay, мой ангел? You are very red?"

He's rubbing the tops of my arms. Crouching slightly to look into my eyes. I put my hands over my face, I'm mortified, I actually found that to be disgusting, but also arousing all at the same time. I just nod. I hear him chuckle. I feel so embarrassed, especially after my confession about kinky stuff in the red room of pain. Him doing anything to me now would be nothing compared to what goes on in his basement.

He puts his arm around my waist and turns us to start walking. We are on an incline as we move up the corridor now and we pass through another set of double doors and we get to a section of more bright white rooms then through more double doors and we are back at the elevators. I don't speak, I'm trying to process it all and wondering now is this really the life I want to be involved in.

"Talk to me, мой ангел, I can see your brain working overtime."

Not here, I'm not going to talk about anything that I'm thinking, only in our room.

"I had no idea we were going full circle. It didn't feel like it. Can I ask you then, all the doors were on the right as we walked, and we were going around, so what is to the left? I didn't see any doors at all."

He pulls me into his chest and hugs me.

"You are so observant. You amaze me. I have men working here who have never realized and have never asked that question. There are only four of us that know. That is myself, Andrey, Ivan, and now you."

We head back to the doors we just exited and go back through them but stop as soon as we pass. He presses something on the wall and another retina scanner appears as what looks like a brick slides up. The wall moves inward slightly and then slides to the left. You would never know it was here. He takes my hand and walks me into the space. I'm stunned to see it's an apartment inside. There's furniture, a kitchen, doors to what I suspect are other rooms, and a bathroom. There is also an elevator. I look at him quizzically. He smiles.

"This is my secret apartment. Like I said, nobody knows about it. If things get bad up top, then I have everything I need down here if I need to hideout. It is fully stocked, and I have the best surveillance equipment there is. I have cameras everywhere, in and around this building, and this elevator takes me up to a secret area on a floor where I can then exit through the building next door. Which I also own. No one would ever find us down here, so I can wait it out for weeks if need be."

He shows me all the video monitors just like in that first surveillance room we went into. Everything in this apartment is state of the art and it's huge.

"Wow, it's like the secret service. You're like a real life badass James Bond. I bet you have loads more gadgets."

We both laugh. I then start to think.

"Igor, surely if the corridor we were just in near the elevators has cameras then your men would see you coming in here, so it can't be that secret?"

He smiles at me.

"You, мой ангел, are meant to be. You fit perfectly, not only with me but my lifestyle, I could never have dreamt of finding someone like you. Your mind works perfectly for my lifestyle. All the corridors have cameras, you are correct, this side is more low-key and doesn't get used very often unless we are at capacity. I have the camera positioned so the entrance is in a blind spot, but as a precaution, as soon as I put my foot on a sensor on the floor near the entrance, it cuts the camera feed just for a couple of minutes, so I can safely get in and close the door. It plays a recording of an empty corridor for those minutes back in the surveillance room."

"Come, it's getting late. We need to get to bed, we have a busy morning with your combat training. I want to take you to our country house this weekend where we can have you do some practice shooting. Is that good for you?"

I nod, it's not like I'm booked up to go anywhere else.

"First though, on Thursday night, I am going to take my future wife out to the theater and for a special dinner at my hotel. Then next week I am taking the week off and we are going to our beach house, just the two of us to get lost in each other. Who knows, we might stop off somewhere and see what we can find to pleasure you with, besides my cock of course."

Could I fall for this man any more than I have? It doesn't go over my head he keeps saying our, when referring to his properties. I still need to think carefully about all this. If I decide now I don't want this lifestyle, then I fear that would be the end of my life. It's something I need to ask him.

Fifteen

Poppy
A year earlier

THURSDAY NIGHT ARRIVED. HE TOLD ME TO WEAR SOMETHING elegant. I chose a long red beaded gown. He had a stylist arrive to do my hair and makeup. My hair is up in a bun on the top with strands left down on the sides but curled up in ringlets. My gown is elegant but sexy, it has a split up the side right to the top of my thigh, the back is so low it stops just barely at the top of my ass, but it has strings of diamantes across from one side to the other all the way down the back. The front has a very revealing V-shape right down to my navel, it's beaded with little diamonds all the way down each side coming to a point with a big ruby jewel at my navel, I have to wear tit tape so it doesn't gape open and show everything I have. I complemented the dress with a ruby and diamond choker with matching drop earrings. I have red satin gloves and have a matching ruby and diamond bracelet. I gasp at myself when I look in the mirror. It's not me standing there, I look like Julia Roberts from *Pretty Woman* only with blonde hair. It fits perfectly, and if I do say so myself, if I wasn't me, I would fuck me.

I'm standing in the closet looking at myself in the mirror when I see movement out of the corner of my eye. I turn and see Igor leaning against the doorjamb with his arms crossed over his bare chest. He's in his tight boxer shorts and his cock is rock-hard. He's looking at me like he wants to fuck me, which is exactly how I am looking at him right now with his cock trying to escape the shorts.

"Потрясающий, чертовски потрясающий, мой ангел, я хочу трахнуть тебя так плохо."

I laugh at him. "Well, I got the 'my angel' part out of all that."

He moves up behind me and puts his arms around my waist and rests his hands on my tummy, pulling me back to his chest, resting his chin on my shoulder. He smiles at me in the mirror and I see the love and lust written all over his beautiful god-like face. He is too gorgeous and he's mine.

"I said, 'Stunning, absolutely fucking stunning, my angel, I want to fuck you so bad.' But I correct myself, I want to make love to you, not fuck you."

I laugh again and swat his hands.

"Later, you are not ruining this beautiful dress or my hair. Now get dressed. You said we had to leave at seven, so we don't miss the start of the show." I tease him and grind my ass into his cock slightly, then I turn in his arms and reach up to kiss his lips. As I move away, I accidentally, on purpose, brush my hand over his cock. He growls at me and I laugh as I sashay out of the closet.

The show was amazing. I didn't realize he was taking me to see an actual Broadway show, it was *Les Misérables* and I loved it. The last time I went to the theater with Aunt Cassy was to see *Annie* many years ago. We had to go to one with sign language, because of course we had to cater to Prim as usual. It actually got on my nerves having someone standing in front of the stage signing.

I'm smiling so hard leaving the theater, but I can't help notice the looks we get from people. Mostly women eyeing Igor. I mean, who can blame them, but he only has eyes for me. I noticed some people saying hello to him, but he ignored everyone. I thought it was very rude, but we just kept smiling at each other. This was the first time I actually saw the presence Igor has in public, he is like a king, I even saw people bowing to him.

We head out to his hotel, it's beautiful, it's called The Dimitri, I know the significance of that name. It's huge and the opulence of the place inside is mesmerizing. The clientele are all well-to-do people. They are people of status, this is the kind of place royalty, dignitaries and stars stay at. I gasp as we enter, and he looks at me and winks.

"Do you like?"

I nod vigorously, my hair nearly falls out of its bun.

"It's beautiful, Igor, and I know the significance of the name."

"Yes, I named it The Dimitri as soon as I bought it. I wanted this to be the place everyone wanted to stay at and I think I got it spot on. We will stay here in my suite tonight. I have some things in there for you." He smiles and winks but it's kind of a mischievous smile.

We head to the elevators and he is greeted by lots of different people. He acknowledges some of them but others he ignores again like in the theater. We enter the elevator on our own, other people are stopped from entering by the elevator operator. As soon as the doors close, he's on me, devouring my mouth and his hands start to wander.

"Igor, do not mess me up until after we have had dinner. I am not your dinner." I laugh, stopping him. "Why do you not acknowledge everyone that says hello to you? Isn't that rude?"

He smiles down at me as he tries to straighten himself out before we reach the floor we need.

"I did not honestly see many say hello. I do not notice a lot of the time, but it seems especially when you are on my arm. I watch you, I love to see your reactions, but I also get very angry when I see men stare at you, I noticed that happened a lot. It makes me want to burn their eyes out for looking at you. How dare they, you are mine."

I slap his chest lightly and he grabs my wrist.

"You, ARE, mine, мой ангел, make no mistake."

He is kind of intimidating when he's possessive like this and it turns me on, knowing this god wants me and only me. I just have insecurities because of my past relationships, thinking it will all end. The elevator doors open and we are greeted by a hostess who asks us to follow her. She takes us through the restaurant to a private room up some stairs. She shuts the doors behind her as she leaves. I stand looking out at the view over LA, all the lights twinkling, and all the high buildings.

"It's beautiful up here, Igor," I breathe out, standing at the window.

He comes up behind me and places his chin on my shoulder, wrapping his arms around me. We sway to the soft music coming in through concealed speakers. Just then the door opens and a man walks in followed by a waiter. Igor sighs and kisses my shoulder. We turn and he pulls out my chair for me to sit. I'm sitting facing the window with Igor in front of me. What a view. The man speaks to Igor in Russian. He introduces me and I find out he is the hotel manager. He leaves and the waiter starts to serve us food. I look at Igor because he didn't order anything.

"I ordered for us both, I hope you don't mind. I did it earlier so it would be ready when we arrived."

The waiter comes in with champagne for us, the entire time servers are coming in and out, although it's a private room, you get no peace, but it keeps the other guests from interrupting Igor. We have dessert brought to us, then as we finish, I notice he keeps looking at his watch.

"What are you waiting for? Are you late for something?"

He smiles at me. "No, мой ангел, I suppose I am eager to get to the suite."

"Do you have a permanent suite here that is just yours, or is it just one of the normal hotel suites?"

He frowns slightly as if it's an absurd question. "I have a place here that is OURS and OURS alone. It is not a normal guest suite. It is OUR suite to use as and when WE please." He sounds a little angry as he emphasizes his words.

"Are you ready, мой ангел?" He stands and comes around to pull my chair out.

It would be tough if I wasn't ready. He seems a little agitated, as though he can't wait. He turns me around, pulls me to him and kisses me hard. I'm not sure what this is about, then he pulls back and he looks over my head. I see a big smile on his face. I go to turn around to see what he is smiling at.

"No, wait one second." He stops me from turning. He removes his tie from around his neck and puts it over my eyes very gently, tying it at the back. "Trust me, мой ангел," he whispers.

He moves us around the table. Then he unties the tie and it falls to the floor. The lights are out in our room. I look back at him and scowl, but he nods to the window. I look outside. I don't see it right away, then it hits me. The buildings in the distance that I can see are all dark, apart from the windows that are lit, and it spells out 'Will You Marry Me, my angel?' with a big heart underneath. I gasp out loud and my hands shoot to my mouth, I have tears running down my face. I turn to look up to Igor but he isn't there, he's down on one knee holding a box with the most beautiful sapphire and diamond ring.

"What is your answer, мой ангел?"

I fly at him, knocking him to the floor. "Yes, yes, yes, a thousand times yes, Igor. I love you so much."

We are both on the floor with me on top of him, peppering him with kisses. The lights come back on and the door opens and there are staff standing outside, all clapping and cheering, I can hear the guests downstairs all clapping, whistling, and cheering. I get up off him and he gets back to one knee and takes the ring and slips it onto my finger. I lean down, taking his head in both my hands, and I kiss him hard.

"Can we go to our suite now, мой ангел?" He laughs and I laugh with him, nodding vigorously with my hair now falling all around me.

I don't care. We head for OUR suite with only eyes for each other and ignoring all the congratulations as we pass the other diners. I feel very rude, but I can't stop staring at my god, knowing he is mine. We have the most enjoyable night in the suite. He said he had some things for me, and he wasn't wrong. After pleasuring each other, he pulled out a cock ring and a vibrator. We enjoyed experimenting with them both and let's just say we weren't very quiet, not that anyone would knock on our door to tell us to shush. I just hope we don't have any neighbors on the other side of the bedroom wall because they would not have gotten any sleep, that's for sure.

We're on our way to Igor's house in the country for the weekend. We didn't do any training this morning, well not that sort anyway, although my legs are like jelly from all the sex and lovemaking. I'm worn out, I must have fallen asleep because I'm being woken up by Igor kissing my lips gently. I open my eyes and see he is crouching at my side in the open car door. I look around, stretching, and I see the front of a beautiful big country house. It looks European to me, maybe Spanish looking. There is no one else around, just the two of us, and he smiles at me.

"Come on sleepyhead, let me carry you to the bedroom where you can relax for a while."

I start to get out of the car, and he stands, holding my hand to assist me. When I stand up straight, he scoops me up and marches up to the house.

"Wow, this place is amazing. Is this your house, Igor?"

He smiles down at me and nods. "Our house."

Yeah, no, I will never get used to the ours business. They are his, not mine, even when we marry, they will always be his. I have money, but nowhere near the amount to buy even a house a tenth the size of this one. He opens the door and we walk into a huge foyer with a sweeping staircase right in front of us. He carries me up the stairs and to a huge bedroom. I'm so tired after hardly sleeping last night, I don't get a chance to take it all in. He gently lays me on top of the bed, kisses my forehead, then leaves.

I must have gone out like a light. I feel the bed dip and then warm lips on mine.

"Good morning, sleepyhead."

Morning, what the fuck. I shoot upright and see that the blinds are up and it's very sunny outside. I look at my wrist for my tracker, but it's not there. I don't remember putting it on again. I think it's in our apartment.

"What time is it?"

"It is seven-thirty in the morning, мой ангел. You were dead to the world yesterday. It must be all the early mornings you've been having and then no sleep the night before, it has just caught up with you. Now it is time for some training. Do you think you are up to learning to shoot today and me teaching you about guns?" He's smiling at me as he pushes my hair behind my ear and leans in to give me a kiss. He then reaches for a tray and passes me the only thing he can cook, breakfast.

"You eat and I will go to the gym for a while. When you are ready, how about you join me, and we can have a swim before you start training? We will walk around the grounds. They are vast and I have wildlife here, we can look for something to use for target practice."

Wow, he has my days all planned out. Do I get a say in anything anymore? Is this going to be my life now? Igor telling me what to do and when to do it. I know he's training me at my request, but it's starting to feel like he needs the control. I know I've been on a high with all the excitement of the proposal, which was amazing, but I think was kinda quick. Even though he said it would happen, I thought it would be a while yet, or rather I think I hoped it would be a while. I wanted time to think about everything. I wonder if he could see my hesitation when he was showing me the basement. I do still need to think about all of this. I do love him, God do I love him, but this is not just some normal man I've agreed to marry, he's a dangerous man, a very fucking dangerous man. Am I ready for a life like his? I do want him to train me. I have to get my revenge on Nick, it will haunt me forever if I don't do something. I dream now of waking up in the grave. I wake up suffocating sometimes. How Igor has not seen that I don't know, but it happens. I nod at him as he waits for me to say something and I start to eat.

It's been a while since Igor left to do some training, I got my swimsuit on and I've just been wandering around the house in awe of it all. It's beautiful and it's huge. I get lost, it's that big. I find his office, there's a library, a home theater, I think three dining rooms, a lounge, a family room, a game room, it just goes on and on. I eventually find my way outside walking through the vast kitchen and see there is a pool, I don't see Igor, so I just jump right in and start my laps. Even the pool is huge. It's sometime later before he joins me, I'm almost finished when he jumps in. Needless to say, he takes me in the pool, stripping me of my swimsuit.

We rest up for a little while on the loungers by the pool. He goes and gets us some orange juice.

"Poppy, I can see something is still troubling you, like it was before, when you told me about Svetlana. I can tell when you have something on your mind. Please talk to me and do not try to hide it. You must always be truthful with me, no matter what. Do you understand me? Never hide anything."

Okay, is that some kind of threat, he's using my name, he does that when he's angry with me for something.

"Does that go both ways, Igor?" I glare at him. I can see he looks hurt.

"Have I not been truthful with you, Poppy? I have shown you all my world and what I do."

"Only in your place, not what goes on out there." I say, pointing to the outside world. "I can only imagine what goes on from films I've seen, I don't know what you do, do you deal with drugs, trafficking in any way, what?" I'm raising my voice and I have no idea where this has come from.

To be honest, I haven't thought much about what he does every day in the outside world, I'm always lost in a little bubble in his apartment. He looks at me quizzically, he's trying to understand me. Well he can't, he's not in my head. I take a sip of my orange juice and avoid eye contact with him. I pull the towel up over my body to cover me.

"Мой ангел, please tell me what is bothering you, anything you need to know I will answer you. I will not lie, ever."

I look over to him and I actually feel bad. I get up off my lounger and I go and sit on his lap facing him.

"The truth is, I'm scared, Igor."

He pulls me into his chest, and he wipes away a tear that has fallen from my eye.

"Is it me you are scared of?"

"Yes and no." I shrug as the tears fall down my face. "I don't know. I love you so much and that scares me, it's not easy for me to talk and tell anyone how I feel. This is all new to me. I'm scared of you in some ways, but it's not that I'm scared of you. Does that make sense? You don't scare me as you, it's more what you do, I think that might scare me. When I was in your basement, I was thinking to myself that now I know all of this, now that you've told me and shown me all this there is no escape whatsoever. If I decided I didn't want to marry you, tha—"

"You don't want to marry me?" he breathes in.

I sit up and look him in the eyes.

"I do want to marry you. Hypothetically though, if I didn't, I was thinking you would kill me

because you've told me and shown me more than anyone else. That scares me. To me if… no… when we get married, and like so many marriages these days fail, if ours fails, that will mean I lose my life. It wouldn't just be a case of me walking away, it would be my life. To know I only have a choice between marrying you and staying with you or dying, that's what it feels like, and that fucking terrifies me, Igor."

I watch him taking in what I am saying. He doesn't move, but his eyes take in all of my face.

"It's like now, you're telling me what to do all day, every day, you have the days planned out, I don't have a say in anything. Yes, I asked you to help me train, and I am so grateful you are taking the time to do that for me. Believe me, I am, but it's coming at a price. One I don't think I can take."

He looks at me with horror on his face. I lean in and kiss his lips gently to try to reassure him. I take his head in my hands and look him in the eye.

"It's like you have started to control me, and I won't be controlled, Igor. I'm a free woman who was almost killed by a psycho, I was buried alive. I did not escape that to be a controlled woman. I love you, I do, so fucking much, but we need to compromise."

He looks at me for a minute, takes a deep breath as though sighing in relief, before he kisses away my tears.

"Okay, thank you, мой ангел, for being honest with me and telling me. That is what I love about you, never change for me, even if you feel like I am trying to change you. I need you to always challenge me. Never keep quiet. When you are quiet, I know something is wrong and honestly, that scares the fuck out of me. You scare me too, мой ангел, I have never been scared in my life, no, my father scared me, he was a very powerful, demanding man, and then when Dimitri died that scared me but other than that, nothing scares me, apart from you."

I stroke down his face to his lips. "Why, why do I scare you?"

"Because I love you with everything I have, and it scares me that you will rip my heart out and throw it away. You're talking about our marriage failing already, we aren't even fucking married yet and that fucking terrifies me. If it ever comes to our marriage failing, promise me, we will try to work on it before we do anything drastic, promise me we will try and I promise you here and now, I would never end your life. No matter what, мой ангел, I could never do that. If your life ended, then my life would have to end with you. I give you my oath here and now. I never want you to fear for your life if you think it's not working, I never want you to live in fear. We are going to get married. That can be as small or as lavish as you want it to be. I don't give a fuck about traditions or anything like that. If you want a low-key ceremony, then we will do that, if you want it in a castle in some country, we will do that. My life is yours, мой ангел, I am sorry if you thought I was controlling you, at this moment, with your training, I just want you to get to the point you are ready for your revenge. I see your nightmares most nights and it makes me so angry and so sad. The fact I cannot help you it drives me crazy, I hurt because you hurt. I want to kill that fucker myself, but that is for you to do and I will help in any way I can. The sooner you are ready, the better. Get him out of your life once and for all."

I couldn't love him any more than I do right now. My heart is bursting with love for him. I feel like a big weight is being lifted from me; him telling me he won't kill me. I believe him because he's told me so many times his oath is never broken. I kiss him hard. That of course leads us to another make-out session on the lounger.

I agreed to getting my training done, the sooner the better. We are just eating deer, it's one we shot this afternoon. I found I adapted to the guns very quickly and I was a good shot, he was really pleased with me. The problem with the deer is it brought back so many memories of Nick and him killing that deer for us to eat. I started having a little panic attack until Igor took me into his arms. I told him what was wrong, he soothed me. I suppose my determination to get Nick is pushing me.

In all, the weekend was amazing. He set up lots of different courses for me to go shooting, luckily there are no neighbors around for miles, he told me that's why he picked the house. It is surrounded by acres of walled-in land. The next few days he was busy making sure everything was set up for us taking a week off to go to Malibu. I haven't seen much of him apart from the training we do in the morning, and it's gone back to me being asleep before he returns.

"Мой ангел, мой ангел, wake up, baby." He's shaking me awake. I sit up and rub my eyes, looking at the time on the clock. It's one fifteen.

"What is it, what's wrong?" I ask as I start to check him over to make sure he's okay. He's fine. He smiles at me.

"I have to tell you, there's been a change of plans. I have some business to take care of and I can't take the week off to go away with you. Not just yet. I don't want you to be angry. Something has come up. I need to be here. I know you were looking forward to it. You can still go if you want to and I can join you when I am able." He looks so sad and sorrowful, he diverts his eyes to my chest. Oh no, he did not wake me up for that. I pull the covers over me and he looks up into my eyes with a now mischievous grin on his face. I stroke his cheek.

"I will be fine staying here. We can go another time. Besides, it will mean I get more training in. We need to start setting up a plan now. It's nearly time, baby."

He nods. "You are not angry we are not going away, no? I would have liked nothing more than to spend the week buried in you and I had some surprises for you. But we can always do that here." He wiggles his eyebrows.

Oh no, what is he up to now? His hand starts to wander up the comforter, but I swat it away.

"No, you did not wake me up for sex. I'm tired, goodnight baby," I say as I snuggle down under the comforter and turn my back on him.

He gets up. I hear the rustle of his clothes being removed and he climbs under the comforter, spooning me. One thing leads to another and he's inside me before I have a chance to tell him no.

The week passes quickly. Igor and I are going to sit and discuss our plan tonight in the bedroom eating our dinner. We've had a small dining table and chairs set up by the window so we can eat in here. His safe place. He also wants to discuss the wedding. I still need to decide on what I want. I know he has a lot of family and acquaintances, but I have no one, not one person on my side. I think we need to have a very small ceremony. I'm not sure he's going to like that.

Sixteen

Poppy
A year earlier

W E'RE AT BEVERLY HILLS CITY HALL, I'M ABOUT TO become Mrs. Poppy Ustrashkins, I cannot wait to marry Igor. We applied for our marriage license, which took a little longer than usual because of Igor's status. He actually has dual nationality because he was born here. It soon got sorted out, as does everything where Igor is concerned. I was able to get a copy of my birth certificate because of the fake ID Igor got me. My life has been a lot easier now that I have my ID again. It's me and him waiting to be called in. We have Andrey as my witness and Ivan as Igor's witness, it's just the four of us. I have been a little upset leading up to this day because I'm missing Aunt Cassy, Uncle Trevor, and the girls, even Prim. I've been remembering when we were little girls, we played dress up and always swore we would have big fairy tale weddings like Cinderella and we would be each other's bridesmaids, it hurts, but now that we are here all I have are butterflies in my tummy.

I turn to Igor and I smile. He looks so handsome in his tuxedo, he always looks handsome. I thought that just because we were having such a low-key ceremony that didn't mean we couldn't still dress for the occasion. He had a designer come in and design a dress with me. I couldn't believe he got Vera Wang herself to come and design my dress. I dread to think what he paid for that, flying her in from New York. He told me he wanted to get Alexander McQueen. He knows I love the McQueen brand. I told Igor no more designer stuff unless it was McQueen, but he found out he was no longer alive, I could have had McQueen house come in and design the dress but he didn't feel it would be the same.

My dress is stunning, it is full-length and fitted, very plain, but it has a detachable skirt to it that is only on the back, making it a long train. Because I am quite quirky, and I love the skulls McQueen does, Vera actually incorporated some into my dress. It's very low cut at the front and backless. I wanted to be sexy but stylish for Igor. I have a bouquet of white and black lilies with feathers cascading down. Igor's tux is also by Vera Wang as a one-off special and it complements my dress with skulls in the fabric. I didn't want the traditional bow that a tux has, I wanted a bow that was just loose around his neck, not tied. He looks like the god he is standing by my side with his piercing blue eyes and his curly blond hair. We almost match, my eyes are piercing blue and I have long blonde hair. I went back to my original color a while back now.

The call comes, it's time for us. I link my arm through his as we walk into the room. Andrey and Ivan behind us, they sit as we stand in front of the Deputy Commissioner of Civil Marriages. She conducts the ceremony and I cry as Igor faces me and says his vows, he promises to cherish, obey and love me for our entire lifetime, his silent oath to me that he will never hurt me. I cry. My vows to him are similar but I don't vow to obey him, I leave that part out and I just vow to love him and cherish him. We both had designer wedding bands made for each other and we exchange rings. The Commissioner pronounces us husband and wife, I throw myself at him and we kiss, hard.

We head to The Dimitri where the restaurant is set up for the wedding banquet Igor wanted to put on. He has a lot of important people he didn't want to piss off so they all got invited. There are dignitaries from all over attending and he points out some of the other godfathers to me. I have no chance of remembering any names. I smile and shake hands as he introduces me as his wife to them all. I play the dutiful wife. It's the best day ever. I'm so grateful to be standing here with this man as his wife. Not the time for Nick to pop into my head, but if it wasn't for him trying to kill me, I would never have ended up with Igor and where I am today. The day is perfect.

We are on our way to Bora Bora for our honeymoon, he's rented an island for just the two of us for a week. He's promised me that he will only use his phone when absolutely necessary, that his time is devoted to me. The setting is perfect. We are on the beach bed, made for couples, holding hands as we lay soaking up the sun. I have on a barely-there white string bikini and he has on the tightest, smallest white swimming trunks I've ever seen. If we were on a public beach, I would make him cover up. We only landed yesterday, so we have been tired from the long flight. He suddenly moves and is on top of me, looking at my face.

"Mrs. Ustrashkins, I love you with everything I am. Give me a kiss, my beautiful wife." He can't stop calling me his wife or Mrs. Ustrashkins, he says he loves the sound of it.

I don't hesitate and I kiss him. It gets heated within seconds. I feel his hands on my bottoms undoing the ties on each side, he then pulls me up to sitting without breaking contact and he unties my top which falls off. I use my hands to try and push his swim trunks down, but they are too tight. He laughs in my mouth at my feeble attempt. He pulls back and takes them off himself, by ripping them off. I laugh at him. He's inside me making love to me in no time at all and it's only minutes before we are both coming one after the other. We're panting away, forehead to forehead, staring into each other's eyes. He starts to feel around under the pillows on the bed, he surprises me by pulling out a small silk bag. I look at him quizzically and he gives me a cheeky smile and winks, I melt. He starts to pull out some sex toys. I stare at him.

"How did you sneak those without me seeing them?" I laugh and take what he has. He takes them off me.

"These are nipple clamps, they are supposed to bring you pain and ecstasy when I fuck you. This is a butt plug, I'm not sure I want to use this on you since I prefer my cock or fingers up there. These here are the pussy balls you told me about. Now with these, I place them in your pussy and you walk around with them in for a while and they are supposed to make you so damn horny, I want to try these, they sound fun. Apparently I have to suck them first, then push them inside you. We will try these later. Now you know this is my favorite from the night I proposed, this little cock ring, but this is a new one, it's not just any cock ring but a stealth one, I quite liked the sound of this as it vibrates on my cock, then when I'm inside you it vibrates on your clit, I like the idea of that as well."

He's like a kid who has just got some candy. I laugh loud at him, covering my face, slightly embarrassed, but fucking ecstatic at the same time.

"Let me just say, Igor, we do not need these toys because believe me when I say your cock, tongue, and fingers are more than enough for me, but I am more than happy to play, I agree the cock ring was amazing and this one sounds perfect." I suddenly think, what if I'm not enough for him? It also reminds me of the day in the basement and the sexual torture that goes on down there. He must see the look of horror on my face

"What is wrong, мой ангел, you look upset?" I cover my face because he reads me like a book.

"I just remembered I was going to have a conversation with you after we left the basement. It kind of upset me, the sexual torture bit, and I was wondering if you had actually tortured anyone like that. I was thinking if you had it kind of put my little snipe about the red room of pain to shame."

He looks at me and tilts his head to the side, but he doesn't smile.

"I have never administered that punishment to anyone in my life, Mrs. Ustrashkins. I am more than eager to help you try out these items though."

"Am I enough for you Igor, do you need to spice it up, is it boring for you now? I know you were sexually active a lot before me. How can I compete?"

He frowns at me, then I see anger cross his face and his eyes darken. "Don't you ever think that. Nothing has ever compared to you, just the taste of you is my drug of choice. You make me mad sometimes with your insecurities, I love you Mrs. Ustrashkins, don't you ever forget that and you are much more than enough for me. I can't get enough of you." He pulls me up onto his lap and he smothers me with kisses.

"Which would you like to try first?" He's all smiles as he plays with the cock ring in his hand. I want to try them all.

"The ring first and then the balls, I want to try them all, wait, can I swim with the balls in? What if they pop out?"

We start to laugh and he shrugs. He puts me to the side of him and he kneels up in front of me. I kneel up so I am facing him. He puts the cock ring on right to the base of his cock and he turns it on. I see the look on his face. I grab hold of his cock and just hold it feeling the vibrations in my hand, he starts to thrust. I flick the little black switch on the side and it vibrates faster, he's breathing hard and I see him gulp over and over.

"Fuck me, this feels amazing, quick, I need to be in you, you need to feel this."

I sit on my ass and move closer to him, he helps lift me up and I wrap my legs around his waist and hold on to his neck, I slowly lower myself onto his vibrating cock and OH. MY. GOD. I can't even move. I freeze on him and let the vibrations work on my clit. I let go of his neck and lean back with my hands behind me for support. I start to move around trying to rotate as he starts to move in and out.

"No, don't move out, it takes the vibration from my clit," I breathe out to him.

He just slams and rotates inside me so I don't lose the contact from the ring, it goes on and on, oh my god, I sit back up grabbing his neck and I start to bounce and dig in deeper on him. I explode like never before. I'm frantic on his cock, clawing at his neck to get him deeper and deeper. I take his mouth and kiss him like never before, I can't come down from the orgasm, I lean back again and keep going.

"Mrs. fucking Ustrashkins, I can't get enough, I fucking love you. This. Is. Fucking. Amazing."

He digs and digs as far as he can, rotating more and more, faster and faster. His cock, if it's possible is bigger than ever, he hits the spot over and over, he's like a madman on steroids. It goes on forever, I must be having multiple orgasms or one rolling one that never stops. The intensity is unreal. I watch his face, it's contorting into so many expressions, he looks ecstatic, then pained, then manic, then he explodes, thrusting harder and harder. I explode again with him. He falls forward onto me and we are panting like we just ran a fucking marathon. It takes us so long to come down and catch our breaths. He is still in me and the cock ring is still vibrating on my clit. He devours my mouth once we catch our breaths and he starts moving again. He's still hard, even though he climaxed.

"Baby, you need to get up, baby, I need to breathe, I need a break. That was so intense I didn't fucking cuss. So I'm doing it now. Fuck me, Igor, that was unreal, baby."

He laughs into my mouth and gently pulls out of me. I think I'm going to be red raw down there. I watch him get up off the lounger and turn the ring off, and slowly and very carefully he removes it. I watch in awe of him.

"Have you ever tried anything like this before?" I'm curious, but I don't want to start crying if his answer is yes. He looks at me.

"Never, I never even thought about it until you mentioned it. But I agree, holy fuck, my cock is bigger, and it took me a lot longer to reach climax but I fucking loved it. Definitely one to try again!" He smiles at me.

"Only with me, Igor."

I see the look on his face slowly turning to anger. Oh shit.

"What do you mean, only with you? I just made vows to you, you are my fucking wife, of course it will only ever be with you."

I kneel up and reach for him, but he steps back. Ouch, that hurt. He didn't get what I meant. I look down to my hands.

"I didn't mean that." I don't look at him, it hurt when he stepped back from me out of my reach.

"Explain," he says authoritatively, this could either turn very nasty with me telling him to fuck off for being bossy with me or I just explain.

I sigh out and look at him. "I didn't mean with anyone else, I meant only with me as in don't you use these things on yourself alone. That was all I meant."

He moves to me and hugs my head to his tummy with his still hard cock sticking in my neck. I lean down and take care of him.

We had an amazing honeymoon, albeit a short one. It was supposed to be for a week but it was cut short by three days because Igor was needed back home. Is this going to be our life? Him always having to run off for something. It caused an argument because he promised me he would devote this week to just me. There will always be something, no matter what.

We have just arrived back at the apartment and he's already rushed out on business. We need to have a conversation on when he is going to let me in on his business and involve me. I'm not going to just live my life sitting in this apartment on my own waiting for my husband to come home. Wow, that feels funny saying my husband as I look at the gorgeous rings on my finger. I feel all warm and fuzzy. Jet lag, I head to bed. I'm not waiting for him.

I feel him get into bed and spoon me, he kisses my shoulder. I'm awake, jet lag, I turn to face him.

"Hey baby, you okay? What time is it?"

He looks at his watch. "It is now one in the morning. I'm sorry if I woke you, Mrs. Ustrashkins." He smiles and kisses me.

I need to talk and plan now, he's not going to plan my life.

"My beautiful husband. I want to start learning about your business, I want to be a part of it no matter what it is. You have me for life and that doesn't mean I'm going to sit waiting for my husband to put in an appearance. I know you are the godfather and you rule, I completely understand that, but I want you to teach me. This lifestyle I'm about to embark on with you is all new to me. Yes, I have been a bitch and can be a bitch, but please don't ask me to just sit at home like the dutiful little housewife. That is not me, Igor. I also now want to put into place my revenge. I want to finish it once and for all so we can get on with the rest of our lives, baby."

He's smiling at me with this great big smile. He leans in and kisses me. "I knew there was a reason I married you, Mrs. Ustrashkins. Let us sleep, it has been a very long day, after training in the morning we will sit and plan. How does that suit you, my beautiful wife?"

"That makes me very happy, my beautiful husband. I love you, Igor, so much." We both fall asleep with me in his arms.

Even though we are jet-lagged he still has me up at the crack of dawn to train. I don't mind, I need this, and we didn't do any training the last week. He worked me hard, I don't know if he was trying to tire me out so we wouldn't discuss what I wanted to at breakfast but there is no way he's getting away with it that easy. I'm pumped and ready for this. We sit and have breakfast in our room.

"Mrs. Ustrashkins, God, I love calling you that, мой ангел, are you not tired? We worked hard this morning. You are almost at your peak. You amaze me, my wife. No matter how hard I push you, you push back harder still. Let's make our plan, but first, what do you want out of this revenge. Do you want to kill him or just harm him?"

Hmm, I have thought about this and to kill him makes me a murderer like him, to harm him or disable him permanently like Prim, then he would suffer for life.

"мой ангел, tell me what you are thinking, talk it out and I can help you reach the right decision for you."

"I've wanted him dead all this time, from him trying to kill me, but just lately I've been thinking if I kill him, he doesn't suffer so much, and that makes me a murderer like him."

I see Igor's face change and he looks away from me when I say that, looking out of the window, he looks hurt. I know he's killed a lot of people or had a hand in killing a lot of people. I squeeze his hand and he looks at me.

"It doesn't matter to me what you have done or do, Igor, I'm thinking out loud like you asked."

He gives a slight nod of his head but still looks hurt. "I know, мой ангел, it's just we are the same this Nick and I."

I shake my head. "Never Igor, you are my husband, I love you and I will stand by your side even if you killed every dignitary in the US. I would join you, no matter what. Do you understand Igor, I will be by your side no matter what. I want to be there in your lightest hour and your darkest hour, I want to be with you, I want to join with you and be by your side in life and in business, I want us to be a force to be reckoned with." I get up and move around to him to sit on his lap. He puts his arm around me, and I take his face in my hands and kiss him gently on the lips. "Do you understand me, Igor? You are my world, my life, and you are nothing like him."

He nods and kisses me hard. "I love you so much, мой ангел. Please carry on with what you want out of your revenge."

"So to kill him means it's over, but I want him to suffer, one way I can do that is to hurt Prim, if they are still together, that is."

He nods his head, what does that mean? I frown at him. "They are together, and he lives with her. I had someone check it for me."

He smiles at me, I'm not surprised he did that, once he found out my full name, it would be easy to find Prim.

"Okay, but you should have told me you did that, no secrets ever, can we make that pact right now? We have the no lies, but I want the no secrets to go with that."

He smiles and kisses me. "You have my oath on that also, Mrs. Ustrashkins."

"You have mine too. Now, I want him to suffer. If I somehow maim him, in a way, he will suffer for life, although he will still be alive, he won't lead a normal life. Like Prim is deaf, I wan…"

"She is deaf? You never told me. Was she born deaf?" I shake my head, slightly ashamed.

"I had a small hand to play in that. It was the first time I did something bad to her, but I didn't know it would damage her hearing. I've told you how much I hate her, and we have never got on. If I hurt her then it will hurt him. I want us to get him and really do some damage to him, give him so much pain he nearly dies from it, maybe shatter his kneecaps. I helped him for a while when he twisted his ankle. He walks everywhere, or he did, so if I do something to his legs, something where he will never walk again, I think he will suffer so much with that." Before I know what's happening, I am being thrown onto the bed and he is stripping out of his sweats and he's in me like a madman.

He's gone to work and left me here again. He said we would talk about his business, but he distracted me instead. Well, if he wants to be like that, then I'm going out. I think I need a little of my own retail therapy. I head out, not having a clue where to go. I walk past the park, which is the area I know, and I just take in my surroundings. I call in for a Starbucks, it's hot out here today. I know one of his men is following me but I just ignore him. I spot a Macy's. Great, I'll go see if I can find any bargains I can pay for myself. Maybe buy Igor something nice, but what do you buy a man who only dresses in the best, most expensive clothes and has quite a few expensive watches. Not the kind of money I have, anyway. I stop to try out the perfumes and I find a nice new one that I buy, and I find a lovely new cologne for Igor, so I buy that one as well.

I head back out of the shop and walk along the street. I am fully aware of my surroundings, one of Igor's training sessions was to teach me to be aware of everything around me. I see an Agent Provocateur shop just up ahead. I want to do something different for Igor and this is the ideal place. I enter the shop. I turn and see his man standing outside. I didn't think he would come in here. I have a good look around and head toward the back where all the naughty items are. I pick up quite a few items to take into the changing room with me. I've picked out a few matching bra and thong sets which are amazing and if he dares rip my thongs off, I will kill him. I laugh to myself. I have just put on the sexiest corset that pushes my tits up so high and really brings my waist in. I put on some matching crotchless panties which also open right up the crack of my ass, and I'm bent over putting on some very fine stockings when the door suddenly flies open. What the fuck, I start to stand up but a hand gently pushes on my back to stop me. I know who it is straight away, I can smell him. I lift my head to look in the mirror and there stands my Russian god of a husband with that look on his face that turns me on.

I stand up and adjust the corset so my tits pop out of the top. I watch him take all of my body in through the full-length mirror in front of me.

"Like what you see, my Russian god?" I lick my lips provocatively.

His hands are on my ass, kneading and spreading my cheeks, he bends down and sticks his tongue inside the hole. His hand wanders underneath to the front, he sticks his fingers inside my pussy. I spread my legs wider and play with my nipples as he's in and out of my holes. I'm panting away trying to get more friction from him and I move a hand to my clit. He stands up, keeping his fingers inside me, and he watches me playing. He growls at me, shaking his head. He pulls his fingers out of me and licks them before taking his trousers off. He moves the cushioned stool in front of the mirror, and he sits on it facing the mirror. He makes me straddle his legs with my back to him so we can both see what's happening in the mirror. He opens his legs more, in turn making me spread mine wider, and he lowers my ass onto his cock. He slams it straight up and I gasp. He sits me down and moves his head to the side so he can see what's going on. He brings a hand round to the front and he plays with my clit with his thumb while inserting his fingers in my pussy. This is fucking hot watching us together like this. I start moving up and down as he thrusts up into my ass, each thrust harder. I play with my nipples as I watch us both in the mirror, we're both panting away, I don't give a shit if anyone can hear us in here and neither does he as both of us start to get louder and louder the nearer we get. I explode on his fingers, I can't help it but I press his thumb harder onto my clit and get him to rub, I bounce up and down and in no time he explodes inside me. He holds my hip down hard with his free hand as he thrust and thrusts to empty himself. He bites at my shoulder as I lean back. His breathing starts to calm as we stare at each other in the mirror. He makes me stand, still facing the mirror. He's on the floor in front of me kicking the stool out of his way, he lowers my body so I crouch above his face and he laps at all my juice while playing with my tits. This is so erotic watching what he's doing in the mirror, he tilts his head so he can watch upside down and it's hot as fuck. I'm exploding on his face once again.

"Fucking hell, Igor, that was hot as fuck," I say, still hovering above his face while he licks me dry.

He slaps my ass then pushes me up. I turn around and kneel over his face, then bend to lick his cock like a popsicle. With his tongue back in my pussy and his fingers in my ass, we both explode yet again. Will once ever be enough for either of us?

"My wife, you will be the death of me, especially wearing outfits like this. It's hot as fuck. I can't get enough of you. I need to buy you everything that makes you look like this. Then I will make sure none of my staff enter our apartment, ever, it will just be the two of us, and you can walk around in this stuff all the time I am home. How does that sound?" I laugh at him and he laughs with me.

He stays and sits on the stool, watching me as I try on the other outfits I brought in.

"We will buy them all. Now come we need to leave. We have a meeting to get to."

What is he talking about? I watch as he gets dressed, not moving. He looks at me and raises his brow because I haven't moved.

"What meeting? You never mentioned we were meeting anyone. In fact, why did you come here? I suppose you were told I was out shopping. You knew I would be safe, why come?"

He raises his eyebrow again. "You always make me come." He laughs at his own joke, but I don't laugh with him.

"I was on my way home when Steve phoned me to say you were here. I couldn't resist seeing you try on lingerie, so here I am. Let me just say any time you want to try on lingerie again, you have to take me with you. This is so fucking hot." He smiles at me then stands and starts to undress me.

We leave the shop with bags and bags of things. He left me in the dressing room to put my clothes on and when I came out the poor assistant was being bombarded with all kinds of things, including pasties for my tits, body chains and who knows what else? He found the extreme naughty section and I can see her packing up whips and paddles, oh no, he is not hitting me, I watch as she puts in chokers and boxes of other stuff. I picked one up that was a love egg. He took it from my hands and showed me the back.

"Look, I can control this from my phone while it's in you. I thought it would be fun to use." He smiles the big goofy smile and puts it in the bag.

Oh lord, what have I created? We head home with all our bags. Once it's just the two of us inside, he takes my hand and we head to the bedroom.

"Oh no, Igor, we are not trying any of these things now. We can play later on. Now, what meeting are we supposed to be going to?" I say as he shuts the bedroom door, smiling at me.

He takes his little bug gadget out and sweeps the room. I sit on the bed watching him.

"All good. Okay, I have a meeting this afternoon with one of my suppliers and I want you to be there. This is a gun supplier." He watches my face for a reaction but I don't give him one.

I know he deals in stuff, but I'm not sure what.

I nod for him to carry on.

"I want your take on this one. I think he is up to something, I just have a funny feeling about him. I have only used him once before, but I don't think I trust him. I would like your opinion. Now I will not put you in any danger. I want you to stay in the car at the warehouse we are meeting, just in case something happens. For this first meeting, I want you safe. Will you agree to that?"

I nod, smiling. He's including me. Is this because I went out?

"Are you doing this because I went out without telling you? You distracted me this morning and then left so we didn't discuss your business. That is why I went out. I was mad at you."

He takes my head in his hands and kisses me.

"No, I was coming back before I knew you were out. I want you involved, but we have to take it slow. Let people get used to seeing you by my side. But I also have to be careful because the more I show you out there the more ammunition I give to my enemies. Until now, there has never been anything they could do to me personally. Now I have a weakness, which is you, and they will soon pick up on that. I want you to be badass in this business like I am. I want you to take control of some of my less dangerous business." He must see me frown.

"Just for now, just until I am happy for you to be exposed. Will you agree to do this with me, мой ангел?"

I do understand and I do agree. I know he just wants me safe and I understand I'm now his weakness.

"One other thing, Igor, when do I get my own key cards to access all the floors." I need to know he trusts me this much. He says he does, but this will put my mind at ease. He gets off the bed and heads to the closet.

"Come," he says, and I follow him. He moves over to where his shoes are and he moves a shoe on the shelf at neck level and presses something at the back. The unit slides completely to the left, exposing a retina scanner. He puts his eye there and the back panel slides up, revealing a huge safe behind it.

"Like I said, a badass James Bond. You have high-tech gadgets everywhere."

He turns and smiles at me. He then puts a code into the safe and puts his forefinger and then thumb on a panel and the safe opens. It's a tall safe with lots of shelves. The top three I can tell are just full of cash. Then he pulls out a drawer and takes out a key card. He passes it to me.

"This is a master card like mine. There are only two, not even Andrey or Ivan have these. It will let you go anywhere in the building, including the safe room in the basement. If I ever message you, or just tell you, to be safe, I want you to go to that room immediately, no matter where you are. Do you understand?"

I nod, wow, he really does trust me.

"I need to also add your retina to all my scanners. We can do that in my office. You will then be able to come and go as you want. Okay, мой ангел, are you ready for this? This is what you wanted, no?"

I throw myself at him. I can't believe he trusts me with everything. This means more to me than he will ever understand.

"Now we go to the meeting. Come." He takes my hand and we leave.

Seventeen

Poppy
A year earlier

WE'RE IN A CAR BEING DRIVEN TO THE MEETING. ANDREY and Ivan are up front. There are three other cars with us full of his men. I feel my adrenaline pumping, he's really doing this. We enter what looks like an old industrial place full of huge warehouses that look run-down. We pull into one and I turn and see the other cars go in different directions. He takes my hand and I turn to him.

"So observant. We arrive early so we have a chance to stake out the place. Always arrive early to get the upper hand. I can have my men in place if anything goes wrong. Now this man we are meeting is Iranian, and he is selling me guns, a lot of guns. I don't know much about him and he sought me out. That always makes me nervous. I used him once as a trial and it worked. I didn't make the pickup that time. He wanted to see me this time, which is one of the reasons I am suspicious. When someone asks for me specifically, I always have to wonder if it is a sting. Either the FBI are involved or if it is a rival that wants to take me out."

I gasp at the thought of him being shot. For some reason, I have tears welling in my eyes. He leans over and wipes a stray tear away with his thumb.

"Мой ангел, what is wrong? Are you scared to be here? Is this too much for you?"

I unbuckle my seatbelt, and I climb onto his lap. He holds me tight. Our windows are all blacked out so no one can see me in here.

"No, Igor, I'm not scared to be here. I'm scared at the thought you might get shot or hurt. I've only just found you. I don't want to lose you. Why could you not just send your men for this? Why show up yourself, even if they asked for you? I would just say no, they deal with my men."

He smiles and kisses my forehead.

"It is not that simple, мой ангел. I have to show my face, or they would think very little of me and think they can walk all over me and my men. When they ask specifically for me, I have to be there, to show I am who I am and to show they do not scare me. I have been dealing with gun trafficking for many, many years, my father had his own contacts who he passed on to me. The last one thought he could get one over on me and it did not end well for him. Some of the other contacts of my fathers are happy to deal with me. They didn't think I was as ruthless as my father, some of them found out the hard way. This new one though, I think he is going to try his luck. I don't think he is working with the FBI but I can't take any chances."

He stills as he listens to something, I didn't realize he had an earpiece in until he turns and moves his hair aside to show me.

"It is my men. They are in position and there is no one else around. They will tell me when anyone approaches. I am always in contact with my men at meetings like this."

I'm getting scared. Not of who is coming, but of what may happen. I cling to him. "Igor, what else do you deal in besides guns? I pull away so I can see his face. "Is it just guns?"

He shakes his head.

"No, most of my business is drugs and money laundering. I know that is bad, мой ангел, but it is what I know. My father was also heavily into sex trafficking. I didn't find this out until he was dead, I was disgraced by it. I don't condone anything like that and in fact, I make it a point now to get rid of anyone I find doing that. I have my own team that hunts sex traffickers out and we dispose of them. It is another reason I have a lot of girls back in our building. They were rescued, I gave them a safe place to stay. We help them back to their countries and for those that want to, we help them back into society. I provide them with a fake ID so they don't get deported and set them up with jobs if I can."

I watch his face as he tells me this and I'm in awe of him.

"I love you so much. You have a good heart, Igor." I tell him about the work I did helping girls on the street and how I thought about talking to him, about setting up a refuge for them. I hadn't told him that before and he pulls me to him.

"You too are an angel for sure, мой ангел."

Just then I can tell I don't have his attention. He starts to lift me off his lap to place me on the seat.

"They are approaching. There are two white trucks and an Escalade. My men don't see anyone else."

I must look worried as he pulls me into his side.

"Wait, there are two more cars approaching. They have stopped outside on the street. There are men with guns getting out of the cars. They don't look like FBI. They all look middle eastern. I have one of my men out on the street as a vagrant. He says there are no Americans and they are speaking Persian. I think we are safe to say it is not a sting by the FBI." Just then Andrey speaks to Igor.

I really need to learn to speak Russian. How can I be by his side and help run the business if I can't speak his language? I look to him, creasing my brow as if asking what he said.

"The trucks and Escalade have just come into view, see."

He nods his head out the front of the car and I look. My heart is beating so fast.

"Igor, will you teach me Russian? Then I won't feel so helpless when I'm with you in meetings."

He smiles and kisses my head. Andrey and Ivan get out of the car and stand either side of it, but behind their open doors.

"The doors are bulletproof, мой ангел, as is all the car. It is to military standard and would take a rocket launcher to damage it." I sigh out, I was worried for Andrey and Ivan. The Escalade pulls up and four men get out of the car. They walk to the front, three are holding what look like machine guns. I look to Igor. I think he is listening to his men.

"Is everything okay?" I whisper to him.

He nods but doesn't speak. I hear someone shout outside.

"Where is Mr. Ustrashkins? I will only do business with him." It is the man who is not holding a gun.

"Is that him, Igor? Is that the Iranian you are doing business with?" He takes out a tablet from the pocket of the seat in front of us and brings up a picture. I look to the Iranian man and back. It looks like the same person.

"Do you think that is the same person, мой ангел?"

I look closely, making the face of the man bigger on the tablet, then look back to the man. I take out my cell and zoom in on the man's face. I shake my head.

"No, this man on here has a scar near his mouth and he has blue eyes, the man standing out there doesn't have a scar and he has dark brown eyes, see." I hold up the phone so he can see.

He smiles. Then he speaks into his hand. I hear Andrey outside telling the man that Mr. Ustrashkins will only speak to Farhad Javid. I look to Igor, he is so calm. I'm a bit of a wreck inside. Knowing there are a lot of men with guns out there ready to shoot at us. The back door of the Escalade opens, and another man gets out. I zoom in on him and I turn to Igor and nod, showing him the image on my phone. He kisses me on the head.

"What are your first impressions, мой ангел?"

I don't trust the man outside. I shake my head.

"I don't trust him. Why send the other man out pretending to be him? He had no intention of getting out of the car. I think they are going to try and shoot you and take your money. I would ask them to bring the cases of guns out and put them on the ground where you can see them clearly and have one of your men examine them. They will no doubt have seen your men behind us up there, I would get one of them to check. Not Andrey or Ivan."

He speaks into his hand again and looks at me. I hear Andrey telling the man outside to do as I just advised. He nods to his men and two of them move to the trucks behind them. I'm scared.

"If it's a trap, Igor, then those trucks could be full of men with guns ready to come and ambush you."

He nods, he knows this could be the case. I watch carefully. I see eight men now coming from behind the Escalade. I grip Igor's thigh tight. He rubs my hand. As they appear in front of the Escalade, I can see they are carrying big wooden crates, which I would hope are full of guns. I look to Igor.

"Is this what you were expecting?"

He nods, then speaks into his hand and a minute later two of his men walk past our car with their guns at the ready and walk to the crates. They say something as they approach and the men with the crates open them up so Igor's men can inspect them. They move forward cautiously. We can't see what is in the crates from here. Igor speaks and Andrey bows slightly and speaks back to him. I look for confirmation to Igor.

"He says it looks like guns, but he thinks something is not right here." Igor opens his door and steps out.

I see the look on the other man's face when he sees Igor. Why has he stepped out now? Igor stays behind the door and speaks.

"Farhad, why did you try to fool me? Do you have any idea who you are actually dealing with here? You had me come out personally to see you, yet you tried to fool me by sending him as though he was you. These crates are not big enough for the amount we talked about. You are trying to take me for a fool, Farhad. Let me just tell you now. No one ever takes me for a fool."

With that, he gets back into the car, as do Andrey and Ivan. Igor's men have retreated, and I see the moment the other men raise their guns to fire. They set off a couple of rounds which hit our car but just bounce off. Igor speaks to Andrey and Ivan, then into his hand. Andrey puts the car in reverse and Ivan starts pressing a lever on the center console. I see bullets rapidly firing from what looks like the front of our car and I see the Iranian men go down. Farhad and his look-alike try to get into the Escalade. His look-alike goes down, but Farhad manages to get into the car. More men have appeared, which I presume are from the trucks. Just then the trucks explode and the gunmen go flying. I look to Igor, who is watching it all play out at as calm as anything.

I hear more gunfire as we start to move toward the exit

"It is okay, мой ангел, my men have killed them all now. No casualties on our side."

I breathe out just as I see the Escalade head straight for us. Andrey manages to swerve and it misses us. It crashes into the wall. Before I know it, Igor is out of the car running to the Escalade with his gun drawn. He approaches the back where Farhad was and opens the door, pulling him out. He doesn't look hurt. The front door opens and a gunman gets out. He looks bloody, he lifts his gun at Igor just as I scream and hear the gun go off. I watch as the gunman goes down and I see Andrey is out of the car pointing his gun. He shot him. Igor has Farhad by the hair and is pulling him away from the car. He then has him facedown in the dirt with his foot digging into his head. He then drags him up by the hair again, so Farhad is looking. I don't get out of the car. I can hear what he says.

"Why would you try to take me on like this, you fucking stupid prick? Do you have any idea who you are dealing with? You came here with the intention of taking me out and stealing my money. Who do you work for? I want names, now," Farhad spits at Igor, who in turn hits him hard in the face with his gun.

Farhad goes down. Igor puts his foot on his neck and points the gun at his head.

"Tell me who you work for and I will kill you with my bullet. Don't tell me and I will torture it out of you."

Farhad doesn't speak. I watch with fascination at Igor in action. He is one scary motherfucker and I certainly wouldn't want to mess with him, but at the same time, it makes me want to jump his bones. Seeing all this play out has my adrenaline pumping. I feel light-headed as though I want to collapse, but I want to see it play out. Farhad doesn't speak. I see movement out of the corner of my eye, it's the look-alike, he isn't dead, he's reaching for a gun. I grab the gun from the floor of the car and get out and I shoot. Without thinking, I shoot the fucker and I get him right in the head. He goes down. Igor and his men swing around and aim at me, thinking it was me trying to shoot at them, but Igor shouts loud and they lower their guns. He sees what I was aiming at and sees the look-alike on the ground with a gun in his hand and a hole in his head. He turns to me and smiles. It's a 'so fucking proud of you smile' and I drop to the floor as I realize I just killed someone.

Igor rushes over to me, shouting orders as he does. He picks me up and checks me over just to make sure I didn't get shot. I'm fine, but he gets into the back of the car with me and I'm shaking. I'm not crying, I'm not upset. That bastard was going to try to shoot my husband. I'm just in shock I actually fucking killed someone.

"Мой ангел, are you okay? Are you hurt?" He's got me on his lap, holding me to him tight. I can't stop shaking. I pull back and look at him.

"J-j-j-just, sh-sh-shock-ed. Ca-ca-ca-can't stop-p-p-p sh-sh-shak-shaking." My teeth are chattering loud. He smiles at me and kisses me all over my face.

"You saved me, мой ангел, you just saved my fucking life. You are in shock, that is all. I need to get you home for a hot drink and a long soak in a hot bath. You amaze me, Mrs. Ustrashkins, absolutely fucking amaze me." He barks out orders from inside the car, I don't see what is happening but I feel the car start to move. I'm buried in his chest.

It's not long before he's carrying me into our building and up to our apartment. He places me on the bed, I'm still shaking and I'm cold. He goes into the bathroom and runs the bath. While that's running, he goes to make me a coffee and brings it with a tumbler of whiskey. I hate whiskey, but he makes me drink it to calm me and warm me up. I sit up, cradling the coffee cup in my hand while he sees to the bath.

He walks back into the room naked. I raise an eyebrow. I've stopped shaking, the whiskey worked. Never underestimate a Russian god. He lifts me and carries me to the bathroom where he places me on the vanity unit and starts to undress me. He puts me on the floor and finishes stripping me. He then picks me up and puts me over his shoulder, he steps into the bathtub and lowers us so I'm sitting on his lap.

"I love you, мой ангел. I'm sorry if I made you a murderer like me. It wasn't my intention. I wanted your opinions on the meet today and you were amazing. Your assessment of the situation was spot on. Using your cell to zoom in was fucking brilliant, and you saved my life. All my men's eyes were on me, not on what was going on around us. You spotted that and you saved me. Thank you, мой ангел."

He's being so gentle with me as he starts to wash me with a cloth and soapy water. I move slowly from his lap and sit at the other end facing him. He looks hurt at my move. I see the confusion on his face. I smile at him.

"I'm okay, Igor, I just wanted to face you. To see you, to look at you. If I'd have lost you today, I don't know what I would have done. You're my life, Igor. In such a short time, you've become my family and my life. It scares the shit out of me thinking back to that and what if. The chances are he would have missed anyway, he was badly hurt, but what if. It scares me, Igor. You say you want me to talk things out with you instead of letting them stew in my head. I don't know if I can do it, Igor, I don't know if I can let you go out that door without me. Worrying if you will be coming back. I didn't think of it like that before, until now, seeing the danger you put yourself in. If you walk out that door without me, I will be fretting nonstop. I don't know if I can live like that." I look down and play with the bubbles. This is the first time I've actually used the bath since living here. We're always in the shower together. But never had a bath. It's nice.

"What do you mean? Do you want to leave me? I knew it would be too much for you to fucking take. I was kidding myself. If you want to leave, I will not stop you, мой ангел. I should have let you fucking see it before we got married. I am sorry. I've now changed your life forever. You killed a man because of me. For that, I am truly sorry, and I hope you find it in your heart to forgive me." He gets up and leaves the bathroom, grabbing a towel as he does, wrapping it around his waist.

I don't say anything. I'm angry, but not at him, I'm angry because now I know what he gets up to. I don't know if I can live like this. I'm angry because he now thinks I'm going to leave him, and he would let me walk away. He promised me he would always let me walk if I needed to, without harming me.

I stay soaking in the bath until I start to get cold. I don't know where he is and to be honest, I'm not in the mood to stroke his ego. He has such a good heart, but he's a villain when all's said and done. I step into the shower and rinse off and get warm again. I grab my robe and head to the kitchen with my empty glass and cup. I pour myself another coffee. I don't know where Igor has gone. I don't know if he got dressed and has gone out or if he's in the apartment somewhere. I want to speak to someone, the only person I can talk to is Svetlana. I don't think Igor would like that, and I wouldn't tell her anything that happened. I think I just need a female to talk to. I leave my coffee, get dressed, and head to the ninth floor.

I'm walking down the long corridor toward Svetlana's and there are a few girls in and out of each other's rooms. They all look good, none of them look ill-treated. I get to the suite at the end and I walk in. There are three girls sitting on a couch. When they see me, I see the shock on their faces. I ignore them and turn to Svetlana's door. I walk in without knocking and I stop dead in my tracks at the sight of Igor sitting on a chair near the dresser. I freeze and look around. Just then Svetlana comes out of the bathroom in just a towel. What the fuck is that about. Did he just fuck her? I don't say a thing and I walk out and almost run towards the elevators. He doesn't chase after me. I get to the elevators and I press the button for the basement and insert my key card. I go to the control room and I make them show me Svetlana's suite from twenty minutes ago. I tell the man to leave me alone. I watch as I see Igor enter the suite. She runs over to him, he looks upset, she then takes his arm and leads him to her bedroom. It doesn't help because there is no camera in her actual room. That would be absurd if there was.

I head out of the door, and Igor is standing near the elevator. He looks remorseful. I don't speak and I hit the button to take me up to his apartment. He tries to grab my arm.

"Fuck off, Igor," I say, gritting my teeth. I see his face turn to anger.

He gets into the elevator with me, but he doesn't come near me and I don't speak. Once the door opens to his apartment, I march to his room to grab some of my things. It's too late to go anywhere now, but I will stay in my old room for tonight. He's watching everything I do but he still doesn't say anything. I storm past him with my bag of things, which includes my purse with my ID and money, so if I get up and leave in the morning, I will have that with me. He tries to grab my arm as I pass him but I wince as he does so he drops it right away thinking he hurt me when he didn't. I knew he would drop my arm. I march into my room, slamming the door, hoping it hit him in the face. It's no use locking it, he has a key to every room.

I get into bed in my clothes. I hear him open the door. I wait to see what he does. I feel the bed dip behind me, and his arm comes around to pull me to him. I shrug him off. He tries again.

"Fuck off, Igor. Fucking leave me alone if you know what's good for you."

He flinches at the venom in my voice. He sighs.

"Мой ангел, please let me explain. Please let me talk to you."

I ignore him. I feel him get off the bed. Good he's leaving, but he appears in front of me kneeling on the floor. I close my eyes. I don't want to look at him. All I can picture is him sitting in her room. Why go to her if she's nothing? Why run back to her? That hurt more than anything. The big fucking godfather running to a little girl he used to fuck as soon as he thinks we're in trouble. I'm seething. I open my eyes as he strokes my forehead, moving my hair.

"Don't. Fucking. Touch. Me. You know what, Igor? You say talk to you about what I'm thinking, so here it is. I think you went and fucked her because you thought we were in trouble. I think the big fucking pussy of a godfather went running to a pathetic little girl he used to fuck because he thought we were over. Not ten minutes after a meltdown and you run to fuck her. That's what I think. If you fucking dare try to scold me for my fucking language, I will fucking commit murder for the second time today. That is what I'm thinking. So fuck you, Igor, and leave me the fuck alone."

He laughs, he actually fucking laughs at me. He sits back on his ass and laughs. He looks at my face then falls back laughing, he's hysterical. I admit I have a smile on my face at him laughing, but I'm fuming. I get off the bed and walk past him to the bathroom. I get a glass of water and I come back where he is still laughing. I stand above his head and slowly pour the water on his face. He laughs harder. I put the glass down and start to walk away. He gets up and grabs me around the waist and pulls me onto the bed. He has my arms pinned down at my sides and he's facing me.

"Now, мой ангел, it is my turn, please let me explain and let you know what I am thinking. I think you are amazing. I know I will love you forever, I think you are a fucking firecracker. NO, I did not run to Svetlana to fuck her or for anything else. I was upset from what you said in the bathroom, yes, in fact, I was fucking raging inside but I was also hurt, I felt like my heart was breaking. I needed to get out because I got mad for two reasons, one I thought we were through, but two, she was unfinished business I needed to sort after the fiasco of today."

I frown at him and try to struggle to get him to release me. It's only a half-assed struggle, I don't want him to let me go. But then what was his unfinished business with her?

"No, Mrs. Ustrashkins, please just listen to me. I have had Svetlana put in one of the dull rooms this time, the bad rooms as you call them. She has betrayed me. She is the one that put Farhad Javid in touch with me. It was on her. The more I thought about it, the more I think she knew, and it was a setup for her getting revenge on me."

I scowl at him, not quite taking in what he is saying. It's her.

"Why would she get revenge? You saved her from an abusive papa. Why would she do that to you?" I'm confused.

"Because she has always wanted me. Every other girl I have been with after her she has had a problem with. The more I think about it and her knowing about the acid vats, I think she may have killed some of them. I've got some of my guys checking the ground that I own near the Port of LA. I'm going to get it out of her one way or the other. I was not there for any other reason, мой ангел, I love you and only you. I told you, I gave you my oath that I would never fuck anyone else. I never, ever break my oath." He strokes down my cheek. I can't help but melt into him. I rest my head on his chest. Could she have done that, could Svetlana have killed girls because he fucked them.

"If she did kill any of them, then I suppose it pissed her off when you married me, huh, knowing she couldn't do anything to me." I shrug.

"Now, can you explain what you meant in the bathtub please, мой ангел, I have to tell you it's scared the shit out of me, and you know I don't scare easy. Did you mean we were over? That you couldn't do this? It kills me thinking I made you feel this way." He closes his eyes and I lean in and kiss each eyelid gently.

I pull back and watch as he opens his eyes slowly and I smile at him.

"I knew you didn't fuck her, Igor. I'm sorry for thinking that. I was so mad, I thought you had run to her because we had words. We didn't even argue, it was just me speaking my mind like you tell me to. You didn't give me a chance to talk to you, you ran out. I needed to think for myself, I don't even know why I went to Svetlana's, I think I wanted to speak to a woman, I don't know, I don't even know what I would have talked about. I certainly wouldn't have mentioned anything about today. Maybe I just felt a little lost and confused."

He watches me closely. "I was wondering why you were there, I'm sorry if I am not enough for you. Was today too much, tell me honestly, Mrs. Ustrashkins, do you want out of this life I've dragged you into?"

I can see the pained and scared look on his face as he asks me, waiting for my answer. I kiss him gently.

"No Igor, I don't want an out. I love you and it would kill me to leave. I just got panicked, I was thinking about you going to meetings and them always being like that and never knowing if you would come back. It freaked me out after going through that today. God today, it was only today, it feels like it was weeks ago." I laugh. I see him sigh out as he closes his eyes with relief.

"Thank you, мой ангел, you have no idea how happy that makes me. Also, not many of my meetings end up like that. In fact, it's very rare they end up like that, so you do not need to worry if I go out without you. I promise I will take you to as many meetings as you want to go to or that I can take you to. I will also teach you how to speak Russian."

I smile at him and give him a kiss.

"I'm just thinking aloud here, but how would Svetlana get down to the basement if she doesn't have access? How would she be able to kill the girls without your men seeing her on the surveillance system? Did you ever take her into the basement and show her what you have shown me?"

He looks at me and he's thinking. I can see he's conflicted.

"I have never taken her down there. You are right, someone would have picked it up on camera. I have thought about this since that day you spoke to her and how jealous she was. I know some of the girls have disappeared, I mean completely off the grid. To me, the only reason would be death. I have got Andrey looking into it for me also because the only conclusion is she has someone on my team who she must be fucking and using to get what she wants. She is very manipulative. That is the only way she could get down to the basement, or she had one of my men take the bodies down for her. With this today I fear her end is near."

I gasp, he's going to kill her.

"It must be if she betrays me, мой ангел. If I have a traitor, I have to dispose of them. I cannot let her stay here, who knows who she is giving information to. Like the shootout here, weeks ago, I think someone inside helped. If it is her, then she has to be dealt with like every other traitor, death is the penalty. There is no other way for someone who betrays you." He looks sad.

I cuddle into his chest. Loving the feel of his big strong arms holding me close. We fall asleep holding each other tight.

Eighteen

Poppy

WHEN IGOR TOLD ME HE HAD SVETLANA IN THE BASEMENT I wanted to help, I wanted to go and talk to her myself and see if she would open up to me. See if I could find out if she did do anything to those missing girls, or even if she did set Igor up with Farhad. In a way, I think I wanted to be her friend. Crazy, I know, but maybe it's because of the lack of females in my life. Igor told me to leave her there to stew for a few days, which I did, then I went to see her.

I peered through the Perspex into her cell. Well, to me that's what these are, cells. Igor had a few people down here going off the noises coming from some of them as I walked past. I didn't peer into any of them. One of Igor's men, Sergei, showed me which room she was in. It was the closest room to the acid chamber, as I call it. I couldn't really make her out as I peered in with it being so dark in there and out here. Sergei gave me a light. I opened the door on my guard, ready in case she pounced. Sergei stayed near, just to make sure I would be okay. I can defend myself, so I wasn't worried.

The light lit up the tiny cell, I saw it was bare, just dark brick walls, no bed or mattress, just a hard cement floor with a drain in the middle. There was only a bucket in the corner which I took to be the toilet going off the smell as I walked in.

"Hey Svetlana, I brought you some hot black tea and some soup. Here, take these. I don't know when you last had anything to eat." I turn to Sergei.

"I bring her bread and water daily under Igor's instructions."

She doesn't stand up. I bend and place the soup cup in her hand and put the flask of tea on the floor.

"Sergei, can you please go and fetch some bread for Svetlana, and from now on when she is in here, I want her to have hot tea and soup three times a day. Is that clear?"

He nods and leaves to get some bread. I watch Svetlana, she looks dirty and only has on what looks like a very thin nightdress.

"Sergei," I shout, waiting for him to appear. "Bring some blankets back with you."

He nods and leaves again. I sit on the floor next to Svetlana. I lift the hand with the soup cup in it toward her mouth, encouraging her to take some. She eyes me warily. I smile. I know Igor is fuming with her and wants to torture the information out of her about Farhad, but I just want to talk to see if I can coach it out of her. I watch as she takes sips of the soup and Sergei arrives with bread and blankets. I pass her the bread which she gingerly takes from me and I sit up and place one of the blankets around her shoulder and the other across her lap.

"Why do you do this for me?" she whispers.

"Because I believe in you, Svetlana, I just think you need some guidance and a chance." I smile softly, trying to gain her trust. I sit back down, the floor is freezing and I'm in clothes so god knows how she feels in just a short nightdress. A sexy short nightdress at that. I look around to Sergei who is standing in the doorway.

"Sergei, I want you to get her some clothes from her suite. She needs jeans or sweats or both and a sweater along with underwear and see if she has a warm coat. I then want you to get the men to bring a mattress from one of the other rooms." He frowns at me. He's not used to taking orders from anyone other than Igor.

"Sergei, I am Mrs. Ustrashkins and you will do as I say, now."

He bows slightly and leaves. I look back to Svetlana, who is looking at me with what looks like a little admiration. I smile again.

"If you are to stay in hear for a little while then I don't want you freezing to death. Igor wanted to come and talk to you, if you know what I mean." I do quotation marks on the talk, not that she understands me going from the confusion on her face. "Let's just say he wanted to take you to the room next door, after he forced information out of you."

She still looks confused.

"Svetlana, I'm in your corner here, I do not want to see you get hurt. If you tell me what happened, then I will speak to Igor. He thinks you betrayed him Svetlana, he is so mad with you right now, after everything he's done for you. He does care for you, believe me if he didn't you would be in the acid vat in the next room already." I see the look of horror on her face, now she's realizing what is in the room next door.

"Please don't let him put me in there, Poppy, I did not do anything. I swear I did not." Her accent is thick, probably because she's scared. She starts mumbling in Russian, Igor has been teaching me Russian the last couple of days as I asked and I've been learning quickly, so I understand a little of what she is saying.

"Просто расскажи мне, что случилось, и я поговорю с Игорем."

She looks at me shocked as I ask her to tell me what happened, and I would speak to Igor.

"Yes, I've been learning Russian, I know some, but still prefer English. Tell me Svetlana, how did you meet Farhad Javid?"

She hesitates, putting her now empty soup cup on the ground next to her and wrapping the blanket around her tight.

"I was out, not working, but out at a bar with a couple of my friends and he had one of his men talk to me. I didn't know who he was, the man talking to me, I just thought he was coming on to me. I get that a lot when I am out. I was with Malvina and Tamila, but he only talked to me. He asked me to go and sit down with him and have a drink, I agreed. He guided me toward the stairs, which I knew led to the VIP level. I thought it would be okay up there. When we got to the VIP entrance, we were let straight in by another man who looked like some of Igor's men, really big and mean. I started to get a little nervous, but he pushed me in gently and I could see other girls and men inside so thought it was safe."

She picks up her tea and takes some of it, looking at me. I wait patiently for her to continue, rather than rush her and have her thinking I'm being demanding. I don't want to play the hard bitch here. I truly think she is just a lost young girl who looks to Igor as her savior. I sit on my ass and cross my legs.

"Once I was inside, he led me to another man, which turned out to be Farhad Javid. I did not know who he was, he introduced himself to me and told me to sit next to him, he was nice and charming. He made the girls that were with him leave. He poured me some champagne, and we just started talking. Not anything in particular he was asking me where I was from originally, I never give any information out to anyone about my life or where I am from or where I live now. I made everything up that I told him. The next thing I knew he had hold of my wrist telling me I was lying to him, that he knew exactly who I was, that I was Igor Ustrashkins' girl. He scared me. He told me things about my family back home, he knew about my dead papa. I looked at him shocked because I didn't know what he was talking about. He must have seen that on my face. He told me Igor executed my papa, that he did it just before he brought me here. He killed him while I was still there."

I can see tears falling down her face. Why would she be upset if her papa abused her?

"Why are you upset, Svetlana, if your papa did bad things to you?"

She looked at me funny, then shook her head.

"He did not do anything bad to me. My mama only told Igor that so he would pay them good money for me and take me to America. One less mouth to try to feed. My family were very poor, I was the eldest of six girls." Wow, I don't think Igor knows it was all a lie. That will make him even angrier with Svetlana.

"Did you never tell Igor it was a lie?"

She shakes her head. "I promised my mama I would not tell anybody. She didn't want it getting out as my papa would have been killed. As it turns out, he was killed anyway, by him."

She's angry as she nods toward the door. I see Sergei standing there. He will tell Igor. I am just about to tell him to leave when I remembered these rooms all have cameras. No doubt Igor is watching and listening, so it makes no difference.

"Sergei, where is the mattress and clothes I wanted for Svetlana?"

He moves, I just wanted him gone. It may help her open up more to me.

"What happened then on the night you met Farhad?"

She looks at me. I think she is gauging if she should tell me the rest. I nod and give her a small smile, trying to encourage her to continue. She sips more of her tea from the flask, watching me, I stay neutral. I don't want to appear hard or demanding.

"When he told me Igor killed my papa, I was so angry with him. I did not know he had done that. But then I wondered if Farhad was telling me untruths. I told him I did not believe him. He pulled out his cell and showed me a video of my sister Vidana. On the video she was crying, telling me Igor had killed Papa while we were still in Russia. I was shocked and in that moment, I wanted to kill Igor." She looks up to me to watch my expressions. I just smile sympathetically at her and nod for her to carry on.

"He told me he wanted to do a trade with Igor, and he wanted me to set it up. I know some of what Igor does, not in detail, so I said I would talk to him. Farhad warned me if I didn't and I betrayed him, then my sister Vidana would get it like my papa. I was shocked and didn't know what to do. Igor had made me mad with yet another whore, so I told him I had a friend that wanted to do business with him and I set up the meeting, I told him I knew Farhad for some time and he was a good man, that is what Farhad told me to say. I did not know what Farhad was going to do, I did not know the man, only from this visit in the bar where he gave me his details to pass on, but I could not take the chance he would hurt Vidana or any of my other sisters. I have been so worried about my family. I have not been able to contact them. I tried, but I don't know what else to do." She looks so sad as she sits huddled on the cold floor, she's now crying hard and I can see her shivering. I think I believe her. I know she loves Igor and I don't believe she would set something up intentionally knowing he would get hurt even after what she had just been told.

I wrap my arm around her, pulling her into me, and I comfort her while she cries.

"I am so sorry, Poppy, if there was trouble for Igor, I am sorry, it is the last thing I would want, even after learning he killed my papa."

I nod and pull her back into me to comfort her. Sergei arrives with a mattress, but he's followed by Igor. I knew he would be watching and listening. Svetlana hasn't seen him, but I smile at him and he nods, acknowledging I did good. He moves closer and crouches in front of us. Svetlana looks up to him.

"I am sorry, Igor. I would never want you hurt after what you have done for me. I am sorry I am a bitch sometimes, but right now I don't like you, Igor. I just found out you killed my papa. It was for nothing, Igor. He was a good man and a good papa. He just wanted to help his family." She's really crying now. She starts to hiccup and tries to catch her breath.

I rub her arm to let her know I am here for her. I feel sorry for her. To be bought like she was and just accept it so her family could be better off, then, to learn her papa who she clearly loved was killed by her savior for crimes he didn't commit. I look to Igor, who looks a little remorseful.

"Svetlana, look at me," he says in his authoritative voice, which seems to work with everyone but me.

She immediately looks to him, wiping the dribble from her nose on the blanket.

"You know I will not tolerate anyone being used or abused sexually. It goes against everything I am. For your mama and you to tell me what your papa did made me so angry there was no way I was letting him live to sexually abuse your sisters. I apologize for killing him, now I know the truth, but Svetlana, you and your mama have to take responsibility for his death. You lied. If they had just told me the truth that they struggled so much, I would have still brought you to America and I would have made sure your family had money each month. I told you, like I tell everyone around me, never tell lies." He looks to me as though he's chastising me, and I scowl at him and tilt my head. What is he trying to say?

She nods her head and looks back down to her hands in her lap.

"You will stay in here until I am ready for you to leave. You need to reflect on what you have done. I still feel betrayed for both the lies about your papa and an innocent man being killed, and also for Farhad. You should have come to me and told me what had happened, immediately. I could have sent my men to check on your family straight away. I have always sent money over to your mama because she lost her husband and she had five more girls to look after, and that money has been used each month by her. I have asked Andrey to check if that is the case this month. As soon as I know about your family, I will send Sergei to tell you. For now, because of my wife, you will be a little more comfortable in here. If I had my way, you would not have any of it. We then need to have a conversation about how you know about the acid vats and what happened to some of the girls I fucked, that are now missing. Reflect on that and I will be back for your answers later on. Do not lie to me, Svetlana, you now know the consequences. I will also do what I can to find Vidana if the Iranians have her." He looks to me and I just glare at him. At least he hasn't undermined me in front of her, which is what we agreed on.

I leave her and walk out with Igor just as Sergei and some other man arrives with a mattress and some clothes for her. We walk out, leaving them to it. Igor takes me into his side as we walk toward the elevators.

"Thank you, мой ангел, you probably just saved her from getting her nails torn out. I would not talk to her like you did. But thank you. You got her to talk so easily, I was watching everything from my office. I got on the phone to have Svetlana's family checked on and I will wait to see what they report back."

I lean up and kiss him just as the elevator arrives.

"You, Mr. Godfather, have a great big squishy heart of gold. I don't care what anyone else says. You sent money to her mama because there was no one to provide for the family after killing her papa. You didn't have to do that, but because of this heart, you did." I place my hand over his heart and he puts his on top of mine and squeezes it gently.

He laughs at me. "Don't ever tell anyone else I have a big squishy heart of gold or that I am soft. I will lose my badass reputation and will be called a pussy." He leans down and devours my mouth.

"I have a meeting tomorrow with the godfathers, and I have to leave tonight. Will you be okay with me gone?"

I hate it when he goes anywhere, and he knows it. I must look sad as he lifts my chin up to look at him, he's still holding my hand on his chest.

"This is one meeting I cannot take you to, мой ангел. This meeting is for godfathers only, no one else, not even Andrey can be there in the room with me. We are meeting in New York tomorrow. I will take the plane tonight and I will come back straight after the meeting. I can't stand being away from you for long." He kisses me gently. I sigh and lean my head on his chest.

"I will miss you, baby."

After spending a boring night on my own, I'm just going out for a run as part of my training, I still trained early this morning, even though Igor's not here. Steve is following me as usual. I finish my run and am bent over catching my breath. I'm still in the park and I stand up and drink my water, ready to do my warm-down exercises. As I stand up straight and start stretching my arm across my chest holding it with my other arm, I suddenly see Prim, I have to do a double take, there really is no mistaking my own fucking sister, fuck, what the hell is she doing here? I move out of sight behind a tree but keep an eye on her. She's just across the street, near the Starbucks. I see Steve look at me quizzically and he follows my eyeline, he does a double take. Fuck, I can't let her see me, she'll call the police. I watch as she looks at her cell, then she looks up and around. I pull back behind the tree so she doesn't see me. What the fuck is she doing here?

I wait for a few seconds and watch Steve. He nods to me with his head in her direction, I cautiously look around the tree and see she's started walking. I wait for a minute, watching until I see she's far away from me, I move to follow her but I make sure there is something I can quickly hide behind if she was to turn around. She stops and I get behind a parked car, I must look really suspicious to anyone watching me. I bend down on the sidewalk pretending to tie my lace on my sneakers but keep an eye on her. She looks lost. She keeps turning around watching her phone. It must be Google maps or something. She starts walking and I stay behind, following her. I turn to see Steve following me and he has a slight smile on his face, the fucker, he's enjoying this.

Prim walks to a high-rise building and looks at the name plaques by the revolving doors. She heads inside. I watch from outside, again pretending to tie my lace. She heads to what looks like the bank of elevators. I watch as she disappears inside. I stand and look at the names on the plaques, she's obviously here on business and she seems to be alone. Just then I look around searching frantically. What if he's with her? What if he's seen me and is following? I start to panic.

I'm not going to stick around. I head back toward home and pass Steve. I don't acknowledge him but quietly ask him to check if anyone follows me. The last thing I want is for Nick to be with her and see me following. I'm a fool to not think about him being near. Igor told me they are together, or they were. He hasn't updated me since then.

I'm back home, showered, and dressed, I'm going to go and see how Svetlana is. I hate that she's got to stay down there until Igor says she can come out. I understand why she did what she did in a way. I think if things had been different with Prim and I then I may have done the same thing. I think I still probably would if it was someone else going to hurt her and not me. I'm a little conflicted because I have these protective feelings all of a sudden, maybe it's because I saw her, and I feel sorry for doing what I did.

I've just stepped out of the elevators and I stick my head into the control room to let them know I'm going to see Svetlana. Sergei isn't around, I head through all the double doors scanning my eyes to open them. As I open the doors to the corridor Svetlana is in, I can see a figure down near her room. I quietly shut the door, not wanting to make a noise. As I get closer, I can see it's Sergei and I see him nodding and he talks in Russian, of course, he's standing in the corridor but as I approach, I can see that the door is open to her cell. I still for a second because he hasn't noticed me yet. I can hear Svetlana speaking, but not loud enough to hear what she's saying. He's nodding and shaking his head. I carry on walking when he suddenly spots me. He steps back as I approach.

I look in to see Svetlana sitting on her mattress, fully clothed, and eating some soup and bread. Glad to see he followed my instructions.

"Hey, I thought I would come and see how you're doing today. Thought you might like a little company, but I see you already have some," I say, looking back to Sergei who doesn't say a word.

Is he the one who's told her things, is he the one she's fucking? I enter the cell and sit next to her on the mattress. She finishes her soup.

"Thank you Poppy, I know it was all you, the food and making me more comfortable, I am grateful to you."

She looks better than she did yesterday. For some reason I feel I want to talk today, maybe it is seeing Prim that's made me feel like this, I think I actually miss her, and I feel a little remorse for attacking her. But then I think back to her and Nick and how they were involved in my parents' death. If that hadn't happened, my life would have taken a completely different path. I know I'm a great believer that everything happens for a reason. I think all that heartache at losing my parents at an early age and going down the path I did, was all to lead me to Igor. I truly believe that now.

"Poppy, why do you look so sad, you are in thought, no?"

I look to her and I move some of her hair that is hanging down and in the way, to behind her ear.

"Yes, I just saw my sister earlier, I haven't seen her in so long and I was just thinking about her."

She frowns at me. "I didn't know you had a sister, why do you not see her?"

I actually open up to her and sit talking for a good hour. I don't give too much away, she's shocked I have a twin sister that I don't speak to. I just told her we don't get on. I leave Svetlana and head back home. Home, it still doesn't feel like my home.

Igor arrives back late, he wakes me up, the way he and I like, by eating me out.

"Мой ангел, I missed you so fucking much. I couldn't wait to get back and have my taste of you."

I smile at him as he climbs on top of me. He makes love to me, he's gentle and slow and we just stare into each other's eyes. When we are finished, I tell him about seeing Prim and that I spent some time with Svetlana. He's surprised Prim was nearby though.

"Are they still together, Igor?"

He nods. "Yes, they are, I have been thinking, and it was something

I wanted to let the other godfathers know. It's time we made our move. I told them I will not be around for a couple of months, just so they know to watch if anything happens while I am gone. I know I won't be far, and I will still run my business as usual, but they had to know I would be out of town. It is time we finished this. Time for you to get your revenge, мой ангел, you are more than ready."

Nineteen

Poppy

IT'S BEEN A FEW MONTHS NOW SINCE MY MELTDOWN AT KILLING A man, I soon got over it, especially as I've now helped on a few occasions. It's easy, you just point and shoot, watch them go down and it's done, there life is over in seconds. After the first one it means nothing, it's just so damned easy to do and if you don't know the person, then it's no hardship on you. You don't even think about who they might have left behind. People die every day, people grieve every day, I say so what.

Igor rented a house for us not far from Prim's and Aunt Cassy's. He actually rented two next door to each other so we would have our own space and Andrey and Ivan would be next door. I loved playing house with my husband when he was with me. He had to travel back to LA a lot for business, but he made sure he checked in on me each day. He was never away from me for too long. He said he couldn't bear being away from me. I felt the same. I loved we had our own space and we could do what we wanted, anytime we wanted, without the fear of someone walking in on us. I loved that freedom. It gave me a taste for what I actually wanted. The house, the garden, and who knows, kids one day.

We'd planned out exactly what we were going to do, I was to hurt Prim, then when Nick was at his lowest and careless, we would grab him, and I could 'let the games begin' Igor said, laughing at himself. Igor had shown me where and how to stab Prim for minimum impact, just enough for her to need hospital treatment. I had to make sure Nick saw me do it. It all went to plan, Igor was so proud when I told him I had signed, 'Revenge will be sweet' to Nick. He thought that was genius. The problem

I had that day though, I was in a lot of pain from striking Prim. Igor was comforting me as I held my side and my head was splitting. It happened a few times, I felt like someone had an ax in my head. It didn't stop me feeling so proud of myself because Igor was proud.

"What if I killed her, Igor? What if I stabbed her too deep? I know he will suffer, but not in the way I want him to. If I did kill her, then he gets a taste of what I went through losing my parents, but I still want him to feel pain, I still want him to suffer for life."

He held me to him all night, never letting me go. I was crying, I wasn't sure for what. I wasn't sure if it was the thought I might have killed her, or if she was feeling this way and that's why I was Did I really want her dead? I've been thinking this for so long and no, I don't want her dead.

The days went on and I was so pleased with myself and how it all went. I hadn't felt anything else and Nick, who's real name is Blaine, was still visiting the hospital daily, Igor said he was sure she must be in a coma, that maybe from what I said about Prim going down and there being a lot of blood, maybe she hit her head which would make sense with my headaches. I agreed with him. I still followed for days, which mainly consisted of me sitting on the bench on the hospital grounds.

The day I saw Blaine cry I was telling Igor about how tired I was feeling. That was the day I followed Blaine to another house, then on to Prims and he saw me and gave chase. I never told Igor about that bit, he would think me really sloppy and I wanted him to stay proud of me, but he did think that if Prim hasn't died then she may be out of her coma with me being so tired.

Igor had me phone up the hospital straight away to find out what I could, letting them know I was her sister, that I was in Europe and couldn't get to see her. I asked for an update on her. I gave them her date of birth, social security number and her address as proof of who I was. They told me she was awake, that she had only just woken up today. I pretended to cry, acting like I was so overjoyed and I asked if she going to be okay. They said from the looks of it, yes, that she just had a slight problem with her vision but they were sure she would be fine. They said that it can be a side effect of a frontal hematoma and that the ophthalmologist was going to see her the day after tomorrow. I thanked her and hung up. I told Igor everything.

He poured himself a vodka and me a wine and we sat planning what we should do. He suddenly came up with the best plan. He got his laptop and searched the doctors at the hospital. He found out who the eye doctor was or the ophthalmologist as he was called. I went online to see where his office was and I managed to book the last appointment of the day, to see him tomorrow. We paid him a visit at his office downtown. It was as easy as that. Igor isn't one for killing for the sake of killing unless the person does something while we kidnap them, but the ophthalmologist did end up dead.

Igor came with me to the appointment with Dr. Benedict, he wasn't really a nice man. He was old and very grumpy. I figured he was annoyed and maybe thought he should be on the golf course somewhere rather than seeing to me. In his office I told him I was having trouble seeing out of my left eye, Igor watched him carefully, watching everything he did and watched him use the little instruments he had. Dr. Benedict got a bit annoyed because Igor was watching him so closely,

"Excuse me, sir, could you please step back while I finish the examination? You're hindering me by being so close," he said to Igor, who really saw his ass, but tried to keep his cool.

"I'm very interested in what you do, tell me what is that you are using to look into her eye?"

The doctor scowled at him and I was trying so hard not to laugh.

"This is an ophthalmoscope, it's a light source that I can magnify to various degrees to examine the cornea, lens, vitreous, and retina. I need to make sure there are no burst vessels in there or that everything looks clear and there are no breaks in the vessels or anything growing. If there was something growing back there that could indicate cancer, if we have subconjunctival hemorrhage that can be caused from coughing and sneezing and unless it keeps recurring we don't need to worry, just schedule more check-ups to keep a good check on it and make sure it isn't anything more sinister."

"What is a subconjunctival hemorrhage, Doc?" Igor asks.

"It is where the vessels burst and bleed. Like I said, this can happen from a cough or sneeze or it could be an indication of diabetes."

Igor watches everything the doctor does and asks questions about different things. I'm in awe that he takes so much in. I can't even remember what the doctor called the bleeds. Not that I have any, my eyes are all clear. When he finishes, he tells me he doesn't see anything wrong with my eyes that maybe I am just tired. We have been in longer than expected because Igor wanted to know every step of what he was doing. He told Igor so many times to back off but more politely. I could see Igor was losing it but trying to keep his calm so he could learn.

Dr. Benedict was quite agitated by the end because we had been so long. He kept looking at his watch. He was obviously running late for something. I see Igor nod, then he turns to the doors and leaves. Andrey must have spoken to him about something. I followed the doctor to the front desk.

"Can you make the payment now using a card, please? I sent my receptionist home earlier along with my nurse, because I didn't think I would be here this long."

He's very rude. I look at him and see his face go very pale as he looks out toward the front doors. I turn to see what he's looking at. I can't see much, Igor has the door ajar but I can't hear what he is saying. I see Igor and Andrey talking to someone. The glass at the side of the door is smoke glass and hard to see through, only the writing is clear. There's a young Asian girl, and I see her through the open door. She looks very young with pigtails in her hair and she looks like she's in a school uniform. She's very petite, I thought I was small but Igor is towering over her, she's very pretty. I turn back to the doctor and he's as still as a statue, but he hasn't taken his eyes from what's happening out there and he looks pained.

"Dr. Benedict, what's wrong, you don't look very well. You look as though you're sick and your brow is perspiring. Do you need some water or to sit down?"

He doesn't even acknowledge me speaking to him, he is too fixated on what is happening out there. I turn and watch, and Igor turns to me. He shakes his head very slightly. I turn and head for the doors to see what's happening. I look at the doctor before I go out, but he still hasn't moved. I open the door farther.

"No, мой ангел, stay there, do not come out, one second, мой ангел, I will be right in."

Well that's a little odd. That young girl was coming to see the doctor, only I was his last appointment, she looks too young to be visiting this old coot on her own, and he just told me he sent his receptionist and his nurse home, I look to the girl and she looks scared. I head back in and stand in front of the doctor who still hasn't moved. His face is so shiny with all the sweat and I see him shaking. The penny drops, he's a fucking predator, I know it, from the look of her and now the look of him. He's fucking terrified he's been caught.

"Can you get me some water please, Dr. Benedict, I don't feel very well."

He doesn't move. I stand right in his eyeline and wave my hand in his face. He blinks and looks at me.

"What?" he snaps.

Well, fuck you.

"Water, I need water, I just said I don't feel well." He moves out from behind the counter and heads back down the corridor to where his examination room is.

I follow behind him. He turns into his room where there is a water cooler and he starts to pour me some water. He turns and drops the water, not expecting me to be right behind him. I saunter over to him, licking my lips. He looks at me confused. I place my hand on his chest and he moves slightly, I start to unbutton his white coat, trailing my fingers down his chest. His eyes go wide at my touch.

"Are you married, Doc? You're a very handsome man."

He fumbles behind him and feels the chair I was in. I push him down and he just about fits in it. I climb on his lap and start to play with the buttons on his shirt. Just then Igor walks in and I turn to him and wink.

"Well hello, husband, just in time, I was just about to ask Dr. Dick here if I was too old for him or did he like them younger."

I love the look on Igor's face. He smiles at me and puts his thumb to his mouth.

"Carry on, wife, I would be interested in hearing what the good Dr. Dick has to say for himself. Please sir, answer my beautiful wife, she gets a little impatient, and she has such a nasty temper when she doesn't get the answers to the questions she asks." I look at the doctor, who is terrified. He knows he's been caught out. I rip open his shirt, exposing his chest to me. He's got to be in his late sixties, maybe even early seventies, he has lots of gray and white hair all over his wrinkly chest and he has huge man boobs. I grab one of his boobs and I squeeze it tight.

"Is this what you like to do to little girls, Dr. Dick? Do you like to play with their barely-there titties? What is it you like about them so young?" He doesn't speak, I grab the other nipple and I squeeze and twist it so fucking hard. He closes his eyes and starts panting. I turn to Igor.

"Oh my fucking god, he's getting off on the pain. Pass me that pen over there please, baby."

He reaches over and passes me the pen, smiling at me. He winks.

"Was I right, baby, how old was that little girl?"

"She was fourteen, and apparently Dr. Dick here pays her a hundred bucks every time she comes to visit him. She and her friends."

"You sick fuck, do you like to plow them or do they ride you? Do you like the young pussy? What, no mature woman good enough for you, so you take advantage of poor teenagers who are desperate for money? What else do you give them to make them keep coming back?"

He tries to speak, but nothing comes out.

"Baby, I think you need to check his computer, if he's into kiddie porn I will cut his fucking balls off and feed them to him."

He starts to cry like a fucking baby. I take the pen and I hold out his nipple and stab it through so it comes out the other end. He screams. I get off his knee and look for something to stuff into his mouth. I kiss Igor hard as I pass him, so hard and heated the doctor stops crying and just watches us. I watch him while devouring Igor. He likes to get off watching, does he? I pull back and turn my head to him, I can see his cock is standing up and his trousers have a big wet patch which runs down his leg.

"Did he fucking piss while I was sitting on him, baby, is my ass wet?"

I turn slowly to show Igor my ass and he feels it nice and slowly as I bend forward, his hand wanders all over my ass and between my legs to rub my pussy, putting on a show for Dr. Dick. Igor grabs my hips and pulls my ass to his groin. He loves my ass at the best of times. I start to wiggle it and I put my finger in my mouth and suck on it facing the Dr. He's really getting off on this but there is no way I will let him get his rocks off watching us.

"I won't be a minute. Be nice, baby. Leave some for me," I say, leaving the room smiling and winking at him.

I find the small kitchen and search in the drawers. I find a towel which will do to gag him, and I find a knife and some scissors, I wrap them in the towel so Dr. Dick won't see them and I head back to the room. Igor has moved over to the computer and is sitting on a stool doing things on it. He's so clever on computers, he knows where to search and find stuff. I have no clue about computers. Dr. Dick is watching as Igor brings up the images he found on the computer. I can't look. Seeing the first one was bad enough. It was Dr. Dick, naked with a red ball gag in his mouth and a young girl who looked very similar to the one earlier was standing behind him with a whip, she was fully clothed but her shirt was open, I turn away.

"What the fuck do you do to them?" I'm mad.

He looks at me in horror.

"Fucking speak you sick perv, what do you do to them?"

"I… I-I like them to hit me. I lik-like them to hurt me." I twist his other nipple hard. "You mean pain like this or more? Why young girls?"

"Yes, pain, but more. I li-like them yo-young, I like them innocent. I don't have s-sss-sex with them but I watch them, I like to watch when there ar-are two or th-th-three of them. I watch them play with themselves and each oth-ther, I watch them lick each other o-out, while I pl-pleasure my… self. Then I get th-th-them to li-li…"

"STOP," I shout at him, I don't want to hear

"Мой ангел, don't look round but do your worst. He is one of the vile ones."

I see the look on Dr. Dick's face when he hears those words. I put the towel on the side next to the chair and I take out the knife and the scissors. He starts to plead with me, crying like a fucking baby. I see some wrap bandages on the tray under the table next to me, and I shove one into his mouth then wrap the towel around his head. Tight, so he can't spit it out. With the scissors, I cut his trousers around his crotch area. His cock is flaccid and tiny now. He likes pain, huh, well here goes. I lift his floppy cock, luckily, I put gloves on, this is going to get messy. He tries to move my hands away from him, lashing out at me, Igor is up and punching him in the face before I realize what's happening. Dr. Dick stops moving, he isn't knocked out but his nose looks broken, with blood coming out of it.

Igor stands and watches, just to make sure he doesn't fight me. I get the knife and I start to cut at the base of his cock. The knife is blunt. Fuck, I stab it into him to make a hole so I can lodge the knife inside and pull up. There's blood everywhere. I throw the knife down and get the scissors. He tries to grab my hands but Igor stops him. He grabs his wrists and holds them above Dr. Dick's head. I take the scissors and I hack away at his cock. I finally cut it off. It took longer than I thought, who knew it was that hard to cut off a cock.

"Igor, how bad, on a scale of one to ten were the things you found on his computer?"

He smiles at me. "One hundred, мой ангел."

That's all I need. I take the point of the scissors and I pierce each of his balls, twisting the scissors inside as I do. I think the good Dr. Dick just blacked out. Igor slaps his face to wake him up. He comes around and looks down. He tries to scream but his mouth is full. He looks at me pleadingly, his eyes are wide like saucers. The sick fuck he is. Igor puts gloves on, and he takes the scissors from me. He then slices down each of Dr. Dick's arms from the inner elbow to his wrists. He slices deep and I watch as the cuts slowly open up. The blood starts to ooze out. There is blood everywhere. Igor moves so he doesn't get any on his suit. I look over myself and I don't see any on me. We leave him there and walk out.

"Do you think he will be able to escape and call the police?"

Igor kisses my head.

"No, мой ангел, he will bleed out in no time. It is a slow death. He will just get weaker and weaker. Remind me never to upset you. I'm scared for my own cock and balls now." He laughs at me.

We find Dr. Dick's office and take his keys. Igor takes me under his arm and we walk out turning all the lights out along the way. He hands the keys to Andrey, asks him to do the cleanup and to contact his staff to let them know the good doctor has gone out of town for a couple of weeks and they would be notified on his return, then to lock up and bring the keys back to him. I look at him quizzically.

"The cleanup is to wipe it all down so there are no fingerprints, he will leave all the kiddie porn and pictures on the computer for the police to find, you never know he may be part of a ring of pedophiles and that may help them. Andrey will just erase any trace we were there. We don't want anyone going into the office until we have finished with it, you never know if I may need it. He will also hack the security system to this building to erase the footage of us being here." He leans down to kiss me, I am in awe of him.

Igor got some false documents and ID sent to him and he is now Dr. Russkett, ophthalmologist. He had someone call the hospital and tell them that Dr. Benedict had to take a sudden leave of absence, which meant the hospital was now looking for a specialist to take his place. Enter Dr. Russkett. He is a genius. He examined Prim, just repeating some of the things he had asked Dr. Dick about, to make him sound knowledgeable. How he got out of doing other appointments I have no idea but that's Igor, he is a master.

He told me Prim was fine. She woke up not being able to see much but that the other doctor told her that was not unusual after a frontal hematoma, that she should regain her sight. I breathe in a little, relieved that she is okay. That time I attacked her at home, I know Blaine said I left her for dead, but I didn't intentionally, yes, I battered her but I knew she wasn't dead. I'm kinda relieved she isn't dead now, not by my hand anyway. Igor said he found it strange being near Prim, knowing it wasn't me. He said she had nothing on me though.

Next part of the plan is to lure them to Dr. Dick's office where we can strike. Igor didn't like Blaine at all. He said he was very protective of Prim and he growled when he went near her. I laughed at him.

"So you're telling me you wouldn't be the same if a good-looking doctor was that close to me?" He shakes his head and I slap his chest.

We then end up having a good hard fuck. When I found out Prim had left the hospital, Igor sent her a message to come to his office for a check-up. She replied and told him she could see much better, which pissed him off. Our plan has to keep evolving. He waited a few days, then texted her again. He said if he keeps texting them maybe Blaine will get so pissed, he will pay him a visit at his office. We were just hoping the plan worked.

PART VII

Poppy

&

Blaine

Twenty

Poppy

I'VE JUST WALKED OUT OF THE ELEVATOR TO FACE BLAINE FOR THE first time. The shock on his face is priceless. I wish I could keep rewinding it to play it over and over again.

"Hello again, Blaine, my old buddy. How's it hanging there?" I stare at him. I can see Igor leaning against the wall with one leg crossed over the other and one hand in his trouser pocket.

"The lady said hello, aren't you going to answer her?" he says to Blaine.

I see the look on Blaine's face, it's turning to hate and loathing. He's not scared, but I figured he wouldn't be, it's not his style. He's a cocky bastard.

"I don't see a lady, so nothing to say."

I watch as Igor gets right up in Blaine's face, There is no difference in them, well except one has black messy hair with green eyes and the other has blond messy hair with blue eyes, but In height and physique they are almost identical, except I think Blaine is just a touch taller than Igor. I look at them both standing toe to toe, Blaine is still beautiful, regardless, but he has nothing on my husband, nothing at all. I feel so proud in that moment.

I see Blaine slowly take his hands out of his pockets and ball his fists up, ready to fight. I look at his face closely and I'm sure I see a little apprehension from him. He sneers at Igor who just laughs in his face, Igor tells him to apologize to me but Blaine just goads him. I watch as Igor reaches into his pocket and Blaine takes a step back. He's scared, he's actually fucking scared of my god. Well I'll be damned. Igor pulls out his handkerchief to dab his face. They stay at a standoff.

216 | LYNDA THROSBY

"Enough of this already. Let's just take him, baby, so we can be done with this and then we can finish her once and for all." I walk up to Blaine while saying this, watching his face change to anger from me mentioning his precious Prim. I'm not going to do anything to her, just him, but he doesn't have to know that.

"You fucking bitch, don't you think you've done enough to Prim, you've failed to kill her twice now. I ought to just fucking wring your neck here and now." He steps up to me, avoiding Igor and bends to my eye level, Igor leans back against the wall and lets it play out. He knows I can hold my own, I know I can, it's just Blaine is a fucking scary guy.

"What happened, Pops, you couldn't have my cock, so you thought you'd get someone else's cock and let them do your dirty work for you? You're an evil bitch, Poppy." He spits in my face. The venom in his voice is scary enough.

"His cock's way better than yours could ever be, BLAINE, you son of a bitch. I'm not the only failure here, am I though, when it comes to trying to kill someone?" I see his eyes quickly look to Igor, he's seeing if he can do anything to me, but Igor would be on him if he did and he knows it. I punch him in the face while his attention is on Igor. His head moves back slightly. Yeah, my punch not so effective on this giant of a man.

"You fucking bitch, you'll pay for that," he snarls at me and suddenly he grabs me around the throat.

Igor steps forward and whistles, fuck, what's he doing? Blaine's squeezing, he's going to fucking kill me. I try to pry his hand off me. I use both my hands and I scratch him, digging my nails right in, trying to get him to drop me. I can feel my eyes starting to bulge, I can't breathe, just then I notice his eyes go wide, he puts more pressure on my throat. I think I'm going to black out just as I see Andrey and Ivan grab him, prying his hand from my throat. He drops me as they grab his arms and hold him. I walk up to him and sign in his face 'Revenge is going to be sweet, so, so, fucking sweet' and I punch him in the mouth. I see his lip bleed and he licks it.

"Tastes sweeter than your pappy's blood." He sneers at me, the fucking asswipe.

Igor moves over to me and to be honest, I'm fucking annoyed at him, but I won't show it in front of this bastard. He wraps his arms around me and kisses the top of my head before looking at my neck to see if there are any marks.

"Are you okay, мой ангел?"

I look up to him and nod, but I hope he sees the anger in my eyes even if I give him a false smile.

"You are so right my love, he will be all yours to do as you wish." He leans down and kisses me full on the lips, making a show that I am his in front of Blaine.

I pull away and see the slight look of panic on Blaine's face. He knows we are a force to be reckoned with. I turn toward the elevator, dropping Igor's arm from my shoulder. I press the button for down and the door opens right away. I step in and hear Igor telling Andrey and Ivan to take the next elevator and take him to the car in the basement and meet us at the warehouse. I smile to myself. Blaine has no way of knowing what's coming. Igor has a warehouse near the industrial side of the port that he owns, which I didn't know about, seems he has places everywhere. He ships in so much stuff to all different ports along the coast. There is so much to learn about his business. As soon as the doors close, he's on me, I push him away, the back of the elevator is mirrored, and I look into it and I can see the bruises around my neck. I turn on Igor.

"He nearly fucking killed me, and you just stood there. I couldn't breathe and my eyes felt like they were about to pop out of my fucking head and you fucking let him do it. He could have so easily have snapped my fucking neck." I'm so angry with him, he starts to walk toward me, but I push back on his chest.

"Fuck off, Igor, don't you even touch me. I'm so angry with you right now. You let him do that to me. As your men approached, he squeezed harder, trying to do as much damage as he could to me, before they got to him. You let him do that, how could you, he could have killed me?" My voice is hoarse, and I'm struggling to shout at him. I cough and put my hand to my throat. It's so sore even to touch.

Igor has me in his arms, cradling me. He hits the emergency button on the elevator to stop it. It jolts to a halt and we both lose our balance and take each other down. He sits me on his lap and holds me to him, and I cry into his chest. I cry out of frustration more than anything. I'm no match for Blaine, no matter what training I've had. Little old me up against a six-foot ripped giant, who probably weighs over two hundred pounds. My punches hardly did anything to him, okay I may have split his lip, but that's just luck. Igor comforts me for a few minutes. I look where we stopped, and it's near the third floor. I pull back.

"We need to get going, this isn't your building, you can't control it and people will be coming to try and rescue us. I'm okay, just a meltdown, I'm so angry at myself and at you. That should not have happened. He is as strong as you are, he could have killed me. Do you get that, Igor? I'm actually scared right now. I'm having second thoughts now I've actually come face-to-face with him. He killed my parents and he tried to kill me and that makes me want to make him suffer, but then do we just leave it for a quiet life and go back home and get on with our lives?"

He holds me close for a few more seconds, then he stands us up and hits the button again to start our descent back down.

"Мой ангел, I truly am sorry I did not stop him from hurting you. I didn't think he could do so much damage to you in such a short time. It's why I whistled for Andrey and Ivan, I thought they would have been a little quicker. I should have knocked him out myself. Please forgive me, мой ангел. This is your call, we will do whatever you want. Make up your mind though because he is on his way to the warehouse."

I nod and the doors open in the basement car park. We head out in our car in the direction of the port. I'm at war in my head. I've killed people now, so it's not that I'm worried about it. I'm starting to feel guilty because of Prim. She's my sister and if being alone, having no one for the last twelve months has taught me anything, it's that I miss her. Even though we didn't speak or see each other very often, which was all my fault. Having Svetlana to talk to, even though it was just random chit chat and not real talk, I always thought of Prim during and after every conversation I had with her. If I let Blaine go, then she will be able to live a life with him. If I kill him, she will be the one to suffer yet again, and Blaine's right, she's suffered enough.

"Мой ангел, did you hear me? You are deep in thought."

I didn't even know he had spoken to me. I was looking out of the window just thinking. I look at him.

"We are nearly there, do you know what you want to do?"

Do I? No. Igor will think I'm going soft and I don't want him to think that. I want to prove to him I can stand by his side. I do want to hurt Blaine, but not kill him. It would be Prim who suffers.

"Would you think any less of me Igor if I change my mind? I think if I just hurt him, a little payback, maybe cut off a toe and shove it in his mouth like he did to me. I don't want you to think I'm not cut out for this. I'm not going to kill him. It will only be Prim who suffers for that, and I've made her suffer enough from us being young and for what? Just because she wouldn't tell me who the boy with the greenest eyes was. She didn't do anything."

He takes hold of my hand and kisses the back of it while driving.

"No мой ангел, I would never think any less of you. You have more than proved yourself to me, you are just like me, I love you with everything I am. Look what you did to Dr. Dick, мой ангел, I have never come across a woman like you, one who is so in tune with me. I told you, this is your call, you do what you feel is right to do. I will not judge you for anything. If you want to walk away from it now, we do that, and I tell Andrey to let him go. If you want to punish him, then we go and you do that. It is your choice. The sooner this is over, the better. We can then concentrate on you learning everything there is with my business. I want you by my side in life and business. There is no one I trust in this world apart from you. I love you, мой ангел."

I have tears flowing down my cheeks. He kisses the back of my hand again, then keeps hold of it as we approach the port.

"I will punish him, then he goes free. I love you, Igor."

We turn down a couple of roads until we are at a warehouse that is standing alone. I see Andrey's car parked outside and I feel a little nervous as I step out of our car. I don't know why, I owe this bastard big time. We walk toward the little entrance door, which is open as we approach. Something doesn't feel right. Igor looks to me, putting his finger to his lips, and motions for me to get behind him. He pulls out his gun as he quietly steps through the door. I follow close behind, my heart is nearly beating out of my chest. I have no idea what to expect. Igor stands up straight and lowers his gun. He speaks in Russian. I understand some of it. He says what the fuck Andrey, why is the door open and where is Ivan and Blaine. I stand at his side, looking around. It's a huge place, no rooms just open plan with windows high up and stairs over to one side that look like they lead up to a mezzanine floor with offices on it. I look to Andrey. He doesn't look right, and he hasn't answered Igor. He motions with his head very slightly and both Igor and I look. I gasp in shock.

"Fucking hell, what happened?" I ask Andrey.

He moves very slightly, and I notice his arm is limp at his side and I see blood dripping from his hand to the ground. I look back to where he nodded to and Ivan is on the floor, there is blood around his head, at this distance, I would hazard a guess he's dead. So where the fuck is Blaine? How the hell did he get away from these two giants. He asks Andrey where he is. Again, he nods in the direction of where Ivan is. I look but don't see him, then suddenly he appears out of the shadows in the corner. Fuck, he looks like he did that day he was telling me about my parents, mean and fucking scary. He's holding a gun as he slowly walks toward us. He looks evil as he smirks. He's going to finish me for good this time. So much for my revenge. Igor still has his gun in his hand and he aims it at Blaine.

"Put the gun down or she gets it right between the eyes." He has it aimed at me as he sneers at us.

"No, Igor, don't put the gun down. If he shoots me you shoot him and kill him once and for all," I quietly tell him.

He doesn't look to me, he doesn't want to take his eyes off Blaine. I look to his face and see how pained and conflicted he is.

"Просто знай, я люблю тебя и всегда буду, детка. Я собираюсь упасть на землю на счет три. Раз, два, три. Теперь стреляй в гребаного ублюдка." I dive to the ground, I just said to Igor, 'Just know, I love you and always will, baby. I'm going to drop to the ground on the count of three. One, two, three. Now shoot the fucking bastard.'

A gun is fired. I don't know who fired. I have my hands over my head muffling my ears. The sound ricochets around the vast empty warehouse as I lay on the ground. I know I'm okay and still alive. Igor is still standing, I'm too scared to look at him. What if he's shot, what if Blaine fired before Igor had the chance? Just then I hear a noise and instinct makes me look up. I see Blaine still standing, but he's not holding the guns any longer. He dropped them. I look up to Igor, who still has his gun pointed at Blaine.

"Мой ангел, are you okay?" He doesn't take his eyes off Blaine while asking me.

"Yes, baby, are you okay?"

He laughs at me asking, when I can see him standing there. I kneel up, keeping my eyes on Blaine. I can see his arm is down at his side and there is blood on his denim jacket. I stand up and look over to Andrey. He looks okay, but I see he has a gun in his hand and he too is pointing it at Blaine. I'm confused, I don't know who shot Blaine and how did Andrey get his gun so quick without Blaine seeing. Igor leans into me, knowing Blaine can't do anything with Andrey pointing his gun at him. He kisses my lips, then he starts walking toward Blaine.

He checks Ivan first, still keeping his gun pointed at Blaine's head. As I thought, he's dead, I see Igor shake his head to let Andrey and me know. He then puts the gun to the back of Blaine's head and tells him to walk toward us. I look to Andrey and I see there's a chair not far from him. I think this is where they were supposed to tie Blaine to originally. Igor makes him sit, he grips the top of Blaine's shoulder, the one I can now see has been shot, then while Andrey points his gun at Blaine, Igor ties his arms behind the chair and ties his legs to the legs of the chair. I walk over to them, knowing Blaine is secured. I listen to Igor and Andrey talking. He said as soon as they got out of the car Blaine took Ivan out with an elbow to the nose and a throat punch, and he must have grabbed his gun, then he hit Andrey over the head with the gun before he realized what was happening behind him. He then took Andrey's gun from him. Andrey turned to fight him but Blaine shot him in the arm then told him to go help Ivan up and to walk into the warehouse, Blaine had two guns on them. He told them to walk farther inside. Once they did, Ivan suddenly turned and charged Blaine, but Blaine shot him right between the eyes before he got to him. He told Igor that Blaine is one mean motherfucker. Andrey did manage to hit him, but because he was in pain from being shot, Blaine managed to knock him to the ground with one punch. That's when he heard us arrive and Blaine went to hide in the shadows, telling Andrey to keep his mouth shut or else, knowing Igor would be armed.

While they continue to talk, I watch Blaine. He has no idea what they are saying, and he doesn't care. He just sits there, all cocky. Just looking at him makes me so angry, remembering what he did to me. How he led me on to get me to his place to try to kill me. I should put a bullet in his head now and be done with it. I can't do it though, all I picture is Prim in that wheelchair as he wheeled her out of the hospital, also knowing she has problems with her eyes, it's her eyes she needs to talk. I feel so bad, full of so much remorse, knowing she was innocent in our parents' death, I knew all along she couldn't have done anything to them, I just needed someone to blame, I was so fucking angry and I had no one else to take my anger out on, then I just lost it knowing she was hiding Blaine and probably screwing him because I wanted him so bad. Now I look at him and Igor, and Igor is who got my heart, and I am grateful for Blaine in that I wouldn't have met Igor if it wasn't for him.

I stand in front of Blaine while the other two talk. He looks up to me and smiles his cocky smile at me. He is so handsome, I'm not surprised I fell hard for him.

"What you smiling at, Blaine?" I lean into his face, watching him closely as I press a finger into the hole where the bullet hit, I wiggle it around a little, watching closely.

He winces and screws his eyes shut, taking in a deep breath.

Good, it fucking hurts. I pull my finger out which is covered in blood and I smear it on his cheek and over his stubble to clean it. There's a table set up to the side with some instruments on it, Igor had it set up ready for Blaine. I move over and see there are pliers, a handsaw, a hammer, some nails, and lots of other things that look like they will hurt. I notice a long poker pole with the hook on the end that was used on that man they interrogated, and it pulled his brains out through his nose. I'm not gonna use that one. I'm looking at them when I feel Igor come up behind me.

"What are you thinking, мой ангел? Do you need help with what some of these are for?"

I pick up a device, not sure what it is.

"That is a mouth spreader, you place it in and turn it to wedge the mouth open. Then you can either use the tongue splitter to remove the tongue which is this device here or you can use the pliers to remove teeth." He picks up both instruments. I look up to him and can see he's in turmoil, Blaine killed Ivan who was not only one of Igor's guards, but he was also a friend to him. I can see he's holding it in.

"Igor, baby, I know he killed Ivan, if you want to do something then that's up to you." I lean up and kiss his cheek.

He looks at me and shakes his head. "No, мой ангел, I promised he is yours to do as you please. I do not go back on my word. If it was just that he had killed Ivan, then he would already be dead by now."

I put my arms around his waist and cuddle him for a minute, and he cuddles me back.

"Fucking hell, you gonna start fucking next? Get on with it already. But Poppy, just remember it's Prim who suffers here."

He's right and I know it. I pick up the mouth opener and stand in front of him.

"Open your fucking mouth."

He wedges his lips shut tight. Igor moves over to us and he punches Blaine straight in the mouth.

"She said open your fucking mouth."

He spits at Igor, and his tongue instinctively comes out to lick his bloody lip, I put the device between his lips so he can't shut them. I turn it so it pries his mouth open, and he tries to fight, but it doesn't work. His mouth is now open wide. I then pick up the pliers and turn to him. I put the pliers in his mouth and clamp them on to a tooth, I'm not sure I'm strong enough for this. I start to pull and try to turn as I do on a tooth. I hear a crack, and the pliers come loose. His eyes are wide and he's trying to scream. I only managed to crack the tooth and pull some of the top off. I look to Igor, who nods to me to try again. I grip his broken tooth and put my knee on his lap and I get in there, twisting and pulling until I fall back as it gives way. I look and see blood pooling in his mouth and see I have his tooth in the pliers. I smile and hold it up to Igor, who in turn smiles back at me with pride.

Blaine is making noises, trying to scream. I move to the other side of his mouth and do the same. This one is harder and takes a few attempts, but I manage to do it. I feel euphoric. Blaine is staring at me, I think he's surprised I've got it in me. I wanted to take two from the top but don't think I can get the leverage on them so leave it at the two I've removed. I don't take the mouth opener off him. I don't want him to speak.

"Igor, can you untie his left hand and hold it for me in front of him so he can watch me, please, baby?"

He does and holds his arm for me. The left is the one where he is shot in the shoulder. I see Igor holding the shoulder and putting pressure on it to cause him pain. I smile at him. I still have the pliers, I take his little finger, wedging it between the blades and I start to press, not too hard at first, then adding slightly more pressure until I see blood, from breaking the skin, I look to his face and take pride in watching this giant of a man watching me, pained. I then suddenly clamp the blades together hard, using all my force, and his little finger falls to the floor. I pick it up and place it in his open mouth. He wriggles and spits it out with his tongue. I grab a cloth and some tape from the table, laying them on Blaine's lap, I remove the clamps still holding his mouth open but just before his mouth closes I shove the finger back inside, then I hold his chin up, to close it tight. As I do this, Igor pushes down on the top of Blaine's head, making it almost impossible for him to open his mouth to breathe. He struggles and manages to open his lips slightly, his face is upward, I quickly take the cloth and shove it between his lips and stuff it into his mouth. I then tape his mouth up so he can't open it.

"Do you remember doing this to me, you son of a bitch? Leaving me to die with my fucking toe in my mouth. You fucking psycho."

He tries to laugh. I can see the arrogance on his face. I pinch his nostrils tightly together, effectively stopping him from breathing. He starts shaking his head from side to side, I can see now his face has changed from an arrogant bastard to one full of fear as he fights not being able to breathe. He starts to get frantic, his eyes going wide, vigorously moving his head. Igor still has his hand clamped on top of Blaine's head. It doesn't stop Blaine from shaking it frantically though. It makes me lose my grip on his nose, he struggles to breathe. I watch as his nostrils flare with each intake of air. He's struggling, like me in that grave, not being able to take in sharp breaths, I know how he feels. I pinch his nostrils together again, knowing he hardly took in any air, I smile at him then get in his face,

"Suffocating, Blaine, that's how you left me in that fucking grave. Suffocating with hardly any air. I guess you wonder how I got out? Well, it seems when you reopened the grave you let air in, and it got trapped in the skull underneath me. Because you put me in facedown, I was able to breathe that small amount of air in, until I managed to move the earth enough to get out. Lucky for me it was a shallow grave, you sick prick." I let go of his nose and watch the nostrils flare again. I remove the tape from his mouth and he spits out the cloth followed by his finger. I stand and laugh at him, watching him gulp for air. I look at Igor and he has so much pride on his face. I see Andrey standing behind watching, and even he seems to be proud of me. I know they both want to kill him for killing Ivan, I would too if it wasn't for Prim. I take Igor's hand and walk away from Blaine.

"Do you want to finish him, Igor? I see the look on both yours and Andrey's faces. I know you both want him dead for what he did." He takes my face and kisses my lips gently.

"What do you want, мой ангел? This is on you, not me or Andrey. We do what you want." I lean into his chest and let him wrap his big arms around me, giving me comfort. If it wasn't for Prim, I would without a doubt kill him. I look up and shake my head so he knows I'm not going to kill him. He nods slightly at me. I move back to Blaine, who is watching each of us carefully.

"I'm not going to kill you, Blaine, as much as I want to, and believe me I would." I lean in, right in his face and whisper, "You wouldn't be my first kill." I wink at him.

As he stares at me, I see a little shock on his face. I look at his hand where I cut his finger off and see the blood dripping out. If I don't let him go, he may bleed out anyway.

"The only reason you get to leave here is Prim. I've put her through so much shit all our lives, I can't put her through any more. Killing you would destroy her. I don't want that to be on me. I hope if she ever gets destroyed it's on you. I will untie you and I want you to just leave. They won't touch you, but don't try anything stupid Blaine or it's out of my hands and they will kill you. Are we clear on that?" He looks deep into my eyes. I think he's wondering what game I'm now playing. He probably doesn't believe I will just let him walk out of here. I stand up straight and look down on him.

"Are we clear on this, Blaine?"

He nods, his eyes going to Igor. I look round and see he has his back to us and is talking to Andrey. I don't hear what they're saying, they've moved away. I start to wonder if they are going to kill him when I let him go or if they are going to just let him walk out. Igor said it was my call. Maybe he's just telling Andrey what is going to happen. I need to make sure Blaine doesn't try anything once I untie him. I need to make it so he is in pain and will only think of getting out of here.

I walk back to the table where the torture devices are to see what I can use. Something that will hinder him from moving fast. Maybe I need to break one of his legs or something like that. There is a hammer, but I doubt I could do much damage with that, I wonder if I could smash his kneecap with it. I know what to do. I take the hammer over to Blaine and I take off one of his sneakers. It's the ankle he hurt when I was looking after him. I look at his face as I lift the hammer and then bring it down hard onto his toes. He barely flinches. I do it again over and over. I hear crunching, I must be breaking his toes. I then swing it at his ankle a couple of times. He pulls a face, but he doesn't scream out, not once. I need something heavier. I look for something but don't see anything. I walk around the warehouse seeing if there is anything heavy lying about. I look back at the three men, Igor is still talking to Andrey, a little farther away from them, Blaine is still sitting on the chair. He's watching me.

I carry on looking around. I spot some pieces of wood just under the stairs, but also some bricks. One of these might do. I go to lift one. They are heavy, not your normal house brick but a much bigger block brick. I turn with the brick in my hand just as I see Blaine rise up from the chair, heading for Igor and Andrey. As Andrey is facing his way, Blaine crouches low behind Igor, I scream out to Igor just as Blaine comes down hard on his back. Dropping the brick I run toward them, Igor goes down in a heap to the floor and I can see Andrey struggling to get his gun, Blaine grabs it before it can be pointed at him and they struggle, the gun goes off. I don't know what happened. As I get near, they are both still standing. The gun goes off again. This time I see the startled look on Andrey's face. He falls forward onto Blaine, his eyes go blank and his head lolls to the side. Blaine drops him, I scream and throw myself to the ground next to Igor.

Blaine turns on me with the gun in his hand. I'm at Igor's side looking him over, I see blood, a lot of blood on his back, I notice a hole, he's been shot, oh god what, no, please.

"What's up, Pops? Your man not as good as you thought he would be?"

I look up at him and he's sneering at me, pointing the gun in my direction. He's using his right hand, but with his injuries to his left arm and hand, how did he do this? How did he use his left arm to untie the ropes at his ankles and get his right arm out of the ropes? He then wipes at his mouth with his left arm, he's using it as though there is nothing wrong with it, yet there is blood dripping everywhere.

What the fuck.

He's also standing there as though I didn't just smash his foot and ankle. I suddenly have a flashback to me being tied up on his bed. He was asking me how the pain felt. He wanted me to describe it to him because he couldn't feel pain. But he screamed and winced as I was inflicting pain on him, pulling his teeth and cutting his finger off, it was all an act to make me think I was hurting him. I didn't remember, I thought I was paying him back, but he didn't feel a fucking thing I did to him. I should have just let Igor fucking kill the bastard.

"Just finish me, Blaine, you know you want to." I have tears streaming down my face as I look to Igor. I feel for his pulse, I think he's dead. If he's dead, then there is no point in me going on. I have nothing without him. I search on his neck for any sign, suddenly I feel his pulse, it's quite a good one. I look at him, but he's out cold. "What you gonna do now, Blaine? Kill me as well as the three men lying here. Is that it?"

He smiles and looks around. I make him think Igor is dead. I don't want him to shoot him again. I pray Igor doesn't move, if he does, Blaine will finish him.

Twenty-One

Blaine

THE TWO BIG MEN HERDED ME INTO THE CAR. ONE HAD A GUN in my side for the ride down in the elevator, but out of sight of cameras. He then sat next to me in the back, keeping his gun pointed at my side. They spoke very little to each other, but anything they did say I had no clue what they said. All I did was sit thinking about Prim, about not having our future we talked about, getting married, traveling for a couple of years, then having kids. Me with fucking kids, but hey, I'm a changed man. We drove for about twenty minutes until they pulled up at a building. I think this will be the end. My only regret is not being able to say goodbye to my Prim. This will kill her if I don't come back, she's going to just think I left her, that I'd had enough. I'm sure these guys are professional enough to get rid of my body without a trace. She will never know the truth.

As we get out of the car, the fucking idiots that they are, the driver goes straight to the door to unlock it, leaving this prick to get me out on his own. What bumfucks they are. I get out of the car, this one has his gun on me, I turn to start walking. I can feel how close he is to me, I take a chance and raise my elbow, throwing it back and hoping I elbow him in the face. It works, I hear the gun drop and I turn quickly and throat punch him. He goes down without a sound. I grab his gun and quietly walk behind the other guy and hit him over the head. He doesn't go down but turns to fight me as he grabs for his own gun. I shoot, I hit him. He holds his arm and I take his gun from him.

"Go get the other one, bring him inside," I tell him. I watch as he goes to help the other guy and they both walk into the warehouse. I have two guns pointed at them. "Move farther in," I instruct. I need to be away from the door so I can see what's happening.

Just then the one I took down by the car turns and charges me, I shoot him in the head and he falls face-first in front of me. I watch as he goes down, then the other one punches me, but it's a feeble attempt, he must be weak from the gunshot to his arm, he doesn't even move me and of course I don't feel a fucking thing. I punch him and he goes down. I tell him to get up and move over to the other side where I see a chair and table. Just then I hear a car approach. It has to be him and her. I head to the shadows in the corner and wait for them to walk in, telling the other guy not to make a sound. I know he will be armed. I watch as he cautiously comes through the door with his gun raised, sweeping it from side to side. He spots the one who is alive, and he speaks to him. I have no idea what they say, he's standing not far from the chair which I take was meant for me. I then see Poppy move from behind him to his side. The fucking wuss that she is. I see the one I shot motion slightly with his head in my direction and I watch her gasp at the sight of the other one dead on the floor.

"Fucking hell, what happened?" she asks the other one.

He doesn't speak but moves so they can see he got shot. I see them looking back to the dead one and decide to show myself. I walk slowly toward them, keeping my guns pointed at them. I have two guns so can take two shots, there is only the one armed, I see him raise and point the gun in my direction.

"Put the gun down or she gets it right between the eyes." I have one gun aimed at her head, I'll do it. If his finger moves on that trigger I will shoot, hopefully before his bullet hits me.

"No, Igor, don't put the gun down. If he shoots me, you shoot him and kill him once and for all." I hear her saying to him.

The stupid bitch, I'll fire both guns, then maybe kill them both. She then speaks to him in his fucking language, then she dives to the floor. I'm slow to react, I'm hit in the arm, I feel the force of the bullet entering my shoulder and I drop both guns. He says something to her as I look up. He has his gun aimed at me, but so does the other one I shot. Where and how the fuck did he get that gun? I don't know which one shot me as I was watching her dive to the ground, wondering what the fuck she was doing. I'm screwed now, I don't have a gun and by the time I bend to pick one up one of them will probably shoot me first.

"Yes, baby, are you okay?" she says to him as she gets up, keeping her eyes on me, and he laughs at her question.

He leans into her and fucking kisses her. Taking his eye off me, but the other one still has his gun pointed at me. Igor, the smarmy bastard, saunters over to the one on the floor. He knows he's dead, you can see all the blood around his head. He still bends down, checking to make sure he's dead. He still has his gun pointed straight at me as he does this. He then stands and comes around me. He puts the gun to the back of my head and pushes it, ordering me to the chair.

I move, but slowly, why rush my own death? As I sit on the chair, he grabs at my shot shoulder. I think he's trying to inflict pain on me, so I wince, just for show. I watch her to see if she says anything or if she even remembers me telling her I don't feel pain, but she doesn't say anything. Igor then gets some rope and ties my hands behind the chair then both legs to it. The other one has his gun pointed straight at my head while I'm being tied up. She's watching everything very closely. The two men start to talk. She moves toward me, watching me intensely as she listens to them talk. I think the other one is telling Igor what happened to them. She tilts her head to the side. She's really examining my face and furrowing her brow. I watch her just as closely and I see her expression changing from anger, hate, to remorse, then anger again. She looks so conflicted. I give her my best cocky smile.

"What you smiling at, Blaine?" She leans in close to my face.

I watch her hand move to my shoulder and I watch as she puts a finger in the hole. Fucking hell, she's doing exactly what I did to her pappy, I put my finger in one of his holes and I did the same, pulling away some flesh which I then kept for later. If only she knew. I wince as though she's hurting me. I screw my eyes shut, that's what some women used to do when I hurt them. I let her think it really hurts. She pulls her bloody finger out and smears it on my cheek and face. She doesn't remember me telling her. Maybe if I keep pretending she's hurting me, it will satisfy her.

She moves over to a table and stands looking at things on it. I don't remember seeing it, to be honest. Igor moves over to her and speaks, but I don't catch what he's saying. They have their backs to me. I don't know what they are doing. She then kisses his cheek, and he looks at me, shaking his head. He says something else to her, and she wraps her arms around his waist and cuddles him. They are fucking weird.

"Fucking hell, you gonna start fucking next? Get on with it already. But Poppy, just remember it's Prim who suffers here," I shout at them, antagonizing him as I see his back stiffen.

She comes at me with some kind of contraption in her hand. "Open your fucking mouth."

I close my lips, shut tight, I watch as Igor moves over to us and he punches me in the mouth.

"She said open your fucking mouth."

I snarl at him. I instinctively lick my lips and she slots the metal thing between my lips before I can clamp them shut again, fuck her. She turns something on it and I feel pressure on my mouth, she's jacking my fucking mouth to open it wide. She takes some pliers out of the waistband of her jeans and puts them in my mouth. I don't feel pain, but I do feel some pressure on my jawline. She must be tugging at a tooth. I suddenly hear a crack, I try to scream at her, she's pulling my fucking teeth out. She takes this as her hurting me, but it's 'my fuck you bitch, get off me,' scream. She tries to pull at it again then smiles at him and he smiles back at her. They are perfect for each other. Maybe I should have stuck with her. I taste blood in my mouth, I try to moan and scream again to try to stop her from pulling all my fucking teeth out. I stare at her as she tries to do more. She then stops.

"Igor, can you untie his left hand and hold it for me, in front of him so he can watch me, please, baby?"

He does and holds my arm out, but as I watch what he does I notice he puts pressure on my shot shoulder, so I wince slightly. She smiles at him then takes the pliers and grabs my little finger placing it between the blades. I watch as she puts pressure on them. I see the skin break and blood comes dripping out, then she puts on more pressure and bang, my fucking little finger falls to the floor. I'm shocked, she actually did it. Who knew she had this much sadism in her. Just then she bends down and picks my finger up and with my mouth still pried open she puts the finger in my mouth. I spit it out with my tongue. This is payback. She walks away, back to the table, she then returns with a rag and some tape.

Fuck.

She unscrews the thing jacking my mouth open and just before my mouth closes completely, she shoves my little finger back in and takes the clamp thing off my mouth. She then holds my chin up as I tilt my head back trying to get her off me, Igor then clamps his hand on my head to help her keep my mouth shut. I just about manage to open my lips to take in some air when she then shoves the rag in my mouth and tapes it up. The fucking bitch.

"Do you remember doing this to me, you son of a bitch? Leaving me to die with my fucking toe in my mouth. You fucking psycho."

I try to laugh at her, but it's hard with your mouth full and taped up, but she's calling me the psycho, she needs to look in the mirror. She then grabs hold of my nose and pinches it, stopping me from breathing through it. I try to shake her off me, lightly at first, but then panic starts to set in. I can't fucking breathe. I shake my head as much as I can, trying to get her to let go. She doesn't. I can feel the panic. Fuck. She's going to suffocate me. Igor still has his hand pushing my head down. She loses her grip on my nose, but it's not enough. I need to take deep breaths to get the air back into my lungs, I still feel panicky. I try to take the air through my nose, it's not enough and I still feel I might suffocate. She pinches my nose together again, stopping the small intakes of air I managed to get. I start to shake my head from side to side. She talks to me, but I don't hear most of it. I do pick up on something about air in a skull in the grave. That's how she survived. Fuck me. What a fucking stupid mistake that was. She lets go of my nose then slowly pulls the tape from my mouth and I spit out the rag along with the finger and I try to gulp in the air.

She asks Igor if he wants to finish me. They just need to get it over with. I'm still trying to get my breath back. I'll give it to her, she's the first one to ever put me into a panic like that. I really thought she was going to suffocate me. I don't look at them. I don't listen to much of what they say, I'm leaning forward, slightly bent over. He let go of my arm so it's still free. They probably think I can't use it from the pain. They let their guard down. She's suddenly in my face again,

"I'm not going to kill you, Blaine, as much as I want to, and believe me I would." She leans right next to my ear. "You wouldn't be my first kill."

She fucking shocks me with that statement, she's a killer, she's just like me. She then tells me I can leave, that they won't kill me. It's because of Prim, she feels remorse. Is this a ploy to make me think I can go, then they kill me anyway? Why not just fucking kill me now? Why would they do that? I don't believe her. I don't believe a word that comes out of her mouth.

"Are we clear on this, Blaine?"

I just nod and look around to the others, who have moved away, talking. Probably talking about killing me. Poppy moves away from me, she heads to the table, when she returns, she has a hammer. I look at her wide-eyed. What's she gonna do? Hit me over the head with it. She bends down and takes one of my sneakers off. It doesn't escape me that it's the foot where I twisted my ankle. She takes the hammer and I watch as she smashes my foot with it over and over and then my ankle. I don't bother flinching or screaming, what's the point? She looks up at me to gauge my reaction. I think she's annoyed she isn't getting one. She stands and moves away, walking around the warehouse as if looking for something.

This is my chance, I untie my legs with my bad arm. It doesn't hurt, so it's easy to do, and then manage to wriggle my good arm out of the other tie. The stupid fucker loosened it when he freed my bad arm and didn't retie it. I quietly get up and crouch as I move toward the two men talking. Igor has his back to me and the other one can't see me crouched behind him. I rise up and bring my fists down hard on the back of Igor's neck. He falls to the floor. I hear her scream out for him and I hear her running toward me. The other one tries to get his gun out of his waistband but struggles and I grab it before he does. I wrestle with him, we both have shot arms, the gun goes off. I have no idea if I've been shot or not, and we still wrestle. I grapple with the gun and I pull the trigger. He falls onto me. I step away and he drops to the floor in a heap. He's dead.

Poppy screams again, just as I turn with the gun in my hand, she throws herself to the ground next to Igor. I watch as she examines him, there's blood starting to come through his suit jacket on his back, I point the gun at her, and I do a quick once-over on myself. I don't have any blood. We must have shot Igor with that first bullet as we were wrestling. She cries over him.

"What's up, Pops? Your man not as good as you thought he would be?" I raise an eyebrow and give her my cocky grin. I wipe at my mouth and I see her eyes suddenly go into slits, she's looking at me oddly. She looks to my left arm, the one I just used to wipe at my mouth, I think she just remembered I don't feel pain. I smile at her.

"Just finish me, Blaine, you know you want to." She's crying as she looks back down to Igor, feeling for a pulse. "What you gonna do now, Blaine? Kill me as well as the three men lying here. Is that it?"

I watch her. Am I going to kill her once and for all? What do I get out of that? I told Prim it was Poppy who attacked her again. They know she's alive. What the fuck do I do? Finish her and burn this warehouse down with their bodies in here? Pile them on top of each other and set them alight. That will do. It could work. I watch as she still feels around for a pulse. Maybe he is dead. Wouldn't she get up and attack me if he was? I think she wants me to just think he's dead. She was going to let me go for Prim's sake. I think that Igor and the other one maybe had other ideas.

"Were you really gonna let me just walk out of here? What about these two? Were they just gonna let me walk away?"

She looks up to me, the tears are streaking down her face, she nods.

"It was my call, Blaine. Igor said it was my choice. It was me that wanted the revenge on you for trying to kill me and causing me so much pain. But it was my choice. I could have killed you, but like I said, Primrose has suffered all her life because of me. If I kill you, she suffers again. I don't want that, Blaine. I'm tired of it. I got married, I wanted a life with him, but you may have just cut that short for me. He's still alive, I need to call 911 now unless you are going to finish us. Decide Blaine, I don't have time." She's crying, trying to get this all out.

"If I leave, do you promise to never come near us again? That you will never try to harm Prim? She has to live in fear all the time as it is. She has nightmares thinking you will come back for her and finish her for good. I need to know, now, Poppy, I need your word you will never come back into our lives again."

She nods at me. "I promise, Blaine, if Igor survives, I will get on with my own life with him."

"And what if he doesn't survive? What if he dies? Are you going to come for me again? I'm not chancing that happening, Poppy. I will not live like that or have Prim living like that. What if he dies?"

She shrugs and looks down at him. I can see him move slightly. He may be coming around.

"I promise, no matter what Blaine, I will not come for you or Prim again. My word is my oath, Igor has taught me that. He never goes back on his word. His word is oath in his line of work."

I furrow my brow. I don't know exactly what his line of work is, I'm sure he's mafia or some shit like that.

I crouch down with the gun pointed at her and I pull my sneaker on. I back away from her. I walk backward toward the door, keeping my eye on her at all times, making sure she doesn't shoot me in the back as I leave. She looks for Igor's phone, taking it from his pocket. I turn and run out of the door. I'm injured myself. I see how bloody my arm is and where my little finger was. I feel my ankle wants to give way on me like last time. I don't know if she broke anything with the hammer. I open the door of the car they brought me in. There is a hoodie on the back seat, I remembered it being there. I take off my tee and rip it into two pieces and tie the bigger one around my shoulder and the little piece around my hand and over my little finger. Fuck, how do I explain this to Prim and Cassy? What the fuck do I tell them? I put the hoodie on so I don't look odd with nothing on my torso, and I start to walk away.

As I walk down a couple of streets heading to the main road, I see the car pass me going at some speed, it's the other car that was outside the warehouse. It must be Poppy driving Igor to the hospital. He's been shot. She has some explaining to do. That's her shit to sort. I just hope she does keep her word and we never see her again.

Epilogue

Poppy

IT'S BEEN ELEVEN MONTHS NOW SINCE MY LIFE CHANGED. ELEVEN long months, in that time so much has happened, I have taken over Igor's business dealings for one. I recruited Steve and Sergei as my personal bodyguards. I kept all of Igor's other men, but those two were the real loyal men, which is why I promoted them. Steve was my bodyguard who Igor entrusted me to, and Sergei was his main man down in the basement who was in charge of all the security.

Igor always said never, ever, trust anyone, no matter who they are or what they do. I don't.

The other godfathers were not pleased, they had never had a female run a territory, especially someone that wasn't even Russian, I had a lot of opposition to my taking over and that's putting it mildly. I had to meet with them and they were surprised I spoke perfect Russian. I had Svetlana teach me more, she's become my right-hand woman. I think it's safe to say we are friends now, although I still do not trust her.

The godfathers refused to meet with me at first. I was doing Igor's business anyway, and they had no choice but to call me for a meeting. I was doing a good job and they knew it. I flew to New York. I met with them and not one of them had anything on my Igor. These were a bunch of aging, cantankerous old men. I think the youngest was maybe about fifty-five. I sat there on my own, and I answered their questions. I did have my husband in my ear. He was listening through my necklace, all James Bond gadgets. Igor used to tell me after his meetings that none of the others ever interfered with each other that there was only one person who could do that, this was the main boss, the Pakhan, of the godfathers. He had a say in everything. I remember Igor telling me that only the godfathers knew who this was, that no one else knew. His identity was a secret. Imagine my surprise, when at the meeting, after they grilled me, and they voted if I should stay or go, it was an even split, but as Igor was the Pakhan of all the godfathers, they presumed I would have his vote so they let me stay and run Igor's territory. I couldn't get over this. I heard him sigh as soon as they said it, he knew he was in for it once I got home, he never even told me, his fucking wife, I felt a little betrayed and hurt, but then I understand why he didn't tell me, it would betray the Bratva if he did.

I've struggled these last few months. I became a wife in such a short time really, but I became a mother also. Little Dimitri Igor Ustrashkins and Nikolai Igor Ustrashkins are now four months old. I didn't even know I was pregnant for some time. Especially not on that fateful day, taking my revenge out on Blaine. Would I have done that if I'd known? I don't know about that. I don't think I would, but I will never know. I know my life would have been so different if we hadn't gone after my revenge.

Then having to take over Igor's territory while I was pregnant was no mean feat. I'm so lucky his men stayed loyal. I did put myself in danger a few times, the farther I got into the pregnancy I had to stay in the car more than I wanted to. I couldn't risk the sons and heirs of Igor Ustrashkins getting hurt. It's also one of the reasons the godfathers let me continue, Igor's heirs were born and would eventually take over, albeit in many years. I love my boys more than anything and would protect them with my life.

I have never been near Primrose or Blaine since that day, I will keep my oath to Blaine. It is the way of the Bratva, the good ones anyway. A couple of weeks ago I felt pain like never before, even though I wasn't hurt or injured. It was like I was giving birth all over again. I'm almost positive Prim has had a baby. I wonder if she felt it when I went into labor with mine. I've had my men check up on them a couple of times to make sure they are still there, and all is good with them. They got married just over nine months ago. I cried at missing that. I then found out that Primrose could hear. I was so elated. Apparently, she had implants put in that made her hear again. I wish more than anything I could have been there when that happened. I hope they had a baby or babies. I will no doubt get told soon enough. I'm really happy that my sister has now found happiness and I do regret making her life hell all those years. If I could take it back I would, I do put a lot of it down to losing Mama and Pappy, but I shouldn't have blamed her.

I think back to that fucking day so much, to how my wanting revenge changed so many lives. It haunts me, it will forever be imprinted on my mind. If it wasn't for me, the others would still be alive. I've felt guilty about it every single day since. It's because I wanted revenge. If I wasn't so fucking selfish, they would still be alive. Igor came around right after Blaine left, he made me call a doctor he's used in San Francisco before. Mafia have doctors they pay good money to for them to keep silent about any treatments they need to do, especially gunshot wounds. I rushed Igor to the doctor, knowing it wouldn't be reported to the police. If I had called 911, then it would have been reported and a big investigation would have ensued. While the doctor was seeing to him, I called Steve and asked him and Sergei to sort out the bodies of Andrey and Ivan for me at the warehouse, to do the cleanup but with respect for our men so we could have proper burials for them. I didn't tell anyone what happened or what happened to Igor. Sitting in that doctor's room was the longest time of my life. I paced up and down for hours. I waited and waited for the doctor to come and see me, to tell me what was happening. When he walked through that door, I took one look at his face and I burst out crying. I collapsed to the floor, blacked out.

I came to with the doctor giving me some water. He asked when I last ate or drank anything, and I honestly couldn't remember. All I wanted to know was, how was Igor? The doctor asked could I be pregnant. I looked at him, startled. It was then I realized I hadn't had a period for a while. I was so wrapped up in getting my revenge I forgot all about it. We didn't use protection either. I must have looked startled because he got a test stick for me to go and pee. I frowned at him, then shouted at him for not telling me about Igor. I knew it was bad news. He was stalling, not telling me now because he thought I was pregnant. He ordered me to go pee. He helped me to the bathroom. I peed on the stick then walked out and handed it to him. I didn't want to know. I screamed at him to take me to Igor. I needed to see him, regardless of whether he was dead or alive.

He led me to a room and slowly opened the door for me. I walked in and I just stood there, speechless. I burst into tears, yet again, I couldn't believe it, Igor was alive. He was asleep, but he was alive, on a machine, but the doctor told me it was only precautionary, to help after the surgery he performed. He managed to get the bullet out, but he's not sure if there will be permanent damage to his spine. Until he wakes and they try to get him out of bed, then they will know more. I stayed with him for eight nights in that room. He didn't wake once. Then while asleep, I felt a featherlight touch on my cheek. I woke up to Igor smiling at me. I wanted to pounce on him but was too scared with not knowing how he was. The doctor came to check on him. He said he was doing well but the test would be when they tried to get him up. I walked out with the doctor after kissing Igor and telling him I wouldn't be long. I didn't like the look on his face. I was right. He was touching Igor's toes as he was talking to him; I didn't even notice. He said he even pinched him hard, but he didn't feel a thing. He feared his spine was damaged and needed to move him to a specialized unit to help with his rehabilitation.

He was right, Igor had spinal damage and his prognosis wasn't good. He was paralyzed from the waist down. This hit him hard. This proud, feared man was now immobilized. How would anyone take him seriously in his business? He went into a depression at first. I didn't tell him right away about us being pregnant, but when I did, he broke down. He was so happy I wish I had told him earlier. It gave him new strength and a new purpose in life. It helped with his recovery and his mindset. We didn't let anyone know about his paralysis, apart from those closest to us. He taught me everything about his business and I did all his meets under his instruction. I was wired for every meet so he could hear everything that went on and he could speak to me in my ear, giving me advice and instructions. It worked perfectly.

He stayed in the apartment. He was in a wheelchair and we had to have round-the-clock nurses to help him. He was a shattered man at first. His dignity went out the window and it killed him being the strong man that he is. He was determined to get out of that chair, even if it killed him. He had a physical therapist in daily to help him.

Igor was more than happy with the reputation I was getting for myself as not being a woman to mess with. There were a lot of rogue mafia that came out of the woodwork to try to take over Igor's business once word did get out about his paralysis. The ones brave enough to try ended up dead by my hand. That seemed to put an end to it. Once they knew Igor was still in control, but with me by his side, it seemed to work.

The first time he left the apartment in his wheelchair was the day I went into labor. He was determined he would be in the delivery suite with me. We knew we were having twins, but we didn't want to know the sex of them. Sex, that's the other thing that got him so mad. He wanted to make love to me or fuck me all the time and it killed him he couldn't. We used Viagra so it gave him a hard-on and I would ride him in the bed like a cowboy, especially as it got closer to me giving birth, I was so fucking horny. He could feel his orgasms when they happened, he hadn't lost that. He used to make me sit on his face as well, he still needed to taste me. We did what we could. He vowed he would walk one day and the day he took his first steps we both cried like babies.

It was so fucking hard once the twins arrived. Looking after them, Igor and the business, it killed me, but I did it. I never knew I was as strong as I was. Igor can walk slowly and with a walking aid, but he can walk. He has defied all the doctors and done what they said may never happen. He won't go to meetings, he leaves those to me. He doesn't want his rivals or anyone he does business with to think he is weak, which they would.

Our business is thriving.

Life is good, pretty fucking good.

Svetlana

I hate her. I fucking hate her parading around like she's the fucking queen, it should be me, not her. I pretend to be her friend, I know the saying 'keep your friends close but your enemies closer', that is exactly what I am doing. It broke me when I heard my love had been in an accident, and they lost Andrey and Ivan also, I never liked them fuckers anyway. My Sergei was sent to help, I made sure he understood he needed to be on the frontline now. To make sure he became the trusted number two to look after them.

I only saw my love once when he returned home, she was pushing him in a wheelchair into the reception area, I couldn't take it, it hurt seeing this powerful man so broken. It broke me again, the love of my life now a shadow of himself, I couldn't watch them, him broken and her high and mighty pushing him. It was enough to send me to my room alone where I cried all night. I couldn't let the others hear me break, if they see me break, they will think I am weak.

I made it my mission to get close to her. The one who stole him from me. Yes, he had others after me and before her, but there was none like her. The others I could take, he fucked them hard, then he got rid of them. It was only me he ever kept around. Me. It is me he wants. I know it is. I am his and I always will be. He is mine, and he always will be. I just need to show him, it is me who should be his queen. After all, I am Russian, it should be a Russian queen sitting by his side, not an American whore.

I have gained her trust, but I will work at making her look weak and feeble. With the help of Sergei, who loves me, I will overthrow the fake American queen.

The throne will be mine.
In time, I will get my king back.
Soon she will know the pain.
The pain from his rightful queen.

The End

Reviews

I really hope that you enjoyed this story. Reviews are lovely! Honestly, they are! And they also help other people to make an informed decision before buying this book.

I would really appreciate it if you took a few seconds to do just that. Thank you!

Find Me and Follow Me.

Amazon—https://amzn.to/2H5QquX

Facebook—https://bit.ly/345Ydlr

Instagram—https://bit.ly/2SZVcwt

Goodreads—https://bit.ly/37di1oI

BookBub—https://bit.ly/3j6AmWV

Lynda XX

Books by
LYNDA THROSBY

Catfish
A dark, gritty, romantic thriller (this book contains graphic scenes) for 18+ only.

The Best Day Of My Life
A sweet, single dad of twins romance.

Chef
A semi-dark romantic thriller.

A Christmas Wish
A sweet Christmas fairy tale novella.

The Pain Series

Book 1—The Pain They Feel
A dark psychological thriller (this book contains graphic scenes) for 18+ only.

Book 2—Poppy's Revenge
You just finished this. Thank you.
A dark psychological thriller (this book contains graphic scenes) for 18+ only.

Book 3—His Rightful Queen
Coming soon.
A dark psychological romantic thriller (this book contains graphic scenes) for 18+ only.

More about Lynda

Lynda lives in Cheshire in the UK with her husband Peter and cat Bailey also with two grown-up daughters and has a twelve-year-old granddaughter and one-year-old granddaughter.

She runs a successful financial business with her husband.

As a young teenager, Lynda used to read horror books with a love for everything Stephen King and James Herbert. She has always wanted to write and even wrote horror stories at age thirteen.

A little later she started reading Jackie Collins and Jilly Cooper and has always had a love of books. This then exploded with Twilight and Fifty Shades of Grey. Oh, and the introduction of e-readers.

In her spare time, she has a season ticket for Manchester City Football Club and goes to all the home games. She loves going to concerts and the theatre. She goes to the cinema at least once a week. When the weather is nice, you can see her gliding down the road on her Harley Davidson 1200T motorbike. Traveling is also high on the agenda, and her dream is to visit every state in the USA.

Acknowledgments

I wouldn't have done this without the help and support I got from friends and family.

First to my husband, who made time for me to write by running our business and the continued support he gives me, encouraging me to carry on.

Thank you to ellie from My Brother's Editor—for editing and formatting my words, you have no idea what your words meant during this process.

Thank you to Rosa from My Brother's Editor for proofreading my words, such a huge huge help as always.

Thank you to my sister Jackie for her feedback. Greatly appreciated as usual.

My family and friends who read the books and give me feedback.

Sybil Wilson from Pop Kitty for the amazing cover as usual.

Thank you to everyone who supports me and reads my words.

Lightning Source UK Ltd.
Milton Keynes UK
UKHW041822080421
381605UK00010B/77

9 781999 315092